HERE YOU COME AGAIN

The Bishop Smoky Mountain Thrillers
Book 7

LAUREN STREET

STERLING & STONE

Chapter One

NUDE PICTURES IN THE MOONLIGHT. Seriously?

It was a bad idea. A monumentally bad idea. Erica had thought so from the get-go, and the closer they got to Buttermilk Falls, the more certain she became. Wouldn't do any good to point that out to Jenna, of course, because the idea had been Jenna's. All the *bad* ideas came from beneath that girl's mane of strawberry blonde curls.

Jenna and Erica had been friends since God was a corporal and they never squabbled about anything, because Erica always did whatever Jenna wanted to do. It'd been settled a long time ago who was in charge. Or as Erica's granny was fond of putting it, "who crowed and who laid eggs" in their relationship.

Clearly, Erica was the egg-layer who had gotten suckered into this like she got suckered into every other thing Jenna decided she wanted to do. And what Jenna wanted to do this time was take moonlit pictures at Buttermilk Falls. *At* the falls, not *of* the falls. The pictures would be *of* the two of them — *naked.*

"You have got to be joking." Erica had been incredulous when Jenna brought it up.

"Oh, come on, Erica." The way Jenna rolled her eyes and said, *come on, Erica* always grated on Erica's nerves. It started probably in fifth grade, when they were still dancing around who got to make all the decisions in their friendship. By junior high, the dance wasn't just over — the band had packed up their instruments and gone home.

For years, Erica told herself that the power structure wasn't based on the fact that Jenna was pretty and Erica wasn't. Or that Jenna could make friends with a poached egg and Erica was socially awkward. Or that Jenna was slender and Erica … *wasn't.*

Like hell it wasn't! That's *exactly* what it was about. Erica gleaned a small measure of personal satisfaction from being willing to look reality in the eye like that. And when you were "plus-sized" Erica Whitmore, you took your meager crumbs of personal satisfaction wherever you could find them.

"This idea slaps and you know it," Jenna gushed. "Just look at that moon."

"Are you sure you know how to take a picture with an iPhone in moonlight?"

"Of course I know how. I Googled it." Jenna returned to the sell job, though the purchase was a foregone conclusion. "Everybody in school has posted pictures like this except you and me."

Translate "everybody" as the dozen or so kids who claimed the high rungs on the social hierarchy ladder of the school. What the rest of the student body did or didn't do was of absolutely no consequence.

"Have you looked at Madison's Instagram page?" Jenna added. "Or Emma's, in that black negligée?"

"At least she was wearing *something!*"

"She could have covered up more with two Band-Aids and a hockey puck. This is our chance to slay everybody."

"Why does it have to be nude pictures in moonlight?"

"Because nobody else has nude pictures in moonlight. The whole school will be wig-snatched when they see it. That moon hanging over the mountain. The waterfall in the background and us lounging around naked in nature. It's a straight-up thirst trap."

"It sounds cold to me."

"Oh, come on, Erica."

She was doing it again. She always did.

Jenna pulled her little Mazda off the road onto the smaller gravel road that led back to Buttermilk Falls. The tourists had taken over everything in Yarmouth County, and Buttermilk Falls was no exception. But the tourists hadn't yet discovered what a fairyland it was at night. The falls sparkled in the starlight, and when the moon was full, it was gorgeous. Buttermilk Falls had more going for it than the waterfall, too. There was the most perfect oak tree you ever saw sitting by the creek that the Falls fell into. In the summertime, soft grass grew at the base of the tree which was usually trampled by the tourists who stood under it gawking and taking selfies with the waterfall behind them.

It was the perfect romantic place to lay on a blanket and screw. On a Friday night, you'd have to take a number, but today was Thursday. Nobody came out Thursday nights, especially not this late. They'd had to wait until late because today was June 20, summer solstice, the longest day of the year, so it didn't even get dark until after nine o'clock — which meant the moon would rise up over the mountain at just the right spot at just the right time.

This was perfect, Jenna said, absolutely perfect. Full stop. End of discussion.

Erica had to admit it was a staggering sight. The water-fall glistening in the moonlight. The black velvet sky with stars as big as chunks of ice. The fat yellow moon — almost full, just a sliver of black on the left side — parked just above the mountaintop. And the gnarled old tree standing watch on the creek bank.

Jenna parked her car. She'd had the presence of mind to bring along a lacy white blanket, and since she was their photographic "expert" in this little adventure, she would take the first round of pictures. That meant Erica would have to strip down to her bare ass first. She would have orchestrated that differently if she'd had a say in it.

They hadn't taken two steps away from the car when Jenna turned to Erica.

"Showtime, G, take your clothes off."

"What?"

"How many things can 'take your clothes off' mean? Four one-syllable words. Unless clothes … is clothes more than one syllable?" She didn't wait for Erica to reply. "Either way, a first grader would understand."

"I meant, why do I have to get undressed *here*?"

"Because I want to get a picture of you from behind, walking toward the waterfall."

"From the back? You didn't say anything about pictures from the back. I've got …"

"There won't be enough light to show the pimples on your back. So, strip."

Oh, how Erica didn't want to do this. But it was a beautiful night and a beautiful sight, and the pictures would be fire on Instagram. And Jenna was right — every-body else did have something, but theirs would be the blue-print from now on. She stripped down to her bra and panties. Jenna just stood looking at her, iPhone in hand and tapping her foot. Erica reached down, undid her bra,

4

slipped out of her panties, and suddenly felt a chill. If it hadn't been cold with nothing on but her panties and bra, why was it suddenly cold when she took them off? It's not like they covered up that much skin or offered that much warmth. But the chill didn't feel like a drop in temperature. It was something else, and she was suddenly a deer with its white tail standing at attention, on full alert as her eyes raked the darkness under the trees.

"Nobody's here. There's nowhere to park but where we did and there was no car besides ours, so how could anybody be here?" Jenna said.

Still, Erica strained to see into the puddles of darkness under the trees — almost thought she saw ... what was that? Movement. She saw something move out there. No, she didn't. She was just nervous. Jenna was paying no attention, focused on her iPhone, changing the settings like Google had told her she needed to.

"Okay, come over here," she said and yanked a naked Erica twenty feet to the left. She backed up, sighted in, and told Erica to move a couple of steps back to the right. Satisfied, she gave the order for the show to begin. "Now walk slow and sexy toward the waterfall."

Erica didn't feel sexy. Erica felt ... She didn't know what she felt, but there was something *wrong*. There was something hinky about this whole thing that didn't have anything to do with her and Jenna. And if she'd been with anybody besides Jenna, Erica would have called the whole thing off on the spot. But one didn't call off what Jenna had planned. It just wasn't done.

"Come on now, cook it, girl, slow and sexy."

Erica tossed her long brown hair over her shoulders so that it would dangle in curls, provocatively, she hoped, to her waist. Then she set out toward the waterfall, pretending she was a model walking down a runway in front of an adoring audience instead of a "plump" 17-year-old girl walking across rocks and pebbles and grass in the middle of the night with no clothes on.

She imagined the runway, and she didn't close her eyes exactly, but she unfocused them, concentrated on the image in her head rather than the reality around her — which wasn't right. Damn it, *something* wasn't right.

She could hear Jenna coming behind, snapping pictures, telling her to "shake your head so your hair is moving, and I can freeze the movement."

Jenna was focused on taking pictures — changing the settings on the iPhone and getting Erica into the right position. Erica was focused on imagining she was on the fantasy runway. She could see, but she didn't *look* at anything.

That explains why they didn't notice anything odd until they were right on it.

"Now, I'm going to switch to video mode."

"You didn't say anything about a video, you just said still shots."

"I didn't think there'd be enough light for a video, but it says there's enough light."

"Just because it says there's enough light doesn't mean there is."

"We'll do it two or three different ways and see what comes out looking best. Right now, it's on video, so swing that ass, baby."

Erica tried to move slow and sensuous, slinky, as Jenna shouted directions. "To the left, to the left. Okay, the waterfall's in the perfect spot. Now sink down onto the ground."

"Sink down onto the—?"

"Just shut up and do it."

Erica tried to sink gracefully down onto her knees, but

she felt awkward and was painfully aware of her big thighs and her wide ass — that Jenna had insisted would look fine, just fine in moonlit pictures. She tried to be graceful and sexy and alluring, but didn't feel any of those things, just creepy. That was it. Something about this place creeped her out and she didn't know what it was. She'd been here a hundred times — in the morning, noon, at night. She'd come out here twice with Jake. But they had been going at it and weren't really aware of their surroundings.

Never one time had Erica felt creeped out like she did now.

Settling down onto the grass as gracefully as possible, she listened to Jenna's movement instructions.

"Now lie down on your back. And don't keep your arms glued to your sides. You look like one of those soldiers in the Nutcracker."

Erica did as instructed. She spread her arms luxuriously out to her sides and took a deep breath.

Splat.

What in the world—? Well, goody.

"I just got shit on by a bird," Erica said, swiping at the wet on her belly.

"I can't see anything, so it didn't mess up the video."

"Well, it messed up my belly." She wiped it off. "Ewww."

"Don't grimace. You look like a troll."

Splat.

Something hit her on the cheek.

"Dammit," she cried. "There must be a crow up there!"

Given the quantity of shit, the bird had to be as big as a chicken. Okay, maybe a pigeon. But there weren't any pigeons in the woods. The only birds out here were little

7

wild birds like wrens and robins, cardinals and bluebirds, and they didn't shit big globs of —

Splat.

That one hit her nose, then ran down over her lip into — she leapt to her feet gagging, coughing and spitting out bird shit!

It didn't taste like bird shit, though. Not that she knew what bird shit tasted like, but this tasted salty and metallic. Like blood.

She looked up, really looked this time to see if she could find the damned *turkey* up there on the tree limb that was—

Erica froze. Literally could not move a muscle. There was a disconnect between the reality her eyes were seeing and what was actual reality, because what she was seeing couldn't be … *couldn't* be …

She screamed then. And when she did, another drop of blood fell down out of the severed neck of the naked corpse dangling over a limb above her. Got her right in the mouth this time.

Chapter Two

IT's COLD. Dark. She's so scared.

The water's rising, or she's sinking down into it. She can feel it moving up her chest and she just wants to go to sleep. Here in Jillian's arms.

Jillian.

Jillian is beside her and they're going to die here. Together. Jillian and Rileigh. And Rileigh has just found her sister again. How can they die now when Jillian just got home?

Ring.

The sound echoes against the sides of the well.

Ring.

Rileigh jerked awake and sat up, panting, tangled in sweaty sheets. She shook her head to clear the gauzy tatters of dream unreality away. Another one of those nightmares about being in the well with Jillian.

Oh, she'd been here often enough in her life that she knows the drill. Something horrible happened and she had nightmares about it. For a while. Eventually the nightmares stopped. The claustrophobia she'd developed after almost being buried alive hung around longer—

Ring.

That's what woke her up. Her phone was ringing. She reached over and picked it up off the nightstand, checking the name on the screen. It was Mitch.

"Mitch? What time is it?" She squinted, trying to make out the numbers on her bedside digital clock. "Two? Three o'clock—?"

"Rileigh, I'm really sorry to wake you up in the middle of the night like this. But I've got a body and two witnesses who won't talk to a man."

"What are you talking about?"

"There's been a murder and the two girls who found the body are refusing to say what they were doing here, say they won't talk to a *man* about it." He paused. "And I *used* to have a female deputy, but she …" He left the words dangling in the air between them.

"Where are you?"

"Buttermilk Falls."

"Buttermilk Falls in the middle of the night?"

"Yeah, with a body dangling from the oak tree."

Rileigh hung up and started to get dressed. She tried to be quiet, didn't want to wake up Mama and Jillian, but she'd only just gotten her T-shirt on when —

"Rileigh?" said a voice from behind her.

Rileigh jumped in surprise, turned around, and there in the doorway stood her sister, Jillian. Every time she happened to catch sight of Jillian — stirring her coffee at the kitchen table or sitting in the rocker on the front porch or gathering eggs in the hen house — every time, her heart leapt into her throat, and she wanted to laugh and cry and jump up and down for joy. Jillian who was dead for 27 years, except she wasn't. Jillian was home.

And Jillian had just scared the shit out of her.

"You know what Aunt Daisy would say, don't you?"

Rileigh gasped. "She'd say you're so quiet you could sneak dawn past a rooster."

The ghost of a smile skittered across Jillian's face. But that was all.

"Where are you going? It's the middle of the night."

"I got a call from Mitch, and he needs me to—"

"Mitch, the sheriff?"

Jillian knew who Mitch was. But she didn't really understand the relationship that Rileigh had with him when it came to helping out on criminal cases. This was the first time it had come up since Mitch had dragged Rileigh and Jillian out of a well that the former sheriff tossed them into so they could die there of hypothermia.

"Mitch needs my help on a case." Rileigh turned and started pulling her jeans up.

"You're not a police officer."

"No. Well, I *was* … it's kind of complicated. I told you that I was a police officer for nine years."

"And you left because you accidentally shot a toddler in a stroller."

That still hurt. There weren't that many people who knew exactly why Rileigh had left her job more than a year ago to come back home to Black Bear Forge and live with her mother. And those who did know didn't toss it out into conversation like throwing feed to chickens.

She swallowed her discomfort.

"When I got back to Black Bear Forge, I got involved with Mitch, helping him out. He was trying to solve a murder case, and he's from away-from-here." Rileigh gave Jillian a knowing look, which didn't appear to communicate. Well, Jillian had been gone for… *almost three decades.*

Rileigh had to swallow the lump that suddenly swelled up into her throat before she could continue.

"Nobody trusted him. They didn't want to talk to an

outsider. So I got swept up in helping him solve the murder case. The victim was Tina Montgomery. Her mother came and asked me to help."

"But that was last summer. It doesn't explain what you're doing now."

Rileigh could see that Jillian was upset, and she wasn't sure exactly why. She and Mama had done everything they could to make Jillian feel at home. Once she and Rileigh got out of the hospital, Jillian moved back into her old room, down the hall from Rileigh. When Rileigh was much younger, she'd get in bed with Jillian when she had bad dreams.

The proximity had been a good thing when Rileigh was seven years old. It wasn't such a good thing now. She had not intended to wake anybody up leaving. And she certainly hadn't intended to upset Jillian by going.

"I guess I didn't explain it really well. Ever since that case last summer, I've been helping Mitch in an unofficial capacity. Because he is an outsider, and people have been slow to warm up to him. Then he deputized me —"

"You said you left your badge on the kitchen table when you came out to that cabin in the woods."

"I did. I knew that what I was about to do, I couldn't do as a police officer. I had to be a private citizen. Rileigh Bishop going to get her sister. I couldn't complicate that with official police procedure and protocol. That's why I resigned."

"You said Mitch offered to hire you back as a deputy and you didn't take it. You didn't want to be a deputy. So why are you running out in the middle of the night?"

"Because Mitch called. He needs me."

"What could the sheriff possibly need you for at three o'clock in the morning?"

"Jillian…"

Rileigh was getting irritated in spite of herself. She didn't have time for this. Mitch needed her *now*. And Jillian was being remarkably unsupportive and stubborn.

"Look, we'll sit down and discuss the whole thing when I get home. But right now, I have to go."

She turned and started putting her shoes and socks on. Jillian remained in the door, just looking at her.

Rileigh wanted to break the awkward silence. But she couldn't think what to say that would appease Jillian.

When she stood and started strapping on her gun, Jillian gasped.

"You're going *armed?*"

"Of course I am. I'm—"

"Don't do this. Please, don't do this." Jillian rushed across the few steps between them and took Rileigh by the shoulders. "Don't go. It's dangerous out there."

Rileigh couldn't imagine what kind of awful horror Jillian had lived through that had planted that kind of gut-deep terror in her. But she would address that. She really would. She just didn't have time to do it right now. She pulled free from her sister's grip.

"I have to go now, Jillian. I will be fine. I'm armed. Mitch is armed. We're not going into a dangerous situation. There's been a murder—"

"*Murder?*"

"Murder. It's over, and there's a body."

"Then why does he need—"

"He needs me because the witnesses won't talk to a man."

"Can't he find somebody else?"

"He doesn't need to, because he called me and I'm coming. I'll be back later on this morning."

Rileigh took Jillian by the shoulders and gently moved

her out of the way, grabbed her jacket off the back of the chair, and hurried out of the room.

Thankfully, Buttermilk Falls wasn't very far from Rileigh's house, and she got there quickly. Could see the flashing lights from the sheriff's department cruisers, the ambulance, and the rescue squad as she got close.

She pulled off onto the gravel road, drove another fifty feet, then parked her car and hurried to where she could see Mitch talking to Deputy Mullins. He looked up and saw her, and she was thrilled at the look of gratitude and relief that washed over his face.

"Yo, Rileigh," Deputy Mullins said, then walked away.

"Beau." She nodded, then turned to Mitch. "So, what have we got?"

Mitch cocked his thumb over his shoulder. Rileigh looked where he pointed and couldn't grab the gasp before it leapt out of her mouth. Hanging from one of the limbs of the gigantic oak tree was a woman's body, naked, hanging head down, and the throat had been … more than just cut. It looked like it had been violently ripped out.

Mitch gave her a second to take in the scene, then pointed to his cruiser, where she could see two girls huddled in the back seat.

"They're the ones who found her."

"What were they doing out here?"

"That's what I want to know, but they won't tell me."

"Why not?"

"It's some kind of girl thing." Mitch rolled his eyes. "Anyway, will you please go talk to those young ladies and find out what they were doing out here and what they saw?"

"On it, Chief," she said, offering a mock salute.

Chapter Three

RILEIGH WENT to Mitch's cruiser, opened the front passenger side door, and slid in, closing it behind her. She turned to face the two girls who were hunkered in Mitch's back seat. "Hi, I'm Rileigh Bishop."

That was as far as she got before the girls started talking over each other, babbling out a tale of how they couldn't talk to that man and all the other officers were men and... and...

"That's why Mitch called me," Rileigh said, holding up her hand. "He said it was a girl thing."

One of the girls rolled her eyes.

"Tell me your names."

The chubby girl on the left said her name was Erica Wakefield. The girl with the mop of curly red hair said her name was Jenna McGraw.

"How about we start at the beginning?"

The girls started talking over each other again. Rileigh stopped them.

"Let me ask questions, and you answer them. That work for you?"

The girls looked at each other.

No, they didn't look at each other. Erica looked to Jenna, almost as if asking permission.

Then they both turned and nodded their heads.

"So, Erica," Rileigh said, "Tell me why you came out here tonight."

Erica shot a glance at Jenna, who answered the question.

"We came out here to take pictures. It's a full moon, and we wanted pictures, you know, with the waterfall in the background."

"So, you came out here to take pictures of the waterfall in a full moon."

Again, the girls exchanged a look, and again, Jenna answered the question.

"We didn't come to take pictures *of* the waterfall. We came to take pictures *at* the waterfall."

"What were you taking pictures of?"

Before Erica could look and get permission from Jenna to speak, Rileigh turned to her and said, "Erica, tell me what you were here to take pictures of."

"Ourselves."

"You came out here to take selfies in the moonlight?"

Jenna sighed dramatically. "Here's the deal. We came out here to take nude pictures. We thought the waterfall with a full moon would be a wonderful background. So we came to take them. Okay?"

Jenna bordered on belligerent, and it seemed clear to Rileigh that Erica had just come along for the ride.

"What do you want nude pictures for?"

"To post on our Instagram accounts," Jenna said, and tossed her head, throwing the mane of red hair back away from her face.

"All right, so you got here, then what happened?"

"I told Erica to take her clothes off—" Rileigh held up her hand.

"I want to ask Erica some questions, and I don't want you to answer for her."

"I wasn't answering for her," Jenna said in a huff.

Rileigh ignored Jenna and looked directly at Erica, who couldn't have looked more uncomfortable.

"Erica, tell me what happened. You took your clothes off, and then what?"

Thankfully, Erica didn't look to Jenna for permission this time, she simply said, "I took my clothes off because Jenna said she wanted to get pictures, you know, of me walking toward the waterfall in the moonlight. So I walked toward the waterfall."

"And then what happened?"

"Well, I got close to the trunk of the oak tree, and then Jenna hollered at me to sit down."

Jenna interrupted. "I'd switched from still to video and I wanted this fluid picture of a graceful girl settling down into the grass."

"Jenna, I'm talking to Erica right now." Again, Jenna looked terribly put out, but shut her mouth.

"I did what she said. I sat down on the grass and Jenna said to lay on my back and spread my arms wide."

And then Erica's face crumpled, and she started to cry softly, shaking her head in disgust.

"Something dripped on me, and I thought there was a bird in the tree."

"You know, up on a branch in the tree," Jenna offered. "Shitting."

Rileigh said. "If I have to talk to you one at a time, I will. Can you please wait until your turn?"

Jenna shrugged. She'd been put in her place and Rileigh suspected that didn't happen very often.

Erica hadn't stopped crying, but she continued the story through her tears. "I felt something, I mean, like, something dripped on me, and I thought, bird shit. It dripped on my belly, and I wiped it off. Then a drip hit my face and it went in my mouth."

She was sobbing by this time, pouring out words, in a torrent. "I thought, I thought it didn't taste like … I mean, I don't know what bird shit tastes like … but what hit my mouth tasted like blood. And then I looked up and I saw, *I saw…*"

Then she was crying so hard she couldn't talk anymore. Jenna patted her on the shoulder in an expression of plastic sympathy.

Rileigh turned to Jenna. "What did you do, Jenna?"

Jenna was glad to have the ball back and she dribbled it confidently down the court.

"Erica started screaming, so I went over there to see what was wrong. I thought maybe a bug crawled on her or something. A bug crawling on you when you're naked, that'd be gross…" She noted Rileigh's get-to-the-point look and went back to the story. "I looked up and I saw that body. So I told her to go back to the car and put her clothes on, because we had to dial 911."

"Did you see anybody anywhere around when you pulled into the parking space?"

"No," Jenna said.

"How about when you got out of the car?" The girls answered at once. Jenna said no, Erica said yes. Rileigh looked at Erica. "You saw someone?"

"I don't know what I saw, but something moved in the trees." She pointed to a spot in the woods behind the oak tree. "Maybe it was a deer. I don't know. I couldn't tell what it was. There was something there."

"You didn't tell me you saw anything," Jenna said it as if she was offended by the omission.

"I tried to, but you—"

"Girls!" Rileigh said and both of them hushed. "So, Erica went from the car to where she sat down in the grass, underneath the body. Did you go any further than the body?"

"No, I ran back to the car," said Jenna.

"So, the only places either one of you has touched is the space between your car and beneath the body. You didn't go toward the oak tree or walk around anywhere else."

"No," Jenna said. "We just ran back to the car and dialed 911."

Rileigh asked them a few more questions, got Erica calmed down, then left the two teenagers in the backseat of Mitch's cruiser and went to find him among the crowd of law enforcement officers, paramedics, and rescue squad.

The rescue squad members were standing around waiting for an OK from Mitch to haul the body down. But he wanted it left right where it was until Gus, the coroner, released the scene.

"So, what was it that they absolutely couldn't tell a man?" Mitch asked Rileigh as she approached.

"That they came out here to take nude pictures."

"Say what?"

"They came out here because there's a beautiful full moon that lights up the waterfall. They were going to stand in front of the waterfall with no clothes on and take pictures to post on their Instagram accounts."

"You're joking."

Rileigh shook her head.

Mitch opened his mouth to say something else, but

instead, he merely smiled at the man approaching behind Rileigh.

Gus Hazelton was a coroner unlike any other in Tennessee. He'd won the state lottery years ago and had used much of the proceeds to build the finest coroner's lab in the state.

"Dr. Augustus Lafayette Hazelton at your service," he said with a slight bow.

Besides the M.D. after Gus's name, he had an alphabet soup of other initials for associated degrees. A well-known forensic pathologist, Gus Hazelton hung out his shingle in Yarmouth County, Tennessee because he liked to hunt and fish, and he figured the pace would be slow. He didn't particularly enjoy spending all his time with dead people. But in the few months since Rileigh had come home from Memphis, she'd watched a steady stream of bodies cross his examining table. A tall, athletic black man with a wide smile that revealed what he called a "Madonna gap" between his top two front teeth, Gus never went anywhere without a cigar in his pocket — kept it handy in case he got stuck examining a floater.

"Not to be Captain Obvious," Gus said, indicating the corpse draped over the tree limb, "but this young woman was killed somewhere else, and the body brought here."

Mitch nodded.

"And that 'somewhere else' is a mess. What'd the killer do with all that blood? Also, the guy went to a hell of a lot of trouble to hang that body up there." He pointed to the gigantic oak tree and sighed. The tree had a huge limb that stuck out at a right angle from it, easy to climb to, like it'd been designed to use for a tire swing ... or to drape a body over. "Always wished we had a tree like that in our neighborhood when I was a kid. Looks like it came right out of Lothlórien."

"And what, pray tell, is Lothlórien?" Mitch asked.

Gus shook his head and nodded at Rileigh. "You tell him."

The pathologist bent to examine the drips of blood on the grass where the teenage girl Erica had been lying, getting down on one knee and using his flashlight to look around.

He stood back up. "I don't think that body's been hanging up there very long. The blood on the grass is still wet. It's not even sticky. Who found it?"

Mitch pointed to the teenagers in the backseat of his cruiser. "They did."

"Well, it'd be my guess that when those girls got here, they just about tripped over whoever was hanging that body from the branch."

Mitch had cordoned off the area with yellow and black "Don't Cross This Line" police tape. Gus was careful to edge around it as he used his flashlight to examine the ground and foliage. There were marks on the trunk of the tree, drawn with still-wet blood — almost certainly the victim's —strange shapes. They appeared to be crude symbols. One of them might have been a pentagram, but the bark of the tree was so rough and uneven it was hard to tell. Mitch pulled out his phone and took pictures of them while Gus studied the ground beneath the tree.

"Aha!" Gus said, nodding to footprints in the damp earth. "I've got some plaster in my truck, I'll make a cast of this. But even without a cast, I can tell you that it's a running shoe. You can tell by the design on the bottom. Adidas. New Balance. Not Nike, I don't think. Maybe Reebok. And they're brand new."

"You know that how?" Rileigh asked.

"See how sharp the edges of that track are?" He held up his own foot to reveal the bottom of his shoes. "Compare that to my shoes." His shoe soles were worn smooth on the outside edges. "I'm a supinator," he said, indicating the wear marks. "Ankle bends outward when I run. Bad form."

By the time Gus was finished gathering the forensic evidence he wanted, the sun was pinking the sky, which in the mountains meant it was long past sunrise out on the flat, but the sun had yet to clear Beaumont Peak so it could shine down into the hollows and valleys beyond.

"You can get her down now," Mitch said, and made a motion to the guys from the rescue squad who had been waiting to collect the body. Two of the rescue squad members set to work while a third — Tim Nicholson — approached Mitch.

"I know there's no ID on that body, but I think I can identify her," Tim said.

The rescue squad lowered the body out of the tree into the arms of the ambulance personnel, who would secure it in a body bag and transport it to Gus's office for an autopsy.

As soon as the body was laid out flat, the face in full view, Tim nodded his head. "I know who that is. Her name is Annamaria Giordano, but she just went by Annie."

"Are you sure on this ID?" Mitch asked. Rileigh knew he didn't fancy going to some poor mother and telling her that her daughter had died only to realize later he'd screwed it up.

"Oh, I'm sure," Tim said. He leaned over the body with its grisly open wound. Up closer, Rileigh could see marks on the skin of the girl's neck, like bite marks where ... maybe a dog had attacked her and ripped out her throat, though Rileigh could see no other wounds, no bite marks or anything else on the body.

Tim pointed out something she hadn't noticed — a spot on the girl's forehead just under her hairline, a mark.

"That's where she burned herself with a curling iron," he said, nodding to what was obviously a recent minor burn. "Annie works in my dentist's office, as a dental hygienist, and she cleaned my teeth Tuesday morning." He shook his head sadly. "I noticed the burn and asked her how she got it."

Tim said he believed the girl's mother lived on Pine Bluff Road, on the other side of Bledsoe Mountain.

"I think she's the only child. Her mother's not going to take this well."

"I've never seen a mother who did take it well," Mitch said,

Rileigh saw Mitch look in her direction, and she saved him the trouble of asking. "Yeah, I'll go with you to tell her mother."

He nodded his thanks.

Chapter Four

RILEIGH AND MITCH rode together in silence for a few minutes. It would take a little while to get to the other side of Bledsoe Mountain, where the grisly job of telling a woman that she had lost her only child waited. Not just "lost," but that her only child had been brutally murdered. The prospect of that conversation weighed heavy on both of them.

"Any ideas?" Rileigh asked.

"Not a clue," Mitch said. "Right now, I only know her name and address. Maybe her mother will have some idea what happened to her."

"Maybe she will, but I'd be surprised if she's able to tell us about it right now," Rileigh said.

They drove on for a while in silence.

"I saw Jillian this morning before I left the house, and she was upset."

Mitch raised his eyebrows. "About what?"

"Upset that I was running out in the middle of the night to help the sheriff in a murder case. She's frightened for me."

"Helping the sheriff *after* a murder isn't often a life-threatening activity."

"That's what I tried to tell Jillian, but she wasn't buying what I was selling."

Mitch let that lie for a few moments. And then asked carefully, "So, how is she?"

Rileigh leaned her head back on the seat. "How is Jillian?" She mulled the question around in her mind. "She's doing better."

Then she caught herself. "Okay, I'm doing it again, rose-coloring everything having to do with Jillian. Acting like everything's pink lace and cotton candy because she's home." She let that lie. "I gotta stop doing that shit. Everything's not rosy and perfect and glorious."

Mitch gave her a look she couldn't interpret. She backed up.

"Oh, it's wonderful. It's the best thing that's happened in my life in three decades. And certainly in hers. But it is far from perfect. Given what Jillian has been through…"

She let the sentence dangle. Mitch didn't probe or ask. But she volunteered what she knew.

"Jillian will tell me what happened to her when she's ready. I just have a vague sketch in my mind, and even that much is just about too much to contemplate."

"How did she wind up in—"

"The answer to all how or why or what questions about Jillian is 'I don't know, I don't know, and I don't know.' She just seems…" Rileigh fought for the right word. "Brittle."

"Fragile," Mitch corrected.

"Yes, fragile. It's like she's as tough as nails. Like she has survived the worst that life can throw at a human being. Survived and conquered and got away. And the flip side of that is she seems like she's made out of blown glass. Like she would break if you touched her wrong."

"Have you suggested getting therapy?"

"I have."

"And?"

"And she said she'd think about it. Then a day or two later she brought it up herself and said that she understood that she needed it. But the thought of digging into all that right now, of picking at that scab knowing what was beneath it … she said she just wasn't ready yet. And she looked at me, almost pleading, like she was begging me to understand."

They were quiet again for a while as the sun turned the sky from black through pink toward blue.

"You know how they say you can't go home again?"

Mitch nodded.

"Well, this is the 'you can't go home again' story on steroids. She left here an eighteen-year-old girl with her whole life ahead of her, and for three decades she lived in hell, and now she's back. I'm sure she doesn't know who she is, what she should do, or how she should relate to anybody."

"And the Jillian who left is frozen in your mind as who Jillian *is*," Mitch said.

Rileigh nodded.

"But she's not that person anymore."

Rileigh nodded again.

"She doesn't know who she is either."

"You're three for three so far," Rileigh said. "I want to be available when she wants to open up … *if* she wants to open up. But I don't want to pry."

"I think it's too soon now to be concerned about a thing like that. But eventually, you may have to pry." Mitch shook his head. "I'm not an expert on these things, but it has been my experience that the longer you wallpaper over something awful, the nastier it gets. If she allows herself to

26

pretend everything's just fine and go on with life because that's less painful than dealing with the past, she's going to hit a wall at some point, and it'll be ugly."

"So, what should I do?" Rileigh asked.

"Just love her. That's all you and your mother can do right now — love her. And know that the road forward is not going to be smooth."

"She didn't deserve all that."

"I'll wager few people deserve the terrible things that happen to them."

Rileigh was sure he was thinking about Annamaria Giordano. And her mother. But acknowledging that Jillian wasn't the only one suffering didn't make it easier to stand by and watch her suffer.

"She's about to get married and go out into the world and … do life, and she comes home and finds my bastard father…" Rileigh didn't complete the sentence. "After that her life exploded. She didn't have a life. Hers was a waking nightmare, and she endured that for decades. I don't know how to even talk to her anymore."

"I think, and this is just my opinion," Mitch said slowly, "I haven't hung out my shingle as a psychotherapist, still shining it up. But I think normal is what she needs more than anything."

"Aunt Daisy always said that normal is just a setting on a dryer."

"Ordinary, then. The sun rises, you get up, you make breakfast, you have an ordinary day, you go back to bed at night. Wash. Rinse. Repeat. I think she needs a whole lot of that as a buffer between her and all the terrible things that happened to her."

Rileigh thought he was probably right.

"You know what happens to most POWs, don't you?"

Rileigh knew, but she let him tell her anyway.

"At some point after being liberated," he continued. "After the initial glorious freedom. After eating good food, getting healthy, adjusting to not being afraid anymore … after the shine wears off all that, most of them spiral down into depression. Because depression is caused by suppressed anger. However long they were captives — every second of that time, they were full of rage. At the system that put them there, at the world, at life, at God. But they could do nothing about that anger, so they stuffed it, and stuffed it and stuffed it way down deep. And eventually that kind of anger comes back and bites them in the ass."

The silence between them drew out, comfortable silence, companionable silence between good friends who didn't need to fill up pauses with a bunch of needless chatter.

"I saw David Hicks the other day in the post office," Mitch said.

Rileigh turned to him. "You did? What did he say?"

"He peppered me with questions about Jillian, wanted to know how she was and what had happened to her and where she'd been. I told him that I couldn't answer those questions. He said he wanted to call her, to talk to her, to see her, but he didn't know how to do that. I mean, how do you call up the woman who left you standing at the altar twenty-seven years ago and spent the last three decades as a…" Mitch let the words trail off. "He doesn't know where to start, he doesn't know what to say."

"What did you tell him?"

"I told him to follow his heart. I told him that when the time was right, he'd know." Mitch shook his head. "I swear, Rileigh, the man's still in love with her."

Rileigh should have been surprised by that, but she wasn't. The thought settled in, sank deep. It felt right.

"Most of what I have seen of him in the last three decades has been in the past week. I'm certainly not prepared to make a judgement about what's going on with him. Still, I think you're right. David Hicks still loves Jillian."

"What about Jillian? How does she feel about him?"

Rileigh turned to Mitch and shrugged. "I don't have any idea."

Chapter Five

THE SUN WAS UP, not over the mountain, but high enough that its rays streamed down through the trees, dispelling the puddles of darkness beneath them, transforming the dew on flowers and branches into sparkling diamonds.

The Giordano home was a tidy, neat house, set back from the road in a stand of cedar trees, built in the 60s or 70s, by the look of the architecture. There was a single car in the driveway. Mitch pulled his cruiser up behind that car and killed the engine.

"I'm glad it's morning," he said.

Rileigh nodded. "Everything seems worse in the dark."

But there wasn't any way that what they had come to say could be any worse, light or dark.

Mitch could hear the yapping of a small dog inside as they approached. The front fence needed repairs and the lawn needed mowing. It was a place in want of a man or a strong boy. Evangeline Giordano, 68, ostensibly lived here alone: her daughter was not listed on the census data for this address, nor did her name show up on the voter registration roll. But Tim had said he was sure Annamaria still lived at home. Apparently, she'd mentioned to him often how much she wanted to get her own apartment and move out.

There was no good way to do what Mitch and Rileigh had come here to do. If the sheriff's office had called ahead and told the surviving family member that the sheriff needed to talk to them, and that it would be a good idea to have a family member present, they would live through seven levels of hell waiting for the ax of bad news to fall. But if you showed up unannounced and the family member was alone — then they got the worst news of their lives with nobody to help them deal with it.

Police officers who worked together learn to read their partners. They fell into a rhythm that they were not even aware of. Things like how they talked to people — who says the hard things? Who has the best shoulder to cry on? Not so much good cop, bad cop, though there was plenty of that when they were questioning suspects, but the more mundane situations in the life of a police officer required a kind of handling that you couldn't teach. The police academy couldn't prepare you, no matter how many grief-whatever classes they taught — to see the look of utter devastation they were about to see on this mother's face.

Mitch reached up and pushed the doorbell button. They heard no sound inside, nothing but the insistent yapping of the dog. He punched the button again and still nothing.

"Must not work." Mitch knocked on the heavy wooden door, forcefully but not aggressively.

A voice came from behind the door. "Who is it? Who's out there?"

"Are you Mrs. Evangeline Giordano?"

"Yes, I am, and who are you?"

"Mrs. Giordano, I am Yarmouth County Sheriff Mitchell Webster. And I need to talk to you."

"Oh."

Just that one sound came through the door, like somebody had punched the woman on the other side in the belly.

"Oh, oh, alright." she stammered, and Mitch could hear her unlocking a deadbolt. That made a statement, that she had a deadbolt, and that she used it. Most of the older people in the county clung to their old ways. But slowly, even here in Black Bear Forge, Tennessee, the custom was fading away. There was too much ugliness on the news, piped into every household through the internet and the television. Nobody felt really safe anymore. And parents who still had adult children living with them, which, thanks to the current state of the American economy was way more of them than it used to be, bowed to the insecurity of the younger generation. Those adult children locked their doors.

The door swung open and a small, plump woman stood before them. It was clear she hadn't been out of bed long, hadn't yet brushed her hair or changed out of her house shoes. The woman had on a simple house dress and the look on her face would fit perfectly beside the definition of "terror" in the dictionary.

"May we come in, please?" Mitch asked.

The woman said nothing, just mutely pushed the door open for them to enter. Mitch was sure she didn't say anything because she couldn't draw enough air into her lungs to speak.

"My name is Rileigh Bishop," Rileigh said.

"Bishop?" The woman recognized the name.

"Yes, I'm Lily Bishop's youngest daughter. Do you know Lily?"

"Oh, she's in the Hester Sewing Circle with me. Sweetest woman in the world. I hear her oldest come home a week or so ago, the one everybody thought was gone forever."

Then the burst of life in Evangeline's face faded like fireworks out of the sky and left behind it only darkness.

"What is it?" the woman asked, her voice as quiet and terrified as a child talking to the boogeyman in the closet. "What did you come here to talk to me about?"

"Would you mind if we sat down?" Mitch asked.

"It's about Annie, ain't it? She never come home last night. Never called or nothing. Has something happened...?" She ran out of air and couldn't finish the sentence.

"Could we please sit down?" Mitch asked. "We'll tell you everything."

The woman walked before them into a tidy living room that was old school. No widescreen TV attached to the wall. Just a couch, loveseat and matching chairs, plus a small television set on a table in the corner of the room.

She gestured toward the couch and chairs but made no move to sit down.

Mitch sat, hoping Evangeline would follow his lead.

Rileigh sat too, then patted the couch beside her.

But the woman stood rooted to the spot.

"What is it? Tell me. Has my Annie been in an accident? Is she hurt?"

Mitch reluctantly picked up the ball and lumbered with it toward the end zone.

"I'm very sorry to have to tell you this Mrs. Giordano, but your daughter Annie died a few hours ago."

The woman wobbled like she'd just been struck in the face by a high wind, and Mitch leapt to his feet to catch her, but she didn't fall.

"Are you sure you don't want to sit down?" Rileigh asked.

"How?" The word was a whisper on a breath.

"Someone killed her," Mitch said. She had to know, but hearing those words… Every grief counselor will tell you that it's easier to hear the truth, plain and not sugar-coated, than to have the process of finding out the worst news of your life drawn out with vagueness and evasions that are all about the sensibilities of the person delivering the news, not the person on the receiving end.

"It was them *witches*," Mrs. Giordano said. "They're the ones done it."

There was a conversation stopper.

The old woman sat abruptly, or maybe her knees collapsed out from under her. But she was aiming at no particular piece of furniture, would have been dumped on the floor if a recliner hadn't happened to be positioned behind where she was standing. She landed on the over-stuffed arm and slid off it onto the seat.

"What do you mean—" Mitch began, but the old woman wasn't listening to him. Her voice remained an airless whisper.

"… told Annie and them others not to get mixed up in that." The woman's eyes connected with Mitch's. "She said she was going to become a witch— can you believe, my sweet Annie, a … a *witch*."

Chapter Six

As MITCH and Rileigh drove the winding road to Jaclyn Milford's house, Rileigh told Mitch that most everyone in the county had believed Jaclyn's grandmother was a witch — a white witch.

"There are other terms for people like Granny Milford, like 'cunning folk'. I'm sure Mama and Aunt Daisy knew a lot of them."

"What's the difference between a white witch and—"

"There's magic ... and then there's *magic*. Harmful magic is black magic, where people use some sort of power to harm others. But cunning folk practice, there's a word for it, give me a minute —*apotropaic* magic — which is the power to avert evil influences or bad luck. Mostly white witches just help people with simple things, like healing, making things grow, finding lost items — and, of course, love potions and fertility."

She would have told him more, but suddenly her phone tweeted like a bird in the woods.

Mitch smiled.

"Georgia," he said.

The bird tweet was the only individualized ringtone on her phone. Rileigh's best friend since elementary school, Georgia Stump, had programmed it in one evening as they sat together in the stands watching a softball game.

Rileigh smiled back at him as she answered. "Hel—"

"You remember when we were in high school chemistry class?" Georgia said before Rileigh could even complete the greeting. Georgia did that all the time. With five kids, she had way too much going on in her life to waste any of it on pleasantries, and she often started a conversation in the middle so that you had an uneasy feeling that there might have been lots of important points made before she even called you, and suspected that she'd hang up before you had a chance to say all you wanted.

A suspicion that often proved accurate.

"I remember we mixed the wrong things together and the combination blew up in our faces, singed my eyebrows off," Rileigh said.

"Yes, *that!*"

"Why are we talking about an explosion in chem class that happened when George Bush was president?"

"Because that's what it was like. It was like that explosion in chem class."

"*What* was like the explosion in—"

"The summer solstice celebration on the square yesterday afternoon. I invited you to come with me, but you said *nooooo*. I was going to call last night and tell you all about it, but Eli ate too much pizza and threw up in Mason's shoe, pieces of pepperoni—"

"Thank you for that visual."

"Girlfriend, you totally missed the party."

"I don't know what there is to celebrate about the summer solstice, other than the Earth is closest to the sun — so yeah, warm! — and it's the longest day of the year.

People have attached all kinds of significance to it that has nothing to do with either one of those things, but I don't understand why you'd want to throw a party."

"Oh, honey, it wasn't the summer solstice *celebration* that was the party. It was everything else. You remember that movie, *The Perfect Storm*?"

"Where are you going with this, Georgia?"

"You remember that scene where the meteorologists are looking at the radar screens and they realize that two hurricanes are about to crash into each other and make the perfect storm?"

"The scene I remember is that little bitty boat trying to chug up a wave the size of Mount Rushmore and flopping over and everybody drowning."

"Well, yesterday afternoon on the square in Black Bear Forge, Tennessee, it was the perfect storm. Not two hurricanes — *four.*"

"Could we dispense with the analogies, the chem lab explosion and the movie, and you just tell me what the hell happened?"

"It was like—"

"Not like. I don't want to know what it was like. I want to know what it *was*."

"Okay. There were people who had come to celebrate the solstice. They got permission from the council to build a bonfire on that little piece of grass out on the front lawn of the courthouse."

"A bonfire?"

"It wasn't much of a bonfire, more on the order of a small campfire, but it was a fire and apparently that was the point, that it was fire."

"So ... what? Did the fire spread to the courthouse?"

"This is my story. Let me tell it."

"Then tell it."

"The people who had come to celebrate the solstice were dancing around the fire and singing songs and chanting."

"That sounds harmless enough."

"I thought so, too, but other people in the crowd were of a different persuasion altogether. I finally figured out what the deal is. The people who were dancing around the fire were Wiccans. Do you know what Wicca is?"

"Wicca is more or less—"

Georgia didn't wait for a definition. "Well, whatever it is, it has something to do with — here's the money shot — witches!"

Georgia was talking so loud that Mitch had heard the whole conversation. He shot a look at Rileigh.

"Witches?" she asked.

"Yup. I think I understand it enough to know that not all witches are Wiccans, and not all Wiccans are witches. But—"

"But *some* Wiccans are witches and *some* witches are Wiccans. I get it. Can we move on?"

"Okay, so, the Wiccans and the witches are one of the storms. The second storm was some dude I have never seen before who reminded me of Gavin Newsom."

"Who the hell is Gavin—?"

"You know, the governor of California. He's slick, smooth, always has an answer — totally Teflon, good in front of a camera. This guy was that. I didn't catch his name, but I did catch what he's here for. Apparently, he bought that little church building out on the edge of town on Donner Pike."

"The old Lutheran church? Doesn't it have a hole in the roof?"

"I don't know about that, but I know he bought it, and I know he's going to build a church there."

"Well, good. I'm glad to hear—"

"No, you're not."

"Why am I not?"

"Because the church he's going to build worships Satan."

"You didn't say that."

"If I'm lying, I'm dying."

"You're telling me somebody's turning that little Lutheran church into a Satanist church? Why in the world would somebody come *here* for that?"

"You got me. But that guy got into it with those Wiccans, or witches, or both. They were going at it."

"Define going at it."

"Getting in each other's faces and screaming."

"Sounds like I did miss a show. That's two storms, witches and Wiccans fighting with Satanists, but you said four storms."

"And then along comes Zeke Wakefield."

"Oh, no."

"Oh, yes."

The right Reverend Ezekiel Wakefield was the pastor of a little Pentecostal — pronounced Penny-costal, of course — church in Juniper Hollow, one of those you-can't-get-there-from-here places. The congregation of the Mountain Shakers Fire Baptized Holiness Church consisted of a handful of people from the lunatic fringe.

Rileigh had heard he conducted snake-handling and poison services. The snake handling was probably just rural legend, but she knew for a fact that Fire Chief Pete Brady had been a member of the rescue squad when they were called to the church to resuscitate a guy who had drunk arsenic. He didn't make it, and Pete said it was an awful way to die.

Rev. Wakefield's son, Ross, had been in an accident a

couple of years ago and was in a wheelchair, paralyzed from the waist down. Zeke was a personable fellow who had an easy smile and a deep backwoods accent, and you could mistake him for a normal person if you didn't listen to him talk. According to Zeke Wakefield, Earth was a battleground where devils were fighting angels in invisible battles 24/7 and every third person you passed on the street was possessed. God himself had commissioned Zeke to seek out the demons behind every bush and exorcise them.

"Oh, it was a sight to behold, girlfriend. While the Satanists were screaming at the witches who might or might not have been Wiccan, Wakefield showed up and started screaming at everybody. Wakefield claimed that the devil was going to take all of Yarmouth County to hell in a handbasket because of that little Lutheran church being sold to a Satanist church. And the Satanist guy, whose name I can't remember, was claiming that the witches and the Wiccans were responsible for the bad reputation of Satanists, that they weren't the same thing at all, and he didn't appreciate being dragged through the mud behind them in the stupid solstice ceremony. And of course, the Wiccans were mad at… well, I'm not sure they were mad at anybody. They were just singing and dancing around the campfire. But—" Georgia paused for dramatic effect. "—that's not the end of the story."

"I await enlightenment with bated breath."

"Yeah, whatever. The fourth storm came roaring down Main Street like Hurricane Katrina. Two words for you. Ethel. Snodmotz."

"I should've guessed! Snoddy wouldn't miss such a fine opportunity to condemn somebody for doing something she didn't approve of."

Nobody called that woman Snoddy to her face and

lived to tell the tale. She was perhaps the homeliest human being, male or female, Rileigh had ever met. Looked like she'd been assembled from left-over body parts in the garage. Her legs were as skinny and shapeless as golf clubs, holding up a torso where eighty or so pounds of excess weight was layered in a slab on her back and a bulge in her belly. Her head was small, and it appeared to rest directly on her shoulders with no discernible neck. And her face…

Aunt Daisy once said that Ethel Snodmotz's face was so ugly, it'd make a train take a dirt road, whatever that meant. Ethel was as mean and spiteful as Aunt Daisy, though probably marginally saner, and there wasn't a person, an idea, an organization, or an activity she couldn't find fault with. She belonged to a normal, mainline independent protestant church, but apparently the minister and congregation there were so cowed by her meanness that nobody dared to tell the old bitch to shut up and mind her own business.

Rileigh supposed it'd be hard to find a more target rich environment for the old biddy than the zoo Georgia was describing.

"She yelled at the Wiccans for being witches and the witches for being Wiccans and the Satanists for being … well, Satanists. You know how she is, though, wouldn't say the word 'shit' if her mouth was full of it." Everyone knew that Ethel never cursed. Cursing was a sin. "She said things like 'those poopy witches.' Poopy, for crying out loud. Said they were 'full of doo-doo.' Then she got up on the courthouse steps and said she'd had a personal celestial visitation from the Archangel Gabriel himself and he had revealed to her who was going to be cast into the outer darkness of hell for their sins. Then she started *naming names*. And those people were *pissed!*"

"I would have paid cash money to have seen that."

Mitch spoke for the first time then.

"Mullins and Rawlings reported they'd had to break up a free-for-all in front of the courthouse yesterday, but I thought it must have been a bunch of drunks."

"Oh, those people were cold sober. But they got so out of control that if they'd been drunk too, they'd have burned down the whole town."

"Sounds like I did, indeed, miss a party."

Georgia's tone turned on a dime. She could do that, be giggling and frivolous one second, then serious and compassionate a heartbeat later.

"You and Mitch are out there investigating that murder, aren't you?"

Of course, Georgia had heard about it.

"Uh huh."

"Was it as ugly as everybody's saying?"

"I don't know what everybody's saying, but it was ugly."

"You be careful."

"Not you, too."

"Me too what?"

"You too with the 'be careful.' I already got that this morning from Jillian."

"Mitch!" Georgia cried, too loud, as if she had to raise her voice so he could hear when he'd been listening to every word she'd said. "You tell her to be careful, too, and that'll be three of us. Three times is the charm." She suddenly yelled out even louder, but obviously at neither Rileigh nor Mitch. "No, Mason, don't you *dare* — I gotta run." Then there was silence.

Rileigh looked at Mitch. "Charms. Magic."

He finished for her, "And witches."

Chapter Seven

Jaclyn Milford lived in a nice neighborhood. Either she had done pretty well for herself or she had a sugar daddy, and Rileigh didn't think it was door number two. She'd known Jaclyn since she was seven years old —Rileigh had been her babysitter. She'd been adorable even then, and unlike a lot of children who were attractive as kids and grew out of it, she transformed from a pretty little girl to a beautiful woman. Her hair was yellow, the color of butter. *Naturally* yellow. Had been that color when she was seven, hung in huge natural curls that framed her face. Big corn-flower blue eyes that turned up at the corners, the kind of heart-shaped mouth that men went all stupid over, and dimples stapled in both cheeks deep enough to eat pudding out of.

Like most high school seniors, Jaclyn couldn't wait to get out of Black Bear Forge, and she was gone for a couple of years, going to college or working. Rileigh didn't know which. Then she came back home and got her own little town home, had to be making good money to afford it. It wasn't in one of the fancy new complexes. It was in an older development with an architect who'd had the good judgment to blend the structures he'd built into the surrounding environment. The buildings seemed to fit there on the side of the mountain like they had grown naturally out of the rocks.

Rileigh was pretty sure Jaclyn worked from home now, built websites and did data processing. Her town home was an end unit, so her front windows had a view down the valley, and her side and back windows looked out into the surrounding woods. It was more private than the ones with neighbors on both sides.

Mitch pulled his cruiser up behind Jaclyn's little Mazda. They didn't know whether or not Jaclyn was aware of what had happened to her friend, Annie. The way word spread in this town, Rileigh would be surprised if she hadn't heard already. But if she hadn't, then they would have the unpleasant task of telling her that her best friend had been murdered, just as they'd had to deliver the same news to her best friend's mother.

They walked up the short set of steps to the front door, and instantly saw the marks on the door, the doorframe, and the walls around it. They'd been crudely drawn using … red paint, maybe. No, not paint. Rileigh thought about Gus's remark. "What'd the killer do with all that blood?"

She shot Mitch a look and he nodded agreement. Maybe the killer had used some of it to make these marks.

Mitch took out his phone and took photographs of the bloody runes. Close-up shots to display the shape of each individual rune. Wider shots to indicate any kind of design in the way they were painted on the door and walls.

Rileigh studied the marks. Some of them were familiar shapes. There was a pentagram within a circle, but it appeared to be upside down. A Celtic knot of three interlocking circles. An Ankh. A stylistic letter "y" with small circles on the ends of the lines. An inverted cross. What looked like a spiral, though the dripping blood had smeared and blurred the shape. A number three, with the top line extended and formed into a small circle, and a line extending down from the bottom line that also ended in a small circle. A swastika, and a triangle with a circle inside it that might or might not have been a human eye.

When he was finished taking pictures, Mitch pulled from his pocket a plastic bag and scraped into it the substance that had been used to make the marks that looked and smelled like blood. Rileigh supposed it could be something else. That would be Gus's problem to figure out.

Mitch punched the button beside the door and a cheery, distinctive "ding-dong" rang out inside. A voice called out, "I don't know who it is, but I don't want to talk to anybody."

Mitch rang the bell again, waited, then knocked and called out, "This is Yarmouth County Sheriff Mitchell Webster, and I need to talk to Jaclyn Wakefield."

They heard the sound of movement behind the door, then a young woman opened it.

She looked awful. Her face was deathly pale, her eyes swollen from crying, her hair, a bedhead tangle. At least Rileigh and Mitch wouldn't have to tell her what had happened to Annie. Clearly, she'd heard about it already.

"What do you want?" she asked. Then she looked from Mitch to Rileigh, and her face changed.

"Rileigh?" she asked.

Rileigh smiled and said, "Hey, Bunny Rabbit."

A ghost of a smile skittered across the girl's pale face and then was gone.

"Bunny Rabbit?" Mitch looked from one to the other.

"When I used to babysit for Jaclyn, I made up this silly nickname. Jaclyn ... jackrabbit ... bunny rabbit. Get it?"

"And you got me a bunny at Easter. Remember that little pink stuffed bunny?"

"I had forgotten about that," Rileigh said. "Anyway, the 'Bunny' kind of stuck."

"Yeah. I've been collecting stuffed bunnies and getting rabbit figurines for Christmas—" She nodded to a shelf on the wall just inside the front door, filled with all sizes and shapes of porcelain rabbits. "—my whole life, thanks to you. I also have a white lop-eared rabbit named Ernie." She gestured vaguely toward the back of the townhome. "He's my famil—" She stopped abruptly and started over. "He's deaf. A lot of lops are deaf. Ear canals are too narrow. My boyfriend got me a little black kitten for my birthday last summer and she'd sneak up on Ernie because he couldn't hear her." She stopped babbling and just stood there, looking shell-shocked.

"Did you make these designs around your door?" Mitch asked.

She looked at them, obviously noticing them for the first time.

"No. I ... what are ... I didn't put them there."

"Do you recognize the symbols?"

She looked closer. "Some of them."

"Do you know what this means?" Rileigh asked, gesturing toward all the symbols.

"No, and I don't know who put it there. Or why. How will I get it off? I don't know ... I don't ..."

She looked like she was about to burst into tears.

"May we come in?" Mitch asked.

Jaclyn nodded and moved out of the doorway, walked ahead of them down a hallway into the living room and plopped down on the big love seat.

"You're here about Annie."

46

It wasn't a question, but Rileigh answered it, nodding. "Yes, we are."

"What do you want to talk to *me* about?"

"How much do you know about how——"

"How she died? I know she was murdered! I know something slit her throat and drained all her blood out. I know——"

"Some*thing*?" Rileigh asked. "What——"

Jaclyn rolled over the question.

"I know the murderer did something with all that blood. What could you do with that much blood?"

Rileigh didn't mention her suspicion that some of it was used to draw symbols on the front of Jaclyn's townhouse. The girl was circling the drain again, about to lose it, so Rileigh steered the conversation in a different direction.

"I remember your grandmother, Granny Milford, was a white witch."

Jaclyn's face softened. "My Granny Milford was the best human being I ever met. All she cared about was helping people. That's what a white witch does. So that's how I started out, as a Hereditary Witch. That's a witch who has witchcraft as their birthright."

Rileigh thought of college sororities and how the girls in the pledge class whose mother, sister or aunt had belonged to that sorority were called "legacies" and they had a lock on getting in.

"So, there are different kinds of witches?" Mitch asked.

"Oh, sure. There are Augury Witches, who foretell the future, and Cosmic Witches, who use celestial and planetary energy. Hedge Witches focus on herbal knowledge and aromatherapy, and Ceremonial Witches specialize in high magic and reaching out to the spirit world through special invocations and rituals."

Jaclyn paused and her face looked drawn. "I started as a Hereditary Witch, but now I'm a Ceremonial Witch."

"You decided to change?" Mitch asked.

"Not so much a decision. It's just that one morphed into the other. I have a gift for—"

She didn't go on. The look of grief that marked her face changed. It became ... was it *fear*? What had frightened her into silence?

"Would you mind telling me what you have to do to become a witch?" Mitch asked.

Rileigh could see he was just trying to keep the girl talking. Jaclyn certainly wasn't the murderer. But if Annie's mother was right and witchcraft had something to do with her daughter's death, then Jaclyn might know something that would give them a clue to find who'd killed her.

Jaclyn tried to focus on the question.

"The first thing is, you have to decide is do you want to be a solitary witch or part of a coven. I started out alone, but then I got three friends ..."

Her voice trailed off.

"Annie and who else? Who were the other two?"

"Veronica Espinosa and Olivia Booth."

"I'm trying to understand this witch thing. What did the four of you have to ... *do*?"

Jaclyn was scrambling to bring her mind to bear on what he was asking.

"You have to make an altar." She pointed to a table in the corner. "That's mine. Other witches have different altars. It's very personal."

The altar was nothing more than a couple of shelves with rocks and crystals on them, plus a bell and a candle and some herbs in a jar.

"You make a besom ... a wand." She pointed to what

looked like a small tree branch about two feet long wrapped with ribbons and beads and colorful tape.

"And you grow your own herbs. I have an herb garden out back with thyme, oregano, parsley, chives, that kind of thing. And then ... you practice ... you know, casting spells."

"Did you and Annie cast spells?"

Jaclyn got instantly defensive. "We all did. That's what witches *do.*"

"Annie's mother thinks her murder has something to do with witchcraft," Rileigh said. "Do you know what she's talking about?"

Rileigh was pretty good at reading people. And Jaclyn Wakefield was lousy at hiding her feelings. Put those together and there was a one hundred percent chance that Jaclyn Wakefield was hiding something.

The girl stammered a little. Stuttered. Then told Rileigh, "I don't know. I do know Annie's mother never liked it. My mother never liked it either. Neither did Ronnie's. I don't know about Liv's."

Rileigh and Mitch allowed silence to coax more out of her.

"I get it," Jaclyn continued. "It's hard, you know. Your kid comes home and says they want to be a witch. That's got to be hard to swallow. But you know, it's just Wicca, just a religion. Like Christianity. There's nothing wrong with it."

More silence.

"I mean, lots of people don't like it. When we did the summer solstice celebration, there were all kinds of people who got their noses out of joint about it."

"Not liking witchcraft, being offended by witches or Wicca — those aren't very powerful motives for murder," Rileigh said.

Jaclyn just shrugged. Time to pull the rug out from under her.

"You're hiding something, Jaclyn. What are you not telling me?"

Jaclyn jumped like somebody had stuck her with a cattle prod.

"I don't know what you mean," she sputtered. "I don't know anything about Annie's murder. I don't know who would want to kill her, if that's what you're asking me. I don't. I can't imagine that anybody would want to kill ... I mean, Annie is ... is..."

Then she burst into tears, put her face in her hands and sobbed.

When Jaclyn finally got control of herself again, Rileigh tried to get a little more information out of her, asked for a list of names of the other coven members. Jaclyn said there were probably a dozen, maybe more than that. She didn't know all of them by name. They just showed up at services.

"Is there some special significance to Buttermilk Falls?" Mitch asked. "Is there a reason that it would be a special place for Annie?"

"Not that I know of. I mean, if I was the one who'd been murdered ..." She shivered when she said that. "Buttermilk Falls is where my ex-fiancé proposed to me. But Annie didn't have any kind of connection to it, other than it's a beautiful place and we went there sometimes, you know, on picnics or just to wade in the creek below the waterfall."

Jaclyn was in no condition to keep answering questions, so Rileigh and Mitch got up to leave. Rileigh hugged Jaclyn and told her, "Look, if you think of anything that you think is important, anything that would help explain what happened to Annie, you give me a call."

"Okay," she said weakly.

"And girlfriend …" Rileigh said, putting her hands on Jaclyn's shoulders, "I know you're holding something back on me."

"No, no, I'm not. I'm just … I'm upset, that's all. I'm just upset."

Rileigh looked at her kindly and said, "Bullshit."

Then she held up her hand before Jaclyn could protest.

"I'm going to let it ride for right now. Just know I'm not going to let it ride forever. I want to know what you're not telling me."

Rileigh and Mitch walked out to his cruiser, and she settled in the passenger seat beside him.

"What do you think it is, what's she not saying?" Mitch said.

"Not a clue. But I'll get it out of her eventually."

Chapter Eight

VERONICA ESPINOSA LIVED in a three-bedroom brick house on Sulphur Springs Road with her parents, and maybe some siblings, the voter registration rolls didn't say. It was an old house but not run down, and the yard was neat, the grass mowed and edged around the sidewalk. A lush flower bed surrounded the porch, and shrubs lined the driveway leading up to the walk beside the house.

There were small trailer houses on either side of the brick. One appeared to be vacant, and an old man sat in a rocking chair on the attached porch of the other one.

There was no car parked in Veronica's driveway. Mitch pulled his cruiser into the driveway, where he could see runes and symbols marked in red around the door and on the door frame. He and Rileigh got out and approached the house. Mitch took out his phone and took pictures of the marks.

"That what you come out here for, that vandalism?" called the old man from the porch next door.

"Did you see who put these marks here?" Mitch asked.

"Nope. They was there when I got up this morning. I

wasn't curious enough to get up and go take a closer look — got bad knees from jumping out of perfectly good airplanes in the Army. Are they letters or words or something?"

"We're not sure," Mitch said, scraping off a sample into an evidence bag.

"Well, if it's some sort of message, ain't nobody seen it yet. If you're looking for the Espinosas, you can forget about it. They're off on a cruise ship somewhere, left a week ago and won't be back for god knows how long. They're retired, travel all the time, just come home every now and then, stay long enough to wash their underwear. Then they're off again."

"Actually, we're looking for Veronica. You got any idea where she is?"

"I don't keep track of where that girl goes and where she don't. Flittin' around the way she does, she's a little hummingbird, going from one flower to the next."

Rileigh and Mitch crossed the yard of mowed grass to the patch of weeds in front of the old man's trailer. The old guy was dressed in a pair of cargo shorts that displayed skinny white legs and knobby knees. His top was a University of Tennessee Volunteer's t-shirt that probably had been orange once. That was the school color, after all, but it was faded now to a blotchy indistinct gold.

"Sounds like you know Veronica," Mitch said as he climbed the steps to the neighbor's porch. The man had an open can of beer in his hand and a cooler full of beer behind him. A ripped garbage bag leaned against the side of the trailer was bleeding empty cans out into the weeds.

"I know Ronnie, in a manner of speaking," the old man said. "What do you want to know for?" Then he looked stricken. "That little girl ain't in no trouble with the law, is she? 'Cause if she is, it's lies, whatever anybody's saying, it's all lies."

"She's not in any trouble, we just need to talk to her."

"What about? She don't have to talk to you if she don't want to. You can't make her say nothing. Imma tell her that. Imma tell her she don't have to say nary a word to the law."

"We're not here because of anything Veronica has done," Rileigh assured him. "We're here to ask about a friend of hers."

"Just 'cause she works in that head shop don't mean she was dealing drugs or nothing like that." He pointed toward the vacant trailer house nearby. "That fellow was a drug dealer. There was traffic going in and out of that place, all hours of the night and day, buying and selling. But then he up and vanished. I don't know where he went. He was here one day and gone the next — likely dodging the landlord, skipping out on the rent. It ain't like that with Ronnie."

"We're here to ask questions about a friend of hers."

"Who?"

"Annamaria Giordano."

"Never heard of her."

"Ronnie has. Annie was a friend of hers."

"*Was?*"

"She was murdered last night."

"And you think little Ronnie's got something to do with that? You've lost your mind. Why that little girl wouldn't swat a wasp if it was stinging her on the nose."

"Veronica isn't a suspect. But she might have information about who would have had a motive."

The old man settled back in his chair then, clearly relieved.

"That what them marks is about — that girl getting kilt?"

"We don't know why the marks are there or who put them there."

"No telling who coulda done it. She runs with a strange crowd. Bunch of weirdos."

"Weirdos?"

"People come to that house at all hours of the day and night. Dressed funny, in long black dresses and black capes. And there are lights blinking on and off all the time. Sometimes I seen a whole group of 'em leave the house and go up in the woods at night, 'specially when there's a full moon. Didn't take no flashlights, just candles. I don't know what they was doing up there. I should've gone and looked. They were singing these weird-ass songs and chanting. Making all kinds of strange noises." The old man stopped and leaned forward. "There's them that says they was a coven of witches. I don't know about that, but they was weird."

"Did you ever have any problems with Veronica or any of her visitors?" Rileigh asked.

"Hell no!" He wallowed the cheek full of Red Man from his left cheek to his right cheek, spit a big gob of juice onto the ground just beyond the porch, and continued, clearly grateful to have an audience to listen to him pontificate. "As neighbors go, she's better'n most. Aw, she puts on airs of being all sophisticated, all grown up and 'different' with them tattoos all over her and them piercings. But she's just a mountain girl at heart, come over one afternoon last summer and said she made a big batch of chocolate chip cookies, was expecting company and they didn't show up. She asked did I want some. Fresh, hot chocolate chip cookies — hell, yeah, I wanted some! She sat down on the porch and we ate cookies and drank lemonade. She's a good girl, and ain't many I'd say that about. It's just them weird people she runs with and the weird shit she does.

You need to go back out in the woods behind that house and take a look at whatever it was they were doing there. They was making so much noise and carrying on, there's bound to be marks of something."

"We'll do that, Mister …?" Mitch said.

"What do you need to know my name for? I ain't done nothing."

Rileigh rolled her eyes. "We can go down to the road and read it off the side of your mailbox or—"

"Herndon. Festus Herndon. And don't you go telling Ronnie I was saying bad things about her. That girl …" he paused, clearly reluctant to say more. "… she helps me out." He made a vague gesture toward his pickup truck, parked in his weedy driveway. "You know, when I can't pass the test after they put that damn contraption on my truck."

Mitch realized what he was talking about then. He knew the state highway patrol used ignition interlocks on repeat DUI offenders. Interlocks were miniature breathalyzers, wired into a vehicle's electronics, that prevent the engine from starting unless the person behind the wheel is sober enough to drive.

When he said Ronnie "helped him out," it was possible the old man meant Ronnie used his truck to purchase alcohol for him when he was too inebriated to drive himself. But he also could have meant that Ronnie helped him game the system, blowing into the device for him so he could pass the test and the engine would start. If that's how Ronnie had been helping him, it was only a matter of time before he got caught. The machine was programmed to perform rolling resets, randomly requiring additional breaths samples to show the driver hadn't been drinking on the road. The resets require the driver to lift a hand off the wheel, pick up the device and blow — hard — into its mouthpiece for several seconds. If the driver failed or didn't comply, the car went into panic mode: its headlights flashed and its horn honked until the driver turned off the engine.

"You tell Ronnie for me that I didn't say nothing about her but good things, you hear. That girl knows how to make fine chocolate chip cookies, pecans in them and everything. One time they had raisins!"

Rileigh and Mitch left the old man on the porch and trekked up into the woods behind Veronica Espinosa's house. They could see where the grass had been mashed down and lots of footprints, but there was nothing else to be seen.

"I'm sure this is a covenstead," Rileigh said.

Mitch gave her a look. "And a covenstead is…?"

"It's a meeting place for a coven of witches."

"And you know that how?"

She smiled and tapped her phone.

"Google is your friend."

Chapter Nine

When Mitch and Rileigh pulled up in front of the small trailer house where Olivia Booth lived on Postal Clerk Lane, the first thing Rileigh noticed was that, unlike Jaclyn's town home and Veronica's parents' house, there were no runes of any kind around the door, on the door, or on the wall beside it.

Strictly speaking, Olivia didn't live in a trailer house, because that term had been cancelled. So had "mobile home" which was knocked off its spot in the lexicon by the current nomenclature — manufactured home.

This particular manufactured home was not a double-wide, but it was large and it fit snug into the little hollow where a creek ran beside the road and under a bridge. When they got out of the cruiser and stepped up on the little attached porch — which wasn't as stable as you'd like a porch to be — Rileigh realized why there were no runes or sigils or symbols around the door. The whole front of the little mobile home had been recently scrubbed clean.

"Do you think there were marks here but Olivia washed them off?" Rileigh asked, and Mitch shrugged.

He knocked on the door, and Olivia Booth opened it before he could knock a second time. Maybe she'd been looking out the window and saw them drive up. Or, more likely, she'd likely had a heads-up from Jaclyn warning her that they were coming.

She didn't look as bad as Jaclyn, but Rileigh could tell she had been crying and that she was nervous and jumpy.

Jaclyn had described Annie as a tiny little thing who had dreamed her whole life of making it to five feet tall. Olivia must have towered over her. She was maybe six feet, with the willowy arms and legs you'd expect on a model. Her skin was a tawny brown, her facial features delicate, and Rileigh guessed she was of Ethiopian heritage.

Her hair was cut so short that it formed a tight black cap on her head.

"I'm Yarmouth County Sheriff Mitch Webster and this is Rileigh Bishop, and we want to talk to you about—"

"I know why you're here," she said. "Jaclyn called and said you'd probably be coming by. But I don't know anything so you're wasting your time asking me questions."

"May we come in?" Mitch asked.

"Suit yourself. But like I say, I don't know anything, so you're wasting your time."

She started to open the door and Mitch pointed to the frame around it. "You washed it all off, didn't you?"

Olivia looked surprised and Rileigh could see her deciding whether or not she was going to lie about it.

"Washed what off?"

"The bloody marks someone made on your front door, just like they did on Ronnie's and Jaclyn's. Do you have any idea who did that?"

"I got a call in the middle of the night about Annie. I was freaked out, never went back to bed. When Jaclyn mentioned the marks this morning, I ran to the door and there they were. It was awful. But the thing was, I was *here*. The whole time somebody was on my front porch drawing symbols with blood, I was here and I didn't hear a thing."

She shivered.

"May we come in?" Mitch asked again.

"Fine. Come in. Sit down. Ask me a bunch of questions, and then will you leave?"

"We won't have many questions."

"Good. Because I don't have any answers." She turned on her heel and flounced back into the living room. Mitch and Rileigh followed.

"Whoa," Rileigh said, and stopped dead still ... staring at a huge barn owl perched on a fake tree limb inside a big cage.

"That's Casper," Olivia said. "My familiar."

Rileigh thought she knew what a familiar was. Just like she thought she knew a lot of things about witches which might or might not be true. She and Mitch needed more and better information.

Olivia's was not as neat and tidy a place as Jaclyn's had been. Clothes were scattered around on the floor. There were dishes in the sink and on the kitchen table. On a table in front of a window, Riley saw what must have been Olivia's altar. Like Jaclyn's, lying on that altar was a stick with ribbons, wire, and beads wrapped around it. What was it Jaclyn had called it? A besom. A magic wand!

There were other things on the table that hadn't been at Jaclyn's house. A small statue of a female skeleton in a purple robe holding a scythe and a globe beside a drum that looked homemade. And a doll of black cloth that was definitely handmade, with pins in it. Was that voodoo?

Olivia saw Rileigh looking at the items on the table. "I'm Cuban," she said. "Second generation American." So much for Ethiopian heritage. "My parents brought the old traditions with them — Santería and voodoo."

She pointed to the doll. "It's not what you think. That's me, the doll is me. The seven colored pins are what I'm seeking. Yellow is for success and confidence, blue is peace and love, purple is spirituality and wisdom."

"You're not from here—" Rileigh began.

"I'm from away-from-here, I know."

"So how do you know Jaclyn, Annie, and Veronica?"

"I spent a couple of hours with them once in a storm shelter. Two, no, maybe three years ago, when that big bunch of tornadoes came through here. Do you remember?"

Rileigh had been a Memphis police officer at the time, but she knew that Mama and Aunt Daisy had been terrified.

"Anyway, there was a public shelter under a bank building in Gatlinburg and people jammed in there, tourists from off the street, store owners. But when the sirens blasted out all clear, they couldn't get the door open. We were all stuck there in there, nothing to do but wait. The four of us got to talking, and by the time they got the doors open, we were exchanging phone numbers."

"So, who started the coven?"

"Jaclyn came up with the idea. She understood witchcraft because her grandmother was a witch. Did you know that?"

Rileigh nodded. "I used to babysit Jaclyn when she was a little girl."

Olivia shook her head. "Seems like everybody around here is connected to everybody else somehow."

"I've noticed that," Mitch said dryly.

"But it wasn't just about Jaclyn's grandmother," Olivia continued. "She'd done all kinds of research on it. We talked and talked about it. When Jaclyn became a witch, Ronnie decided to become one, too. Then so did Annie. I was the holdout."

She looked around her, then pointed to the figure of a skeleton in a purple robe. "That's Santa Muerte." Saint Death. "When I was a little girl, she was like a Barbie Doll to me because Mama was always changing her robe — different colors according to the ritual she was performing. My grandmother used a doll to change her life — she'd ask the voodoo spirits, the Loas, to help her be stronger or calmer. She had a temper." Olivia made a gesture encompassing the room. "The others didn't believe much of anything, you know, they were just Christians. So it took me longer than it did them to figure out how being a witch could pull everything together in my life."

It was becoming clear to Rileigh that the four witches had mashed together the doctrines and ideologies of various religious practices — a buffet of beliefs where they picked and chose the ones that suited them.

Olivia got up off the couch and began to pace. "Look, you've come here to ask me what I know about Annie's murder. And the answer is, I don't know anything about what happened to her, but it scares me to death."

That seemed an odd remark to Riley, *scares me to death.* The murder of a friend is not upsetting, but frightening?

"Why does that scare you?"

"Because I don't want the same thing to happen to me, that's why!"

"And why would it?"

Olivia got a spooky look on her face and closed up like a clam.

"You know how it is, random violence like that. You never know where it's going to strike."

"You're saying you're afraid that what happened to

Annie might happen to you because the same random violence that struck her might strike you?" Rileigh asked. "That would be quite a coincidence, wouldn't it?"

"Look, I'm afraid. Who isn't be these days? What is it you want to know about Annie?"

"Do you know if there was any special attachment she had to Buttermilk Falls?"

"Not that I know of."

"Do you know if she had any enemies, had received any threats, had—"

"Let me save you the trouble of asking all these stupid questions, okay? Annie was the kindest, sweetest, most adorable human being on the planet. She never made an enemy in her life and certainly hadn't pissed off somebody bad enough that they'd murder her."

Rileigh did her best not to roll her eyes. "Well, somebody did murder her, so apparently she pissed somebody off."

Olivia opened her mouth to speak, then closed it again.

"Yeah, I guess she did. She pissed somebody off bad enough that they killed her. But I don't know who it is. I don't have any idea. And you need to quit wasting your time and mine. You need to be out there talking to people who do know something about who might have killed her."

Riley and Mitch tried for another five or ten minutes to get information from Olivia, but she had shut down. She wasn't just uncooperative, she was practically mute, answering their questions with one- and two-syllable words. Finally, they gave up and left.

Riley slipped into the passenger seat of Mitch's cruiser in the driveway of Olivia's trailer house as Mitch started the engine.

"What did you notice in there, besides the fact that there's an owl in her living room?" he said.

"She said the owl was her familiar. I think that's what Jaclyn was about to say about the rabbit, Ernie, that it was her familiar."

"No, I mean on the wall. Those pictures."

"Yeah, Santeria. Did you notice the statue, Santa Muerte?"

"I definitely noticed the voodoo doll," Mitch said.

"She was obviously into magic of some sort before she ever met Jaclyn and Annie. What else I picked up on was how scared she was."

"Like Jaclyn, she knows more than she's saying. And what she's *not* saying is important."

"I think she has an idea who killed Annie. She's afraid that whoever killed Annie is going to kill her, too."

"What connects the two of them?"

"They're both witches," Mitch said. "All four of them are witches. According to Georgia's description, that pissed off a lot of people at that summer solstice ceremony."

"Enough to commit murder?"

"That's what we need to find out."

Chapter Ten

It was the middle of the afternoon before Rileigh got home, and she was exhausted, mentally, physically, and emotionally. The day had started long before the rooster crowed with a call from Mitch asking her to come to Buttermill Falls. And for the rest of the morning, she had talked to the friends of the girl whose throat looked like it had been ripped out.

She pulled off the road and up into the driveway with the lump at the top, then sat for a moment in her car, getting her head together. Jillian hadn't wanted her to go when she left this morning. Rileigh didn't want to come back all frazzled and upset, because that would make it harder for Jillian to accept what she was doing.

She came in the front door and called out, "Hello, hello!"

Jillian came running to the top of the stairs. She had paint splatters on the smock that Rileigh had gotten her. Rileigh smiled when she saw it.

"You've been painting," Rileigh said, as Jillian came down the stairs.

"How about we don't talk about what I've been doing," Jillian said. "What have *you* been doing this morning?"

No way in hell was Rileigh going to tell her what she'd been doing, not specifically.

Thankfully, Mama came out of the kitchen then, drying her hands on a kitchen towel. "Are you hungry?"

"No, I'm not hungry, Mama."

"Aw, come on, you've got to eat something."

The very thought of food turned her stomach. But she knew Mama needed to look after her, and one of the ways that she expressed her love was to cook.

"Okay, Mama, sure, I'd love a sandwich. Would you mind?"

Mama had already turned on her heel and was headed back to the kitchen. "I got ham and cheese and some tomatoes out of the garden. They're fresh and they taste so good. You want some cucumbers on that sandwich?"

Mama continued talking and asking questions as she walked into the kitchen, even though Rileigh couldn't hear what she was asking anymore and Mama couldn't have heard her answer.

"I want to see what you've painted," Rileigh said to Jillian, starting up the stairs.

"You have yet to answer my question," Jillian remained at the bottom of the stairs, unmoving. "Come on, what have you been doing this morning?"

"Let's make a deal. I'll tell you what I've been doing, and you can show me what you're painting."

Jillian sighed and followed Rileigh up the stairs to the last bedroom on the end.

It had been Rileigh's idea, the studio. She remembered that Jillian had always drawn cute little pictures of rabbits and squirrels and such to put on Rileigh's walls. It seemed to Rileigh that Jillian had always been sketching something.

So she suggested they turn the empty bedroom at the end of the hall into a studio and get an easel and some paints for Jillian.

Jillian had protested all the way, of course. She didn't know how to paint. She didn't know how to draw. This was a waste of money. But Rileigh and Mama pretty much ignored her and made it a studio anyway, stocking it with all manner of art supplies. To Rileigh's utter delight, Jillian had sat on the porch swing that night with one of the sketch pads and a pencil. While Mama and Rileigh had talked, Jillian sketched Mama's face.

It wasn't very good. Maybe Jillian had never had any talent, or perhaps she hadn't been able to practice what she could do for so long, she'd forgotten how. Rileigh gushed over it anyway, and so did Mama. The next day, Rileigh found Jillian in the studio, with paints and a palette, plus Rileigh's laptop sitting on the chest of drawers that they had scooted out of the way to clear space for the easel. There hadn't been any other furniture in the room, just stacks of flotsam and jetsam that Rileigh hadn't yet got around to hauling up to the attic.

Rileigh looked at the screen of the computer and discovered that Jillian had called up an art lesson on YouTube. She'd been watching them and trying to absorb what they were teaching.

That had been several days ago. And Jillian had spent a lot of time in the studio since then.

Rileigh was delighted to see the bowl of flowers that Jillian had painted on the canvas on the easel. It was intricate and colorful, but not particularly representative of the bowl of flowers that Jillian had set on the top of the dresser as an inspiration.

"I love the colors," Rileigh said. "The red and the yellow—"

"Stop avoiding the question. Where have you been?"

There was no sense in not telling her, but Rileigh certainly didn't intend to get into detail.

"The sheriff's department was called to the site of a murder last night. Two teenage girls found the body and they refused to talk to Mitch about what they'd been doing there."

"Where did they find it?"

"Buttermilk Falls."

"What were two teen girls doing at Buttermilk Falls in the middle of the night?"

"That's what they wouldn't tell Mitch." Rileigh turned and walked toward her own bedroom, talking as she went. "They were out there to take nude pictures of each other in the full moon with Buttermilk Falls in the background."

"Seriously?"

"That's why they didn't want to talk to Mitch about it."

"So, you've been at Buttermilk Falls all this time?"

"Oh no, the rescue squad came and took the body and gave it to Gus. You met him, remember?"

Rileigh had invited Gus to dinner with Mitch one night last week, to introduce him to Jillian.

Jillian hadn't wanted to go out much since she got home, and Rileigh and Mama certainly didn't push her. But they didn't want to isolate her either. So Georgia had come over and brought the kids one afternoon. They played in the yard, made mud pies, and tracked mud all over the floor. And she'd invited Gus to dinner.

Jillian had been quiet, meeting people she didn't know. But she seemed to enjoy having somebody around besides Mama and Rileigh.

"So, Gus was there?"

"He's the coroner. Didn't we tell you that?"

"Yeah, you told me. Gus and Mitch were there, and there was a dead body."

Jillian was trying to get way more information out of Rileigh than she wanted to give.

"And then Mitch and I went to tell the victim's mother that she had been murdered."

Jillian didn't ask who the murder victim was or how she had been killed. And Rileigh was enormously grateful for that.

"Her mother gave us the names of several of her friends and we went to talk to them."

"Talk to them about what?"

"About Annie, the girl who was killed. It's Mitch's job to find the murderer, and asking questions of these girls was the place to start."

"Why did you go with him?"

"Because ..." Rileigh let the word hang out there for a few moments. Why *had* she gone with him? She'd gone with him because that's just the rhythm they had worked out, the two of them, ever since she got home.

"I went with him because that's just what we do. It started when Mitch got here. I told you about that. About how him being away from here, nobody wanted to talk to him. And—"

"I get that part, but why *you*?"

Rileigh had been taking her muddy shoes off carefully, exchanging her running shoes for a pair of white sneakers, but she stopped and looked at Jillian.

"Jillian, you have to understand this. I was a police officer for nine years."

"I know, you told me,"

"I said it, but I don't think you heard it. It's what I was trained to do. I enjoyed it and I was good at it. And I am grateful to Mitch for the opportunity to help out." She paused. "I'm a damn good cop, Jillian. I really am. I will be helping Mitch find this killer because he needs my help."

"But doesn't he have any deputies?"

"He has deputies. They're very good. They're all men. And that's why he called me in the middle of the night to talk to these girls. Mitch still needs me to—"

"There's something going on between the two of you, isn't there?"

Jillian wasn't stupid and Rileigh was sure that it was obvious to most people that, yeah, there was something going on between her and Mitch.

"There is, but neither one of us knows what it is yet, or what to do about it."

Jillian actually smiled at that.

Mama called from downstairs. "Lunch is ready."

The sisters went downstairs, where Mama had placed a sandwich she'd made for Rileigh on a plate. Rileigh had to take it apart and remove several of the ingredients before she could eat it, though.

A ham sandwich with tomatoes and lettuce and pickles and mayonnaise made sense. But Mama had put cucumbers inside the sandwich too. She'd even sliced up some carrots, and butternut squash, along with a piece of celery.

Rileigh removed the extraneous items without comment and dug into the sandwich.

Mama bustled around the kitchen putting on a pot of pinto beans.

She had soaked the sack of dried pinto beans on the stove overnight, setting them on the stove above the pilot light, and that was enough heat to get them ready for Mama to load bacon and tiny pieces of onion into the pot and then cook it all for the rest of the day. She stirred the pot, the aroma drifting out into the air, and said she'd be making fresh cornbread tonight. She'd fry a mess of squash too.

Jillian had been home long enough to realize that Mama was not dragging a full string of fish anymore. She looked at Rileigh and Rileigh shrugged. Maybe Mama would make cornbread and squash. Maybe she wouldn't. They'd hover around to right the ship if it strayed too far from port.

"Millie called me this afternoon and was telling me about that old Lutheran church. Have you heard about that?"

Rileigh nodded and Jillian shook her head, so Mama continued.

"Well, there's some fella from away-from-here who bought that old Lutheran church building down on Donner Pike. And he's renovating it, turning it into a church."

"Do you know what kind of church?" Rileigh asked. "*That's* the interesting part."

"Millie told me. That's why she called. He's going to make it a church of Satan."

Jillian looked up. "You're joking."

"Millie said that Harriet told her that—"

Rileigh interrupted. "How about we skip the whole line of transmission explanation? We know it was a reliable source. Just tell me what Millie said."

If you let Mama go off on who told who told who about information from the telephone tree, she could talk all day.

"Well, whoever the man is, they're mad at him."

"Who's mad at him?" Jillian asked.

"Everybody."

"Yeah, Georgia told me about that on the phone this morning," Rileigh said. "She told me there was a bit of an altercation yesterday at the summer solstice celebration downtown that we didn't go to."

"Well, I don't know about any alterations, I just know there was a fight," Mama said.

Jillian and Rileigh exchanged small smiles.

"Zeke Wakefield was there spitting hellfire and brimstone. And there was all these women and girls dancing around a fire, and then Snoddy shows up."

"Snoddy!" Jillian asked, "Are you talking about Ethel Snodmotz? She was a senior when I was a freshman."

"Sounds about right," Mama said.

"I think she was the ugliest girl in high school. In the whole history of the high school. But you couldn't feel sorry for her because she wasn't just ugly, she was a bitch."

"She's even meaner now, and just as ugly as she ever was. She got together with Zeke Wakefield's bunch, and they was raising a holy stink about that church of Satan."

"The people who were dancing around the fire were Wiccans," Rileigh said, "Do you know what a Wiccan is?"

"Only wick I know is one you put in a candle."

"Wiccans are witches," Rileigh said. Then she stopped. "No, not all Wiccans are witches, and not all ..." There was no sense in getting into the weeds about this with Mama. She wouldn't remember anyway. "But some of those people dancing around that fire were witches."

"You mean like Granny Milford and that woman over in Baxter County who growed the biggest tomatoes you ever seen?"

"Not quite like that."

"You remember the time we went out to Granny Milford's house and took her those plants that were dying?" Jillian said to Mama. Then she looked at Rileigh. "We took you with us. You were maybe five years old. Do you remember?"

Rileigh loved it when Jillian did that. She'd only done it a handful of times — "remember when" — since she got home, but she always said it with a kind of wonder in her voice, like she was unearthing some long-buried treasure and was surprised at finding it. Rileigh believed it was a good thing to get Jillian to bring up memories of her life before it fell apart. To build some kind of bridge between the girl who went running out of her bedroom on the night before her wedding and the woman who had returned twenty-seven years later, an entirely different human being.

Slowly the images formed in Rileigh's head.

"I *do* remember," she said.

Chapter Eleven

THE IMAGES WERE BLURRED around the edges, and the light was a little too bright in them, and it had a golden quality. That's the way all old memories looked to her — not faded, but translucent. Most of the time, they mixed reality with fantasy. But that was okay. Everything Rileigh saw with little girl eyes had been real to the little girl looking out through them.

RILEIGH SITS between Mama and Jillian in the pickup truck as it bounces up the road to one of Rileigh's favorite places in the whole world. Rileigh loves Granny Milford's house because it's so interesting, so many things to look at and ask questions about. But more important, the most important thing of all, is that Granny Milford has goats. Oh, they're mean as snakes, and you can't get in the pen with the billy goat or he'll knock you down and step on you. That's what Mama says. But there are always baby goats around, too, in a special pen all by themselves. They're "kids", just like Rileigh, and Granny Milford lets Rileigh play with them.

"Granny Milford still has goats, doesn't she?" Rileigh asks

74

Mama and Jillian when the thought strikes her that maybe the baby goats have all grown up to be grown-up goats, and they'll be mean and she can't play with them anymore.

"Granny Milford always has baby goats," Jillian says, and pats her on the knee. Rileigh smiles wide and bright.

When Rileigh climbs down out of the pickup truck, she smells honeysuckle and frying bacon and some other stink that's animal poop mixed in with all the others. Rileigh thinks animals should have to go to the bathroom to do their business, like people do, instead of leaving it all stinky on the ground.

She doesn't even go into the house with Mama and Jillian, just rushes around the back to where the farm animals are kept and hurries to the pen with the baby goats. She climbs quickly up over the fence and drops to the ground. The baby goats come to her like puppies, nudging her with their heads and nipping at her with their little mouths.

There's a solid black one, except the tip of his tail is white and one of his feet is white. There's a brown and white one, all spotted like a dog. And a smaller one. It's a girl goat, she thinks, but she's not really sure how you can tell the difference between boy goats and girl goats. They both have those nubby things on their heads that will grow into horns someday.

The littlest goat is white with black feet.

She doesn't think you call a goat's feet 'feet'. They're something else. They're hooves. Around the little white goat's hooves is black fur that makes the goat look like it's wearing socks.

Rileigh picks the goat up and snuggles her face down into its neck.

"Rileigh!" She looks up when she hears her mother calling. "Rileigh, where are you?"

"I'm here with the baby goats."

Jillian comes around the house to the goat pen and looks over the edge at Rileigh with the baby goats.

"Want to come in the house and have some cookies?"

Rileigh loves Granny Milford's cookies. She makes the best

cookies in the world, even better than Mama's. But Rileigh doesn't tell Mama that, because that might hurt her feelings.

"And she has fresh, cold goat's milk."

Rileigh doesn't really like goat's milk, it has a funny taste. But Granny Milford doesn't have any cows. So maybe Rileigh will just say she wants cookies and a glass of water or lemonade.

Rileigh climbs the fence and hops down on the other side, then goes into the house with Jillian. There's a honeysuckle arbor over the gate in the front yard fence. The smell of it is one of Rileigh's most favorite smells.

Granny Milford's house looks like something out of a storybook. Jillian reads to her sometimes from books like Dr. Seuss, who writes about green eggs and ham, and Sam I Am. But there are fairy tale books, too. They don't have pictures like Dr. Seuss books, but there are descriptions in the storybooks without pictures. And the way Jillian reads them, Rileigh can see in her head what it must look like. This house looks like one of those houses out of a fairy tale. There are pots of flowers hanging from the ceiling of the porch. And there's a porch swing and rocking chairs and a brass thing like a jar that Mama says is a spittoon. Jillian told her that's where men who chew tobacco spit. Rileigh always stays away from it because that's gross.

Granny Milford is just pulling cookies out of the oven as she and Jillian enter the house. They smell so good Rileigh's mouth waters, and she isn't even hungry.

Granny Milford looks like Tweety Bird's grandmother in the cartoons. She is small and round and she wears glasses that don't have any rims on them. Her hair is pure white, parted in the middle and made into a bun behind her head. She always has an apron on. And her skin has wrinkles all over it, but they're not ugly like some old people's wrinkles are. Granny Milford's skin looks like tissue paper that you wadded up and then smoothed back out.

She's missing some of her teeth, but she doesn't look ugly without them. It's just that her mouth caves in a little.

"Why Rileigh girl, you want some of these cookies? I bet you do. I got some cold goat's milk to go with 'em."

"I want some cookies," Rileigh says, and tries to think of a way to say she doesn't want the goat's milk without hurting Granny Milford's feelings. She hopes when Granny Milford opens the refrigerator, she'll see some lemonade inside and she can ask for that instead. But there is no lemonade in the refrigerator, so she smiles as Granny Milford pours her a big glass of goat's milk.

The cookies are just about the best cookies Rileigh ever put in her mouth. She eats two of them, but when she reaches for a third, she sees the look on her mother's face and Jillian shaking her head. Rileigh pulls her hand back. But Granny Milford pushes the plate toward Rileigh and tells Mama, "Let her have as many as she wants. She don't come here that often. She ain't gonna get sick or nothing."

So Rileigh has two more cookies. Well, she has one more cookie, and she puts another cookie in the pocket of her shirt to eat later. Or maybe to feed to the baby goats.

Mama and Jillian had come out to Granny Milford's house because they wanted her help with something. Mama put some potted plants that are wilted into the back of the pickup truck. One of them, a tomato plant, has holes in its leaves. Mama doesn't know what's wrong with them, but Granny Milford will know.

Rileigh knows they'll ask Granny Milford questions about how to plant things and how to make things. Mama never asks her for recipes, though, because Granny Milford doesn't know how much of anything she puts in her cookie dough.

While Mama, Jillian, and Granny Milford talk in the kitchen, Rileigh wanders around the kitchen and the living room of the old house. There are shelves everywhere in the kitchen, with lots of little bottles with labels on them that Rileigh will learn to read in first grade this fall.

But right now, she doesn't know what the words mean. She just sees bottles that have plant stuff, like pieces of parsley or twigs or dry grass. One of the bigger jars has cattails in it.

Several of the others have seeds, and she recognizes sunflower seeds but not the others. Maybe Granny Milford keeps the seeds to feed the birds. There are always birds around Granny Milford's house. That's one of the reasons Rileigh likes to come here, just to listen to them sing.

Granny Milford has a huge garden behind her house. She grows everything — tomatoes and cantaloupe and watermelon and green beans that climb up a pole and black-eyed peas and corn that grows so tall Rileigh can hide between the rows.

Rileigh watches Jillian's face as she talks and thinks how beautiful she is. Rileigh wishes she was that beautiful and wonders if maybe she will grow up to be beautiful like Jillian. But she doesn't think so, because nobody is as beautiful as Jillian.

Or as kind. Her voice is kind of deep, not like a boy's, but not high and squeaky. It's comforting in the middle of the night when Rileigh runs into her bedroom and climbs into bed with her. She always tells Jillian that she's had a bad dream, and sometimes she has, but other times she just likes to sleep next to her.

Jillian and Mama bring the flowers and the droopy tomato plant with holes in its leaves up onto the front porch. Granny Milford goes into the house and comes back out with some powdery stuff that she shakes on the leaves of the tomato plant. The little rose bush has a couple of buds and one rose on it, but it's all droopy and not pretty, and Rileigh doesn't think the roses smell good at all.

Granny Milford snips off the rose and takes it into the house. She gets one of the jars that has powder in it off the shelf and she sprinkles some of the powder into a glass of water and stirs it around until you can't see the powder anymore. She puts the pitiful little wilted rose into the glass, then they go back out onto the porch. Rileigh asks if she can go play with the goats again and Mama says yes, so she runs back out to the pen and climbs over the fence.

She's decided to name the goats. The white one with black on its feet is Socks, and the spotted one is Spot, and the other one is Elmer, for Elmer Fudd, because she likes the sound of that word, Elmer.

The goats are such happy creatures. They jump around and kick their little feet up into the air like they're having so much fun just being alive. They remind her of butterflies. Butterflies hop from one flower to another, having so much fun in the sunlight.

She plays with the goats until Mama calls her, then she goes back into the house. Mama and Jillian have already loaded the plants they had brought Granny Milford into the back of the pickup truck. Rileigh goes into the kitchen and asks if she can have one more cookie, please.

She shared the cookie that is in her pocket with the goats. Granny Milford says goats will eat anything.

Then Rileigh spies the pitiful little rose in the glass on Granny Milford's table, except it's not a pitiful little rose anymore. The rose has straightened up tall. The petals that were dark and wilted are not wilted anymore, and they're a beautiful red color. The leaves on the stem of the rose are bright and shiny green. And Rileigh runs to the table and sticks her nose up to the rose, and it smells better than any rose she has ever smelled.

"I REMEMBER that I played with the goats in a pen behind the house and I gave them names," Rileigh said, smiling.

Jillian smiled too. "I remember that tomato plant we took there that was sick. That plant made more tomatoes than all the other plants in the whole garden. Them tomatoes was as big as your fist."

"I remember the rose in the glass," said Rileigh, loving that her sister seemed to be enjoying the memory as much as Rileigh was. "How it perked up and smelled good. When we got home, we planted that rose beside the back porch. You remember? And it grew all around the side of the house."

"You know when you buy roses in the store, cut roses, there's a little packet held to the stem with a rubber band,

and the instructions on the packet say you're supposed to pour that powder into the water before you put the roses in, to keep them from wilting? Maybe that's what Granny Milford did. She had some kind of concoction that's like the little granules in that packet."

Rileigh conjured up the memories again and examined them in their blurred-edge beauty. Then she said softly, "I don't think that's it. I think Granny Milford knew magic."

Chapter Twelve

RILEIGH STEPPED up onto the kitchen chair, from the chair to the table, and from the table to the countertop in order to reach the highest cabinets in the kitchen.

The old house had tall ceilings, like all old houses did when there was no air conditioning, so the heat could rise up to the ceiling.

But what that meant was that the tallest cabinets in the kitchen were so high up you couldn't reach them without a ladder.

That's where you kept things you didn't use very often. The prime real estate in the lower cabinets were for cups, saucers, and bowls. The higher cabinets were where Mama kept light bulbs and the reading light and other seldom-used things.

Rileigh reached into the cabinet, hoping to find a 40-watt bulb. 60 watts was too bright and 75 watts was like a torch.

She didn't even realize that she'd knocked anything over until she heard it ring. She looked down then and saw that she had knocked out of the cabinet something Mama had stuck up in there. It was a Christmas bell, made of silver metal, with a circular handle on top, shaped like a holly garland. Etched on the front were garlands and holly. She didn't know why Mama had stuck it up there and was about to ask her when she noticed the look on Jillian's face.

Jillian was frozen. All expression had drained out of her face, along with all the color in it. She had that thousand-yard stare that Rileigh recognized. She'd seen it before. It was PTSD. Jillian wasn't here in this homey kitchen in the mountains of Tennessee. Jillian was somewhere else, where something *really bad* was happening.

Mama didn't notice, her back was turned. She kept babbling on about her recipe for stew and whether or not she ought to pick peppers out of the garden or let them ripen a little more.

Rileigh climbed slowly down off the cabinet and went to Jillian. Reached out to put her hand on her shoulder. But as soon as she touched her, Jillian jerked back like she'd been stuck with a cattle prod. She made a noise, too. A tiny noise. A pitiful noise. Like a noise a baby rabbit might make if it got run over by a tractor.

Then she sank down to the floor next to the wall and made herself as small as she possibly could.

Mama noticed then. Turned to her and said, "Jillian, what are you doing?"

Rileigh grabbed Mama's arm, and shook her head, mouthing no. And Mama hushed. Then Rileigh got down onto her knees on the floor beside Jillian, scooted up close to her but didn't touch her, and started talking.

"It's okay, Jill. You're gonna be just fine. You're home now. You're home with me and Mama. You're home in the mountains. And later tonight, we'll go out in the backyard with a mason jar and see if we can catch some fireflies.

Would you like that? Would you like to go out into the backyard and catch some fireflies?"

Rileigh kept talking, keeping her voice absolutely even and being careful not to touch Jillian. She watched her eyes, watched the faraway look begin to fade, watched her until eventually she saw Jillian's pupils dilate. Jillian blinked. She was back.

"Jillian, are you alright?" Rileigh said in the same tone of voice she'd been talking in for the last ten minutes. Jillian snapped her head toward Rileigh and then shook her head violently. "No. No. No." Then she got quickly to her feet. "I'm sorry. We were washing the dishes. I'm sorry. I can't."

"Jillian, it's okay," Rileigh said. "I know what's going on with you. I've seen it before. I've had it before. It's PTSD. Soldiers coming out of Afghanistan broke out in an epidemic of it. I know what it looks like and what it feels like. There's always some kind of trigger. What triggered you, Jillian?"

Rileigh was careful not to ask what Jillian had seen in her flashback, not wanting to re-trigger it.

Jillian looked around until she saw the silver Christmas bell lying on the floor. "The bell."

"The bell triggered you," Rileigh said.

Jillian could only nod her head. She got to her feet, shaky, and Jillian and Rileigh couldn't contain Mama any longer. Mama rushed to her oldest daughter, threw her arms around her, hugging her and crying and telling her everything was fine, everything would be okay. The absolutely wrong response to a flashback of post-traumatic stress disorder. But Mama didn't know that.

"Mama, did you feed the chickens before you started supper?"

The non-sequitur didn't bother Mama at all. She

thought in non-sequiturs often. "Yeah, I'm sure I did. I fed them."

"I don't think you did, Mama. I think you need to go check."

"Are you sure?"

"The only way to know is to check."

Mama got to her feet and rushed to the back door, mumbling something about needing more chicken feed. Rileigh looked then at Jillian, and a ghost of a smile, slithered across Jillian's face. "That was good," she said.

"Since she got dementia, I have developed all sorts of intercommunication skills I never had before."

Rileigh reached over and carefully picked up the Christmas bell off the floor. She was very careful not to let it ring, and she held it up to Jillian. "You remember this bell?"

Jillian nodded her head, staring at it as if it were a tarantula spider.

"Aunt Daisy got it somewhere, I think. I have no idea why it's not in the box of the other Christmas decorations."

Jillian reached out with trembling fingers and took the silver bell out of Rileigh's hands, as careful not to ring it as Rileigh had been. She held it up and examined it, as if she'd never seen anything like it before.

"This isn't the same kind of bell, but it makes the same kind of sound," she said.

Rileigh asked no questions. She could say as much or as little as she wanted to.

Then Jillian spoke again, but Rileigh didn't understand what she said, and realized she was speaking, what, Arabic maybe?

Duh. She'd lived in the Middle East for years. Of course she could speak Arabic. It just never occurred to

Rileigh that her sister was bilingual. Shoot, she might be able to speak four or five languages for all Rileigh knew. And that was a big part of the problem, maybe most of the problem — that Rileigh didn't have any idea what Jillian could and could not do. What she did and did not like, or had and had not done. That huge gulf of thirty years between them. Somehow, they had to figure a way to bridge that.

"He rang it when he wanted me," Jillian said, not looking at Rileigh. "Any time, day or night, when that bell rang, I went to him."

Rileigh felt a cold rock in the pit of her stomach. A horror crept over her, and she both desperately wanted to know what had happened and absolutely could not stand hearing the story.

"Who was he?" Rileigh asked, but if Jillian didn't choose to answer, that was just fine.

"His name was Kalil al-Amin, and he was in the carpet business. The rugs he sold were beautiful."

Jillian turned and looked Rileigh in the eye. "I belonged to him for five years."

Belonged to. The words echoed around in Rileigh's head, banging against the sides of it like a bowling ball in an oil drum.

"He wasn't bad," Jillian said, "not as bad as some of the others."

She wasn't looking at Rileigh now, and Rileigh suspected her sister couldn't meet her eyes.

"He traveled all over the world selling carpets. That's how I managed to get away."

Rileigh looked a question at her.

"I couldn't just run. There's nowhere a white, blonde female can run and not be spotted instantly. I had to have an identity. I had to have papers. I had to have clothes. I had to," She stopped. "It took me three and a half years to gather what I needed to escape, and I'd been plotting out what I needed for a long, long time before that."

Jillian held the little silver bell up in the air in front of her and moved it slightly so that it dinged. Just a small little ding. Even so, a shiver ran up Jillian's spine that Rileigh could actually see. Jillian swallowed and rang the bell again. Louder.

Rileigh could see she hated every second of it, but she rang it again and again. Finally, she simply sat in the chair in the kitchen ringing the bell over and over. Mama came in, lips pursed.

"I fed them chickens. Why did you think I hadn't fed them chickens?" she asked Rileigh. Then she took the bell from Jillian.

"You know whose bell this is?" Mama asked, blowing right by the look of horror and shame and anger and every other possible human emotion that was registering in Jillian's face.

"Daisy got this when she went to Niagara Falls," Mama said. "She brought it back from there. Daisy went to Niagara Falls all by herself, as far as I know. All I remember is she brought back something for everybody. A gift for all the bouquet. For the whole bouquet." Meaning, of course, all of Daisy and Lily's sisters who were named for flowers. "And this is what she gave me. But it don't say Niagara Falls on it. She brought Rose back one of them little globe things that when you shake it, it looks like it's snowing. And it said Niagara Falls on it."

"Why did you put it up in the cabinet instead of with the Christmas decorations?" Rileigh asked.

"Well, it's a Christmas decoration, but that's not what it was for. It was just a gift. It's all tarnished now. I bet if I shined it up, it'd be pretty, though."

"You like it, sweetheart?" Mama said to Jillian, held it in front of her face and dinged it back and forth. Jillian flinched like she'd been slapped. But otherwise, she showed no response at all. "If you want it, I'll give it to you."

"That's okay, Mama," Jillian said. "You keep it." She drew in a breath and let it out, shaky. "I don't much like bells."

Chapter Thirteen

RILEIGH LAY in the dark in her room, staring up at the ceiling, listening to the sounds of Mama puttering around in the kitchen downstairs. It was a lot like having Aunt Daisy back in the house, she thought. Mama had taken to getting up in the middle of the night and wandering around several months ago. The first few times it happened, Rileigh got up and went to Mama, took her hand and put her back in bed.

But she had seemed to know where she was and what she was doing. She said she got up because she wasn't sleepy. Just because she had dementia didn't mean she didn't know whether she was sleepy or not.

Rileigh was considering whether or not to go downstairs and have a talk with Mama. Jillian was asleep in her room and now was a good time to do it. The thing was Rileigh didn't know whether it would do any good if she did.

She was considering having a talk with Mama about PTSD.

Mama had been so freaked out by what happened to

Jillian tonight. She didn't understand and it scared her. What would happen if Mama was here by herself and Jillian had a flashback? What would Mama do? Rileigh couldn't be here every minute of every day. Given that Mitch had a new case, she was likely to be gone a lot.

Rileigh's conundrum was that she didn't know how much Mama would remember tomorrow morning about what Rileigh said to her tonight. And there was the fact that having to talk to her about Jillian's PTSD would require Mama to acknowledge that terrible things had happened to her daughter while she was gone. Mama appeared to have been able somehow to ignore that reality. She treated Jillian as if she'd been off on a cruise some- where or vacationing in Europe. For almost thirty years.

Either Mama didn't know what had happened to Jillian — and it had been discussed in front of her often enough that she should have — or she had just flat out decided not to allow that to be true.

If there was any upside to having dementia, it was that you could twist and change reality to suit your own fantasy.

Mama's dementia was not like Aunt Daisy's dementia. Mama was sweet and kind and wanted to believe that the world was full of roses and butterflies. Anything that made her see the world differently, she pretty much chose to ignore. Rileigh sighed, sat up, swung her feet over the edge of the bed and into her slippers. Mama couldn't ignore Jillian's PTSD if it happened when Rileigh wasn't there. Rileigh had to at least try to prepare her for it.

As she slipped quietly out of her room and tiptoed down the hall to the stairs, Rileigh let her mind flit to memories of her own episodes of PTSD, but wouldn't let it linger there.

After her first tour in Afghanistan, everything in her environment triggered her. It didn't have to be something as obvious as a car backfiring. Rileigh could squirt ketchup onto her french fries in McDonald's, and suddenly it was blood. Not just anonymous blood, the blood of somebody she knew. She could hear a child crying, and she was back there, gunfire everywhere, and little kids right smack in the middle of it.

She could feel the hot sun on her skin, and she'd be back there. Or be startled by somebody coming up unexpectedly behind her. Or see movement out of the corner of her eye. The whole world was dangerous, and Rileigh was on guard 24/7. It had taken years for those flashbacks to subside. But she remembered what they were like when she lived them. How viscerally real they were. How it felt being transported back to that place. Not *remembering* it, or *thinking about* it, but *re-living* it, being there in that reality, smelling those smells, seeing those sights, hearing those sounds. It was absolutely real.

But she hadn't been at home when she was having PTSD episodes, so Mama never saw them.

But there was no way Mama could live in this house with Jillian, and not see Jillian's flashbacks. And Rileigh suspected there would be lots of them.

Her older sister had not even begun to unpack the baggage she carried with her from living twenty-seven years in hell. Rileigh had spent *months* in Afghanistan. Jillian had spent *years* in captivity. Rileigh knew Jillian would never be who she had been. The very best that she could hope for was that Jillian would be somebody, *anybody*, who was emotionally healthy.

Jillian had yet to agree to go to counseling, but Rileigh was going to put the full court press on her as soon as this case was over. She had to get help.

But counseling wouldn't prevent the PTSD flashbacks. It would teach her how to deal with them and make them less frequent. Eventually, hopefully, they would go away altogether. But there was no guarantee of that. The only guarantee the situation offered to Rileigh was that Mama was going to see Jillian behave like she was crazy. And Rileigh needed to help Mama cope with that.

When Rileigh stepped into the kitchen, Mama was putting butter on a saltine cracker. Then she set another cracker on top of it, and popped the sandwich of buttered crackers into her mouth.

"Ain't nothing in the world better than butter crackers and milk," she said, as if being up at three o'clock in the morning eating crackers and drinking milk were the most ordinary thing in the whole world. "Do you want some?"

Rileigh shook her head, went to the refrigerator, got herself a cool glass of Mama's legendary lemonade, and went to the table, sitting down opposite Mama.

"I was watching Family Feud the other day," Mama said. "You know they got reruns in the daytime, now, and Steve Harvey had on this pink suit with—"

"Mama, we need to talk." Rileigh made her voice as firm as she could without being harsh.

Mama stopped her babble in mid-word.

"What do we need to talk about," she asked. But Rileigh thought she knew.

"We need to talk about Jillian and what happened earlier tonight."

Mama leapt up out of the chair, sending crumbs from her cracker all over the floor. "Oh, that wasn't nothing. She was just upset about—about—"

"Mama, sit down. We *have to* talk about Jillian."

Mama looked at her, and you could see on her face the war going on within her. The battle to hang onto the fantasy of butterflies and sunshine, and the understanding that she needed to deal with reality.

She sank down dejectedly into the chair.

"Mama, what happened to Jillian this evening was a flashback. Do you know what that is?"

"I heard about it, but I ain't sure."

"People who have been through a great trauma often have flashbacks. It's part of something called post-traumatic stress disorder."

"PTSD, them initials. Yeah, I heard about that."

"The reason people who have been through something really terrible have flashbacks is way too complicated to explain. You just need to understand that it happens, and that it's what happened tonight."

"Okay, I understand now, and I don't blame her. It's—"

"Mama, I'm not just explaining what happened to Jillian tonight. I'm warning you that this is the first time, but it will *not* be the last time she has a flashback."

Mama's eyes grew wide. "You don't know that."

"Yes, I do. You weren't there, but when I got back from Afghanistan after the first tour, I was at Fort Campbell. Remember, you couldn't understand why I didn't want to come home?"

"Yeah, I remember that."

"PTSD is why. I didn't want you to have to suffer through it with me."

"You had that thing, that PTSD?"

"Most soldiers do who've seen combat."

"But Jillian wasn't in no war. She was just—" And Mama stopped there like she had run into a brick wall, because to continue that sentence was to go into that dark place that Mama didn't want to go.

Rileigh plunged ahead, watching her mother's eyes to see how much of what she was saying was sinking in.

"Mama, terrible things happened to Jillian while she was gone. You know that."

"Oh, she was just—"

"Mama, stop it. You can't wallpaper over this. Jillian was kidnapped when she was eighteen years old, and she was forced to do terrible things."

Mama just looked at her, eyes huge.

"I don't know what specifically. It doesn't matter. What matters right now is that she has PTSD from all those awful experiences, which means what happened this evening is going to happen again."

"Oh, no," Mama said, and put her face in her hands.

"And it's going to happen when I'm not here."

"Well, you just need to stay home, because —"

"Mama, I'm not going to stay home. I have work to do, and you know it. Besides, even if I was here every minute, you'd still have to learn how to deal with what's happening to Jillian."

There was no way that Rileigh could explain PTSD to Mama in a way she could understand or remember, but that didn't matter. She just had to prepare Mama for what would happen and give her a first aid kit, so she'd know what to do.

"When you have a flashback, it's not like you're remembering something bad that happened to you. It's not the same. You *relive* something bad. You literally think you are there, in that place, in that time, living what's happening. And if what's happening was really bad, you respond to it the way you responded to it when it really happened."

Rileigh paused, let that sink in.

"You saw that on Jillian's face. How terrified she looked."

Mama nodded.

"It won't always look like that, Mama. PTSD manifests

itself in all kinds of ways. But there are signs, things you can look for."

Rileigh described what Mama might see, told her that if Jillian were experiencing a flashback, she'd seem disoriented, like she didn't know what was going on.

"She won't look at you, won't look into your eyes. She'll probably just be frozen, her eyes squeezed shut. She could cry out. She could sob. She could yell, no, no, no, and run away. She'll respond to things that aren't really there, because what Jillian is seeing is not what you're seeing. She's seeing something terrible."

"So, I just got to sit there and watch her suffer?"

"No, there are things you can do to bring her back. To help her get out of the flashback and back to the real world."

"Tell me what them things are."

This discussion was going better than Rileigh had expected. Mama wasn't in denial, at least she didn't appear to be. She was leaning in, engaged.

"One of the most important things is, Mama, don't touch her."

"Don't touch her?"

"She's not where you are. I know you want to run to her and grab her and hug her, but you can't do that, because she's not here."

Rileigh fought for a few seconds before she said it, and then went on.

"And much of what she is flashing back to … has to do with human touch. That's bound to be a trigger. You need to understand, Mama, that just putting your hand on her shoulder while she's washing the dishes might trigger a flashback."

"You mean I can't never touch her? I can't never—"

"I'm not saying that, Mama. What I am saying is you

have to be prepared for the fact that Jillian is very, very wounded. And it's our job to help her heal."

Mama nodded her head. "Help her heal. That's our job."

"When Jillian has a flashback in your presence, you can't touch her, but you need to talk to her."

"What do I say?"

"You tell her who you are. Remind her that she's safe where she is. Say something like, 'Jillian, it's Mama. It's me. Mama. You're here with me and Rileigh at home, in the mountains. And you're safe here.'"

Mama repeated the phrase. "You're safe here. Ain't nothing gonna hurt you here. We will protect you."

"If she has her eyes squeezed shut, ask her to open her eyes and keep asking her until she does. What will bring her back from a flashback is for her to reconnect with the real world. And keeping her eyes shut keeps her locked in unreality. What you have to do is help her gradually realize that she's here and not there. Ask her to look around the room. Say something random like, 'tell me the colors you see' or 'name the objects you see.' Just keep talking. Don't sound frightened."

"But I will be frightened."

"I didn't say don't *be* frightened, Mama. I said don't *sound* frightened. That time when I broke my arm, remember, and I came running into the house with my arm dangling, you were as calm as if I'd come to show you a bouquet of flowers. You had to be scared and upset. But you didn't show it. That's what you have to do for Jillian. Don't show what you're really feeling."

Mama nodded.

"Then just talk to her. Babble. It can be nonsense. Like you'd talk to a frightened child. Say, 'It's okay. You're here with me now. It's all over. Nobody can hurt you anymore.

You're safe. You aren't in danger anymore. You're not in that awful place. And nobody can hurt you.' And don't worry about sounding like a broken record. Keep talking. Keep telling her she's safe. Keep telling her she's here. Keep telling her you'll protect her. Over and over and over."

"When it's over … how do you know?"

"You'll know when she comes out of it when she makes eye contact. When you can tell that she's seeing the same things you're seeing. Then you can touch her. Don't run over to her and hug her. But put your hand on her shoulder. Tell her everything's fine. And don't ask her what she saw. She'll tell us about those bad things someday. Or she won't. I don't know. But we don't ask. We wait until she shares."

Rileigh stopped talking and studied her mother.

"So, when that happens to my Jilly, I'm not supposed to be scared, or leastways, not let her know I'm scared. I'm supposed to be real calm. I can't touch her. I can't throw my arms around her or hug her or nothing like that. I just got to talk to her. I got to tell her she's here and tell her she's safe and tell her everything's okay and tell her who I am in case she don't remember who I am. And just keep talking and talking and talking. Is that right?"

Rileigh was proud of her Mama, might never have been as proud of her as she was right now. Her mother had been willing to open that door into ugly and go there because she loved her daughter.

Reaching across the table, she took Mama's hands in hers. "That's right, Mama. That's what you do."

Mama had a determined look on her face Rileigh hadn't seen in a long time. "We got to help Jilly get well. If that's what I got to do to help her get well, that's what I'll do."

Chapter Fourteen

Mitch stared at the white rhino.

The white rhino stared back.

The beast glared at him through eyes that looked too small on its monstrous face. It appeared to be squinting at him as if it were sizing him up before it charged. It was enormous. With all that body armor, it looked like a Sherman tank with legs.

"Holy shit, man," Mitch said when Gus came into the waiting room from his laboratory in the back of the coroner's office building. "That thing looks real."

"It looked pretty damn real when I was taking its picture. I tried to get it to smile, but it wouldn't even give me one of those little-kid, bare-your-teeth smiles, the kind they stick on their faces when they get their school pictures made."

Mitch tilted his head to the side, studying the life-sized picture of a rhinoceros on the wall of his waiting room.

"I suspect that creature doesn't do a lot of smiling. Not with that pointy lip," Mitch said.

"A factoid for you to file away for the next time you're

playing some kind of trivia game. Rhinoceroses stink, smell like a dirty fish tank with dead fish in it. I am here to tell you, you do *not* want to be downwind of that sucker, its breath smells so bad it needs prescription Tic Tacs."

Mitch crossed the lobby and had the uncanny feeling that the eyes of what looked like a prehistoric creature followed him all the way.

"When you said you were going to put a life-sized picture of a rhinoceros in your waiting room, I thought you were kidding."

"You don't like it?"

"*Like* it? It's a good thing all your patients are dead."

Gus had called Mitch first thing that morning to tell him that he had the results of the autopsy on Annamaria Giordano. And that Mitch might want to come out and have a look.

Of course, Mitch hadn't wanted to go out and have a look, but he went.

That was one of a thousand things Mitch didn't understand about Gus Hazelton. The man *enjoyed* digging around in the bowels of dead bodies. Well, maybe enjoyed wasn't the right word. But he had picked it as a line of work. He was a medical doctor with two or three different specialties. He'd told Mitch over a beer once that he had settled on forensic pathology for two reasons. Reason Number One was that the patients a forensic pathologist dealt with didn't give him any shit.

"When I was interning, doing my shift in internal medicine, I got so damn tired of listening to people bitch about what ailed them. I know they came to the doctor because they were sick. They wouldn't have been there otherwise. But whine, whine, whine."

Reason Number Two was that being a forensic pathologist meant that none of his patients were going to die if he wasn't there. And he wanted to be *not there* a lot.

Gus Hazelton had won the Tennessee State Lottery several years ago. Mitch didn't know exactly how big the prize had been, but he'd heard the story of how Gus had won and it made him smile every time.

"Most people who win the lottery do it because they bought hundreds and hundreds of tickets," Gus told him. "Like all the employees on a certain shift in a factory will put up money and they'll buy four or five hundred tickets and split whatever they win."

"I won on a single ticket, and I didn't even want to buy it.

Gus had gone into a convenience store because he needed to go to the bathroom. Key words in that sentence were "needed to go." As in bad. But the fellow on the register said the bathroom doors were locked unless you bought something in the store. So Gus had looked around, frantic and spotted a rack of Bugles — Bugles being the single best snack chip ever manufactured. It came in half a dozen different flavors, among them cinnamon toast and ranch dressing, but the very best one was caramel.

He was about to purchase a bag of the caramel ones when he realized he only had a dollar or two stuffed down in his pockets, poor last-year-medical-student that he was, and he couldn't afford the three dollars the bag of chips cost. Time was running short in his "need to go" emergency, so he looked at the fellow behind the counter and told him, "Just sell me a damned lottery ticket."

The rest, as they say, was history. Gus had used his lottery winnings to build a state-of-the-art coroner's lab in little Yarmouth County, Tennessee. He had settled there because he loved to hunt and fish, which was reason number three that he had become a forensic pathologist.

No, actually that was just an extension of Reason Number Two. He wanted a medical practice where he could take off for a week or six weeks to hunt moose in Alaska and not be concerned that any of his patients would die from his lack of care.

The last time Mitch had seen Gus before he showed up at Annie Giordano's crime scene last night was when he'd appeared in Aunt Daisy's room to confirm that the woman who'd been murdered there wasn't Aunt Daisy. At that time, Gus had just returned from a six-week safari to Africa. A photographic safari. And his prize picture was of a white rhino. He told Mitch that day in Aunt Daisy's room that he was going to blow that picture up and put it on the wall in his waiting room. Mitch had thought he was joking.

Mitch followed Gus down the hallway to his examining room where the body of Annie Giordano lay on a metal table covered up with a white sheet. Gus began rattling off information as soon as they walked into the room. Mitch had always been surprised at the lack of stink he found in Gus's office building. Every other coroner's office he'd ever been to had reeked of formaldehyde or some toxic cleaning agent or just "dead body." Gus told him once that he had installed a you-don't-want-to-know-how-much-it-costs air filtration system in the building before he ever hung out his shingle and examined his first patient.

"So, cause of death … drum roll, please…exsanguination from a wound to the carotid artery in the neck."

They stood on opposite sides of the girl, who at this time yesterday had probably been getting ready to go to work at her job as a dental hygienist in Dr. Bolesky's office.

"Tell me about that wound. If it was some kind of animal, a dog or a wolf that ripped out —"

"I'm thinking more 'garden claw'."

"Garden claw?"

"Yep. Somebody killed her by slicing her throat. The edges of the wound in the artery were smooth. It was cut with a knife. Then, for reasons unknown, the killer wanted to make it look like some huge canine had attacked her. So they used a garden claw to dig huge chunks out of the girl's neck."

"Garden claw." Mitch wallowed that around in his head.

"I'm not so much wondering about the garden claw as I am about the blood," Gus said. "Where in the hell did all that blood go? In the average human body, there's between 1.2 and 1.5 gallons of blood. *Gallons.* Think about a gallon of milk. Where could you go that you could turn a gallon of milk upside down and pour out the contents without making a mess?"

"You got me. Where?"

"I asked you. I don't know. What I do know is that when he slit her throat, her heart was still beating, pumping that blood out through the wound. Then at some point, he hung the body upside down." Gus shook his head. "I don't think she was still alive, and she certainly wasn't still conscious when he did that. So all the blood would drain out of the body. That suggests to me that the killer wanted the blood. But what for? What could you do with a gallon and a half of type O-negative blood?"

"I'm not even going to say vampire," Mitch said.

Gus turned from the body on the table to the countertop on the other side of the room and gestured for Mitch to come and look.

Mitch added, "I know one thing the killer did with that blood. He used it to mark up the doors, door frames, and walls of two of the victims' friends."

"So that was Annie Giordano's blood?"

"Yep."

Gus turned away from the slides in the microscope and showed Mitch the plaster cast he had made of the footprint he'd found at the murder scene.

"I was right about the running shoe. It's a New Balance. Size ten and a half. Brand new."

Gus paused. "So, walk with me through this deranged mind and see if we can make some sense of it."

Mitch loved it when Gus did this. He was absolutely brilliant. Saw things that Mitch never would even have considered. But more than that, when he was working on a case, Gus wanted to find the killer just as bad as Mitch did. For all his protestations about not wanting live patients because they whined, Gus Hazelton was a compassionate man and a fiercely-determined scientist. When you coupled those two things together, you got a coroner who would run through brick walls and parked cars to figure out how a victim died — the compassionate part of him. And you got a man who loved the puzzle of figuring out a murder. Gus loved putting the little pieces together to form enough evidence to send somebody to prison for the rest of their lives — the scientist in him.

"So, I'm the killer. And I grabbed this girl either because I have a motive—" Gus looked at Mitch, who shrugged "—which we have yet to figure out. Or because I selected her at random, maybe looking for a body type like Ted Bundy picked his victims."

"Whoa, whoa, whoa," Mitch said and held up his hands. "Ted Bundy was a serial killer. Are you suggesting—"

"I'm just running with the facts. This was such a violent crime that the person who committed it either had a real axe to grind with Annie Giordano or is a real sicko. And I think the answer is behind door number two."

Serial killer. Two of Mitch's least favorite words.

"But back to the supposition. So I pick out Annie Giordano. I kidnap her. I slice her throat. I do something with her one-and-a-half gallons of blood that doesn't make a mess. Saving some to finger-paint with later. Then I get a garden claw and gouge out the remainder of her throat and … do *something* with it. Then to round out the night's activities, I drape her body over a tree limb, and make a little circuit around to the houses of the victim's friends, using her blood to put marks on their doors."

"The girls live a considerable distance apart, so that took him awhile," Mitch said.

"And not just any marks. Oh, no, no. Weird-ass marks that looked like something you'd see carved in the forehead of one of Charles Manson's followers."

"The marks weren't just random marks. They meant something. Annie Giordano was a witch."

Gus looked down sadly at the corpse on the table and shook his head. "Ding, dong, the witch is dead."

Chapter Fifteen

"ANNIE WASN'T A 'LONE WITCH,'" Mitch said. "There was a coven and the girls with marks on their doors were members."

"In Black Bear Forge, Tennessee." Gus mused.

"There's more going on than just witchcraft. The last girl we talked to — her name was Olivia Booth — she had all kinds of other magicky things around, including voodoo."

Gus's head snapped up at that. "Now you've got my attention. I don't know much about witchcraft, but I studied at Tulane University in New Orleans, and that place is plumb broke out with voodoo."

"Olivia had a doll with pins stuck in it."

"The girl I was dating when I was at Tulane was really into voodoo, and she made dolls."

"You dated a girl who made voodoo dolls?"

"I was young and foolish." Gus sighed. "But she had the cutest little ass you ever saw."

"Olivia Burke said that her voodoo doll wasn't about

hurting anybody, that it was for, what did she call it? Positive intentions."

"Elise had a doll for that, too. You make a doll of yourself if you want to change. You put a piece of your hair or something else in it and it becomes a symbol of you to the gods in voodoo land, I guess. You use colored pins, and the different colors give you different things —like blue is peace and love, I think, or maybe that was greed. Black, I remember, was repelling negative energies. But Elise was way more into negative energy than positive energy."

Gus described how his girlfriend made an altar, lit a candle and incense, then dipped her hands in salt water and did something with crystals that he couldn't remember.

"But the pins were the main thing. To control somebody, you inserted a pin in their head. I think it had to be a red one. To block somebody, you used a black one. Elise was a nursing student and she got crossways with the dean of the department. Dr. Hellman."

"As in mayonnaise?" Mitch interrupted, couldn't resist. Gus ignored him and went on with the story.

"She made a doll of Dr. Hellman, stuck it with pin after pin, tied a rope around the doll, dangled it in the toilet and flushed. She said she was afraid to do something really violent to it, like run over it with a car or set it on fire, because what goes around comes around and she didn't want the 'karmic backlash.'"

"Which would cause ...?"

"Something really bad could happen to her."

"Did it?"

"Absolutely—I *dumped* her." Gus grinned, revealing his "Madonna gap."

"I've been thinking about those signs and symbols that

were painted in blood on their doors," Gus said, going off in a different direction. "I know somebody who might be able to help you figure out what they mean. The man owns a place called Moonstone, and he knows all manner of things about crystals and witches and Wicca. It's in Gatlinburg."

Mitch shook his head. "I've driven past it, but I've never stopped."

"Well, I've been inside often enough for the both of us," Gus said. "It's all I could do not to buy every damn rock in there."

"It's a store that sells rocks?"

"Oh, not just rocks. We're talking *rocks.*" Gus had a dreamy look on his face. "I love rocks," he said, in the same way a man might say, 'I love pizza.'

"I don't think I ever met anybody who loved rocks," Mitch said.

"I didn't have anything else to love," Gus said. "I grew up on the prairie. Have you ever been to what's called the American plateau? Oklahoma, Kansas, Nebraska. Flat as a Barbie doll's belly. And when they say featureless, they're not kidding. My grandmother came from the Texas High Plains. A little town called Amherst. I remember her telling me once that where she grew up was so flat, when your dog ran away, you could see it for three days."

Mitch chuckled. Gus had told him that story before, and Mitch cut Gus slack for little lapses like that. He figured that Gus's mind was so full of so much, that pieces were bound to fall out of his ears now and then.

"So, on the flat nothing, the only pretty thing there is rocks?"

"Yep. And when I was a kid, I loved them. Picked them up everywhere I went. Geodes were the best, of course. But you don't find one of those very often."

"I think I know what a geode is, but—"

"A geode is an Easter egg. No, not an Easter egg. A geode is a chocolate-covered cherry. The outside's dark, probably ugly as sin. But inside, when you bite into that thing, it's ambrosia. Geodes are like that. My sister and I used to sit out on the concrete driveway with a hammer, banging it on every rock we found, hoping that we'd come up with a geode, and every now and then we did. Inside a geode is crystal. Some of the most beautiful crystal you ever saw, like you'll find in Moonstone."

"I'm surprised by that," Mitch said. Gus looked at him. "I don't know why you don't have rocks around every-where if you think they're so beautiful."

"I've got shelves of them in the den. Ones I found, not bought."

It had been a while since Mitch had visited the house Gus had built out behind the coroner's office —a beau-tiful ranch home that looked like it grew out of the mountains like a fir tree. It wasn't a log home, but it was made of slabs of native wood with the bark not cleaned off.

"When you can buy all kinds of stuff, you make little rules for yourself. And one of my little rules about rocks is that I can't keep it unless I find it. Like I wouldn't put up a life-sized picture of a white rhino unless I took the picture. Make sense?"

Gus didn't wait to find out if it made sense to Mitch or not.

"The fellow who runs Moonstone knows me like a brother. I'm sure he gets annoyed as hell that I never buy anything, though I have sent a whole lot of customers his way. But I just go in there to hang out, like it was a museum or a library. I just wander from one of those gorgeous rocks to the next. Wishing I could find one like that."

"Are there like ... I don't know ... rock *safaris*, like animal safaris?"

"I hired a guide in Colorado once. That's how I got most of the geodes on the shelves in my den."

"Surely there are rocks here in the Smokies."

"I go walking around in creeks whenever I get a chance. Mostly I find pieces of granite worn smooth by running water." Gus shook his head, like he'd just remembered why they were talking about rocks in the first place. "Rupert sells a lot of rocks to the woo-woo people. I've seen symbols on the walls of Moonstone like the ones that killer wrote on the doors of the murdered girl's friends. I bet he could tell you what they mean."

Chapter Sixteen

Mitch called Rileigh on Saturday morning to tell her that he had been to Gus's office and had gotten the results of the autopsy on the body of Annie Giordano.

"Cause of deathe: exsanguination," he said.

"Now there's a big surprise," Rileigh said.

"It's more surprising than you think."

"How so?"

"Gus said that somebody slit her throat with blade of some kind, sharp, left no jagged edges."

"There were plenty of jagged edges on her neck."

"That's the surprising part. He said those marks were likely made with a garden claw. The killer used it to dig out a good portion of Annie Giordano's neck."

"Why do a thing like that if she was already dead?"

"Gus got hung up on what happened to all the blood — a gallon, maybe a gallon and a half of it. What use would the killer have for that much blood?"

"Maybe they didn't want to use it for anything. Maybe they were just making some kind of point by draining the blood out of her."

"What would be the point?"

"I have no idea."

"Gus told me way more than I want to know about voodoo dolls, and he knows somebody who might be able to tell us what the symbols mean. Have you ever heard of a place called Moonstone?"

"Yeah, it's in Gatlinburg. They sell rocks."

"You've been there?"

"Of course. Haven't you?"

"Been a little busy to go rock shopping since I took over this job." Rileigh could tell Mitch was grinning, even though she couldn't see him over the phone. "He said that the person who runs the place, a fellow named Rupert Boemig, might be able to tell us the meaning of the symbols."

"When are you going to Moonstone to talk to him?"

"ASAP. Would you like to come along? I was thinking we could try out that new Mexican restaurant afterward."

"If it's Mexican food, I'm in!"

Rileigh drove from Mama's house to Mitch's office in the courthouse, then on the ride from Black Bear Forge to Gatlinburg, Rileigh told Mitch about Jillian's flashback the night before.

"A bell?" he said.

"Uh huh. She didn't tell me much about it, and I didn't ask. But apparently, she was…" Rileigh took a breath. "She was owned by some guy who summoned her when he wanted her by ringing a bell."

Mitch shook his head. "God only knows what that woman has gone through."

"God and Jillian, and I'm not sure I want to get on that mailing list."

"Do you think she'll tell you?"

"She'll tell me if she decides to, and I'll listen if she

tells me, and beyond that, I don't have any idea what happened to her. Have you ever had a flashback?"

"No," Mitch said. "But I've been good friends with a lot of people who have them, and I'm sure the only thing worse than watching one is living through one."

"You got that right,"Rileigh agreed.

Mitch was quiet for a little while.

"Did you have flashbacks when you got back from Afghanistan?"

"Yeah, for a while."

He said nothing for a few moments, then, "I'm sorry."

That wasn't the response she was expecting, and it so surprised her that she didn't know what else to say.

Mitch drove down one of the main thoroughfares in Gatlinburg, or at least, he tried. Nobody drove down it. You *inched* down it. Watched the red light turn green and then red again, then green, then red again before you actually got to the intersection. This was June in the Smoky Mountains, which meant sunshine and tourists. After the ordeal of driving down the street, the task of finding a place to park was somewhat mitigated by Mitch's police cruiser. He parked in front of a fire hydrant, got out, and grinned at her.

"Rank hath its privileges."

Mitch and Rileigh stepped into the cool interior of the Moonstone store. "No wonder Gus said he would cheerfully buy every rock in this place."

"So would I," said Rileigh.

"I didn't know you had a thing for rocks."

"You don't have to have a thing for rocks to think these are among the most beautiful objects in the universe. Just look at them."

The store was filled with thousands upon thousands of stunning rock crystals. Rileigh couldn't have identified what most of them were. But she didn't have to know their names to admire them. There were clear crystals as big as your fist. Giant geodes, bigger than a refrigerator, broken open to reveal the crystals inside. Yellow crystals and blue crystals and milky-white crystals. Some had been carved into various shapes. A dolphin made out of jade. A mermaid on a rock carved from some stone Rileigh didn't recognize, as red as a drop of blood. The store also sold the kinds of items that Rileigh had seen on the altars in Jaclyn's and Olivia's houses. Plus, all manner of other strange artifacts that she didn't know the names or the function of. Taken all of a piece, the store overwhelmed the senses with beauty and ... she had to admit it ... creepiness.

The man who ran the store called Moonstone looked just like a black Santa Claus. He had the big bushy hair going and the huge beard that came all the way down his big round belly. But it wasn't just those traditional things that made him look like Santa. It was his eyes. Just like in that *'Twas the Night Before Christmas* poem, his eyes *twinkled*. They were merry. He had a button nose and a mouth that spread across his face in such wide smile, it felt like a hug. The fellow waddled out to greet them with his large hand extended to Mitch.

"I'm glad to meet you, Sheriff." His name tag identified him as Rupert Boemig. "Gus has babbled on and on and on about you."

"Said good things I hope."

"Rest assured, Gus Hazelton holds you in high regard, and I suspect there aren't many people you could say that about."

Though the compliment caught Mitch off guard, you could tell he was pleased.

"That man completely confounds me. I've never met a

man who more enjoyed minerals more than I do. And I also never met a man with his kind of money. But he never buys anything."

"He told me it was because—"

The man named Rupert held up his hand. "Unless you find it, it's not yours. He's told me time and again." He made a sweeping gesture around all the beautiful crystals in the store. "I didn't find all these, but by golly, they're mine. You don't need to go trekking up and down mountains with a sack. All you need is a credit card. Now, how can I help you fine folks today?"

"Gus told us you were an expert on Wicca and witches and Satanism and—"

"And Gus is full of shit. I'm not an expert on any of those things. I know a thing or two because I've sold so much merchandise to those people. But I'm not an adherent." He grinned again. "First Baptist, Gatlinburg."

"We're investigating a murder case and some of the evidence involves symbols that were written on doors and door frames and walls. We'd like to know what they are and what they mean."

Mitch pulled his phone out of his pocket and called up the first photograph of the picture of Jaclyn's door and walls.

"What's that drawn in?" Rupert asked. "Red paint?"

"No, it's blood."

"Let me take closer look."

The man who looked like Santa Claus poked his chubby finger at the first image, a triangle, with what appeared to be a human eye inside.

"That there's the eye of providence," he said. "It's a Satanist symbol indicating that an all-seeing eye has unlimited access to us. They believe it represents God watching over everything and seeing everything. But it can also represents the third eye that allows you to see the truth. That's why it's wide open, and surrounded by light."

The next image the man identified was an upside-down triangle with lines intersecting it and a V at the bottom. "That's the sigil of Lucifer. Even though some people consider Lucifer a symbol of evil, the Satanists think he's a symbol of freedom and independence."

In the next picture Mitch showed him, there were three interlocking circles.

"That's a Celtic knot. The use of three circles is an important concept in Wicca."

The man looked from Mitch to Rileigh and back. "You do know that Wicca and Satanism are two entirely different things, right? You need to know that to understand either one of them. In the Celtic knot, the three circles represent the three stages of the goddess, but also the three stages of life. Birth, life, and death. It's used, I think, as a protective symbol in Wicca's spells and rituals."

Rupert looked at the symbol that looked like a number three with circles on the ends of the lines. "That's an angelic symbol."

"Christian?"

The man nodded.

"It belongs to the choir of Seraphim. It's an angel. And as I remember, that particular angel has the gift of triumph over adversity and maybe protection from weapons and dangerous animals. But I could be wrong, I'd have to do some research."

When he saw the picture of the spiral, the man said, "That's another Wiccan symbol. Representing the energy needed to make changes."

What looked like a stylistic letter Y with small circles on the ends of the lines represented the angel Raphael.

"He's about longevity and health. He heals diseases

and transforms souls from evil to good." He pointed to the inverted cross. "Of course, this one is a satanic symbol. Turning it upside down is meant to disrespect Christ. And the whole point of that is to represent the choice to rebel instead of submitting and obeying God. It doesn't make sense to put them together."

The man identified all of the rest of the symbols, one by one. Some of them were Wiccan. Some of them were witches' symbols, some Christian, and some Satanic. It became clear to Rileigh and Mitch that the killer who'd drawn those symbols in blood on the outside of Jaclyn's door was simply throwing paint on a wall to see what would stick, only in this instance the paint was blood. They were so random, it was clear that the person who'd put the symbols there knew nothing about any of the religions or practices they represented.

When Rileigh and Mitch left Moonstone, they decided to walk to the restaurant, since it was only a couple of blocks away.

Rileigh's stomach rumbled. She considered herself something of an aficionado of Mexican food, particularly tacos.

"This place better be good," Rileigh said, "and it's a high bar. Tortilla Tantrums is to die for. So is Guac and Roll." Then Rileigh spotted the building and smiled. "I don't know if the food's good, but I like the name — Tacosaurus Rex."

Chapter Seventeen

A LITTLE BELL above the door dinged when Rileigh and Mitch stepped into the cool interior of Tacosaurus Rex, and the smell of Mexican food almost overwhelmed her. Rileigh had loved Mexican food since she was a little girl, the hotter the better. She loved jalapeños. Fellow soldiers used to shake their heads in disbelief when she gobbled them down, asking, "How can you tell what they taste like while they're causing third-degree burns on your tongue?"

In fact, she had once entered, and lost, a jalapeño-eating contest. The fellow who beat her had cheated. At least she felt like he had. He had thrown up at one point during the competition, and she thought not keeping the jalapeños down ought to be grounds for disqualification, but the judges saw it differently. She remembered the medics stationed at both ends of the table where the contestants sat. Some substance in jalapeños, or maybe just the fact that they were so hot, raised a person's blood pressure precipitously high, and one contestant was disqualified when a medic took his blood pressure and said he was in danger of an imminent stroke.

The waitress showed them to a little table by a window where they looked out on the unending stream of tourists cruising the street up and down. "They look like salmon swimming upstream," Rileigh said, nodding to the tourists.

No, that wasn't right. Few people in the living wedge of tourists swam against the current. As if by some unspoken agreement, the crowds flowed up one side of the street and down the other, with the street in the middle acting like the median of a divided highway.

"Lemmings, maybe?" Mitch said.

"I have a theory," Rileigh said, as the waitress came and brought them glasses of ice water. "I think there are only about a hundred people, really. They march down one side of the street, change clothes, and march back up the other side. It's all the same people."

"And they do that because…"

"Because they're tourists."

Rileigh and Mitch poured over the menu, with Rileigh pointing from one dish to the next, saying "ooh, I want that," and "oh, that sounds good."

You would think, from listening to her, that she weighed a hundred pounds more than she actually did. As Georgia had pointed out on many occasions, there are people who eat when they're upset and people who don't eat when they are upset, Georgia being the former, and Rileigh being the latter. But Rileigh always figured the flip side of that was also true, which was that when she wasn't upset, she ate like a field hand. Or a trucker, or a lumber-jack. Take your pick.

"The fish tacos sound glorious," Rileigh said. "Fried tilapia topped with ancho chipotle sauce. Served with rice and pico de gallo."

Mitch was leaning toward the pollo mexicano, mari-nated grilled chicken strips topped with a red sauce, medium to hot, and served with rice, refried beans, tortillas, and a salad.

But when the waitress actually arrived, Rileigh selected a fajita quesadilla. A tortilla grilled and stuffed with shredded cheese, sauteed onions, bell peppers, and chicken or steak. She chose steak, with a side order of tacos.

Rileigh settled back in her chair. "I'm like Gus, I want everything in that Moonstone store. So if you're wondering what to get me for Christmas, get me a rock."

She said it in the light-hearted way that you say that kind of thing. But suddenly it felt awkward. It implied Christmas presents and birthday presents. And one didn't get Christmas and birthday presents for casual acquaintances. Usually not even for good friends. Georgia and Rileigh never got each other anything for Christmas. On birthdays, it was gag gifts. One year, Rileigh got Georgia a calendar with different pictures of dogs taking a dump for each month. Georgia retaliated with rodent earrings that looked like a rat was jumping through Rileigh's earlobe.

But if you were in a romantic or even semi-romantic relationship, you had to think about birthday presents and Christmas presents and Valentine's Day flowers. That had never happened between Rileigh and Mitch before. She didn't like that she'd brought it up, but didn't know how to make it un-awkward.

"When is your birthday?" Mitch asked.

"July the 25th."

"Coming up soon. I'll remember."

Rileigh kept herself from blurting out something that would make it even more awkward, such as, "I wasn't hinting for you to get me a present." Or, "You don't have to get me anything. We're not *that* kind of friends."

But the truth still in the husk was that she didn't know what kind of friends they were. She didn't know exactly what was going on between them. All she did know was that something was, and the something made her smile.

Mitch finally leapt over the gulf of awkwardness that had stretched out between them.

"I hope you're planning to go with me to interview the third witch in Annamaria's quartet."

He stopped and thought, "I wonder what the collective noun for witches is. You know, like covey of quail, flock of pigeons, pride of lions."

"How about black cat of witches?"

"Black cat doesn't sound like a collective noun."

"Murder doesn't sound like a collective noun either, but that's what a group of crows is called."

"Broomstick of witches?"

"Maybe." Then she smiled, looking over Mitch's shoulder at the waitress carrying a tray laden with deliciousness toward their table.

Rileigh was chewing a mouthful of taco when Mitch dropped the bombshell. Alright. It wasn't a bomb. More like a firecracker. But it did go off with a bang.

"You know that time I invited you to dinner? Right before—"

"The guy tried to kill me. Yeah, I remember."

What she didn't say, what she'd never said was that she had been thinking about Mitch's invitation to dinner and what it might mean when her side window blew out from the sniper's rifle bullet. And she still didn't know how she felt about it.

"The invitation is still open," Mitch said, studying his fork as he dipped a chip into salsa so hot it was in danger of melting the bowl. He didn't look at her, but sounded casual. "I'd just like to have dinner together, you and me, and not talk about dead bodies or blood or witches or any other ugly thing. Just enjoy."

Rileigh swallowed the taco bite and opened her mouth to reply when the mic on his shoulder crackled.

It was the dispatcher.

"Unit one, units three and four request back-up on Donner Pike. Disturbance reported."

Donner Pike was where the little Lutheran church was located.

Mitch had a quizzical look on his face and she knew he was thinking: *Why do they need back up? A protest isn't exactly a shootout.*

"A man has barricaded himself inside the church and is demanding to see the sheriff."

"Ten-four, tell them we're ten-twenty-six," which meant *on the way.*

Rileigh looked longingly at the food on her plate.

"Wrap a taco up in a napkin and let's go," Mitch said, and got to his feet.

When Rileigh and Mitch rounded the bend on Donner Lane and headed toward what had once been a little Lutheran church, Mitch had to blip his siren and turn on his lights to get the crowd in front of the church to part. Rileigh looked out the windows at the people who were protesting. None of them were carrying signs, so this might have been an impromptu protest that hadn't given the crowd time to prepare. She recognized a lot of the people in the crowd, mostly from Zeke Wakefield's church up in Juniper Hollow. But there were other people there as well. Folks you'd call normal people. Plus the strident minority of self-righteous Christians who saw it as their mission in life to find fault and point it out. Thankfully, Snoddy was nowhere in sight. That was the good news.

The doors to the church were closed, and the protesters were standing outside screaming. Chief among them was Zeke Wakefield, yelling about hellfire and damnation and the condemnation of souls to the fiery pit and demanding that the Satanist church leave this county immediately. He was in preacher mode as Rileigh and Mitch approached, sounding like he was giving a sermon in the rhythm of call and repeat, as if he were waiting for somebody to yell, "Amen" whenever he paused to draw breath.

"You are not going to drag the good people of this county down into hellfire with you," Zeke cried. "We're good people. We're God-fearing people, and we stand here in mighty opposition to the Devil and all his tricks."

"Get out of town," somebody yelled.

"Your kind ain't welcome here," somebody else yelled.

"God threw Satan out of heaven — like we're gonna throw you out of Yarmouth County."

The crowd wasn't as ugly as it could've been, they seemed more offended than angry. But Zeke was doing his dead-level best to whip them up into a frenzy. Two Sheriff's Department deputies' cars were parked on the roadside. Mullins and Rawlings stood in front of the church door, keeping the crowd at bay. When they got closer, Rileigh could see that Zeke's son Ross had come with him and was screaming right alongside him.

Ross was a good-looking young man. Had all of Zeke's good features and none of his bad, plus he was graced with a head of curly brown hair that made him look perpetually like a little kid as he sat in his wheelchair beside his father. Rileigh and Mitch made their way through the crowd that didn't exactly part before them like the Red Sea but did allow them to pass. Mitch got to the church door, joining the deputies on guard duty, and turned back to face Wakefield and the crowd.

"The First Amendment of the Constitution protects your right to peacefully assemble, so I'm not going to make you leave," Mitch said. A grumble of approval rumbled through the crowd.

Then Mitch pointed out, "But you have to back up to the road. From this church building to the road is private property. It belongs to … whoever has bought this building, and if you remain on it without the permission of the landowner, that's trespassing." There was a grumble of disapproval that was much louder than the grumble of approval had been.

"You're not siding with them Satanists are you?" Wakefield said. "You're the elected sheriff of this county and it's your job to—"

"It's my job to keep the peace," Mitch said, "and it's my job to make sure nobody gets hurt and everybody's voice is heard."

"But that man's a Satanist. Do you understand what that means?"

"I know exactly what that means. I'm not sure you do, but I do."

"He worships the prince of darkness. He worships the personification of all evil. He worships the father of lies. He worships Satan, Lucifer, the fallen angel who was expelled from heaven for his disobedience. And he has come here to lead all these good people astray, to take the innocent people of this county into the embrace of a church founded on disobedience to God. He's here to take all of these people to hell with him."

Mitch held up his hand.

"Look, all you got to do is back up. Stand out there on the side of the road and yell all you want to. But I have to ask you to move off of this property now."

He glanced from right to left, from Rawlings to Mullins, then the three of them began to move the crowd back while Rileigh watched from the church steps. The crowd was disgruntled and angry and as sour as any crowd is at a protest, but they didn't fight back as they retreated. The altercations with police that often happened at an event like this didn't materialize; the people allowed themselves to be moved, grumbling and mumbling back to the road where they continued to shout.

That was when Deputy Rawlings leaned over and spoke into Mitch's ear. "The guy inside that church is demanding to talk to you. Nothing Beau and I could say would satisfy him."

"Fine," Mitch said and shrugged, then turned and walked back across the little strip of weedy grass to the front door of the church building. Rileigh noted that she'd been mistaken. There wasn't a hole in the roof of the building. There was just a big limb laying there from the latest storm.

Mitch rapped with his knuckles on the door and called out. "This is Yarmouth County Sheriff Mitchell Webster. I understand you want to talk to me. Open the door."

The door slowly opened and a man stepped into the doorway.

"Hello there, Mitch," he said. "Long time no see."

Chapter Eighteen

"You've come up in the world since the last time I saw you," the man standing in the doorway said to Mitch. "You were a lowly patrolman then, and now you've made it all the way up the ladder to Sheriff."

"And you were a low-life bastard the last time I saw you. Doesn't look like you've changed a bit."

"Tut tut tut. Such a terrible thing to say about an old friend."

"We were never friends, Pierce."

"Um, that's another thing I've changed — my name." Then his eyes slid sideways to Rileigh at Mitch's side, smile widening. Mitch resisted the urge to step in front of Rileigh.

"I believe introductions are in order," the man said. "Hello, my name is Gilchrist McPherson."

Mitch interjected, "That'd be Gilbert Pierce."

"There's some things in life you can't change, but your name isn't one of them," the man said and smiled even wider. "Legally changed, on my drivers' license and social security card."

"I didn't know criminals paid social security."

Pierce looked just like he always had. Older, but the maturity suited him; he wore it like a Gucci suit. When Mitch knew him in Nashville years ago, he had always dressed to the nines. Looked sharp because that was what con men did. That part hadn't changed. Today he wore a three-piece suit and tie when everyone within rock throwing distance had on a T-shirt and shorts.

His hair had grown gray at the temples, which only made him look more distinguished, and he had a white streak down the top of his headfrom his widow's peak in the front to his hairline. It looked natural, though it probably wasn't — it was too perfect to be real. But that's the way Pierce had always been. A little too perfect.

Mitch remembered that Georgia had described the new pastor of the Satanist church as looking like Gavin Newsom, the governor of California. He did bear a striking resemblance to the man. He was tall and slender and lithe, moving like a former athlete. His eyes were large and expressive, a shade of brown that could look kind and gentle when he turned on that particular faucet.

He was handsome, all the way down to the cleft in his chin. And he was on the short list of the most despicable human beings Mitch had ever met.

"Please come in," Pierce said. He stepped back and opened the door wide. Mitch followed Rileigh into the building, which was currently a construction site. Somebody had replaced a part of the entryway with new drywall. Other walls had been ripped out to reveal the electrics behind switches; the floor was missing in places to reveal the plumbing.

"As you can see, I'm not exactly ready to entertain yet."

"What are you doing here, Pierce?"

"Hey, I just heard you tell those people it's a free country."

"I asked what you're doing here."

"I've come as an emissary of the fallen angel Lucifer. And I'm calling his children home."

"Got two words for that, Pierce. Bull shit."

Mitch had lots of memories of Gilbert Pierce because he was the fish that got away. Mitch was never able to nail him for anything. He'd caught him bilking old people out of their life's savings, but could never get enough evidence against him to make the charges stick.

Turning to Rileigh, he said, "This man is a master of his trade. I have to admit, I've never seen better. He could sell screen doors to submarines. I went to school on him though. Learned how to spot a con man under the goal posts from the fifty-yard line. He sold some kind of stocks, bonds, and securities to elderly people who didn't have any idea what they were buying. And what they were buying was a handful of nothing."

"Now, Mitchell ..."

"And oh, was he smooth. This guy is one of the best liars I have ever seen. He blends in with any group, like an ink spot spreading out through a blotter. He was forty years younger than the people in the Hillsdale Senior Living facility where he plied his trade, but you'd think he was a peer to them all. He could read people and he brought out the worst in them — fear, greed, insecurity. He preyed on those. And like a fashionista has shoes to go with every outfit, he had a line to go with every con."

Mitch stood back and thought. "'I just got a hot tip from an inside source that this stock will go through the roof.' He used that one lot. And 'Your return is guaranteed. There's no way you can lose money.' He'd tell old people, 'You gotta get in on the ground floor now or you'll be left out in the cold.' And he always sent a messenger to their home to collect their checks, so he couldn't be brought up on federal mail fraud charges."

Pierce/McPherson merely stood and listened as Mitch described his techniques. He never took his eyes off Rileigh either. Mitch did not like the way he looked at her.

"Are you done yet?" McPherson asked. "Because if you're not, I'll wait. I don't mind at all listening to somebody describe the man I used to be. Because I'm not that man anymore."

"You may have changed your name and moved to a different town, but it's just the same con, different day. But Yarmouth County isn't Nashville. These people all know each other. And you're an outsider. Good luck trying to wrench their money out of their fingers. A con man could starve to death real quick here."

"Why a Satanist church?" Rileigh asked. It was the first time she had spoken. Pierce regarded her with a look of kind affection, which would be totally appropriate for a minister looking at a member of his congregation. "What kind of con can you possibly run out of a church dedicated to the devil?"

McPherson shrugged. "It's not like I have any choice. I have been called. Commissioned." He held up his hand as soon as he saw the smirk begin to form on Mitch's face. "I know it doesn't sound believable. It doesn't matter whether you believe me. Truth is truth."

"And you wouldn't know truth if you found it in your underwear drawer."

"I had a miraculous experience. Something happened to me that changed my whole life."

"It certainly needed changing, but I doubt it changed for the better."

"I was visited by the Lord himself. The Lord *Lucifer.*"

There was something about the way he said that. Some light in his eyes. Some fierceness in his voice that put chills down Mitch's spine. "He commissioned me to start a church that would honor him and glorify him. Show people the way to the true God."

"That's got a nice ring to it, though the people out there on the road would argue about the identity of the 'one true God.'"

"There are any number of different Satanists or Luciferians, as we are sometimes called. Just as there are any number of different denominations worshipping God. For some, Satan and Lucifer are merely a symbol of the values that they champion — independence, rebellion against unnecessary authority. But there are others of us who know that Satan is real. He lives. And those of us who worship him understand that, one day, we will rule with him over the earth. And that we must stamp under our feet any religion that venerates any God other than our master Satan."

"That's a pretty impressive speech. You give it often?"

There was a light in MacPherson's eyes now that might have been anger at Mitch for making fun of him. But he turned it aside.

"All through history, we have been maligned by those who don't understand. They claim that we engage in incestuous sexual orgies and sacrifice children. Just like the Romans said of Christians in the early centuries. But the worst thing that has happened to Satanism since Satan voluntarily left heaven behind — because he was greater than the god that ruled it —is the association between Satanism and witchcraft. There is no association between Satanism and witchcraft, no alliance, no connection of any kind. Witchcraft is stupid magic tricks. Witchcraft is pointy hats and broomsticks and black cats. Satan is real, alive, in control of the universe. And yet people associate him with little kids in Halloween costumes. You saw what happened at that Wiccan ceremony, didn't you?"

"Missed the show," Mitch said.

"It's their fault!" The man's eyes were black now, not brown, darkened by unspent fury. "Those … cartoon characters are keeping people from seeing the light of truth. Witches make a mockery of who we are and what we represent. They must be stamped out. The inquisition had the right idea, they just didn't take it far enough."

"So, you believe witchcraft should be stamped out?"

"It should be eradicated from the face of the earth."

"What about witches? Witchcraft is a set of beliefs. Witches are human beings. What happens to them?"

"They must all die."

Mitch felt the hair on the back of his neck begin to stand up. "So, you're saying Satan sent you here to do his will — which is to stamp out witchcraft and kill witches?"

"Satan sent me here to found a church. And as long as those witches are distracting them with candles and crystals and stories about their made-up gods, ordinary people will never hear the message."

"You didn't answer my question. I asked if Satan sent you here to stamp out witchcraft and kill witches?"

"If he had, I would obey." Then McPherson bowed at the waist and gestured toward the door. "I invited you in, I'm now inviting you out. Leave my church and don't come back."

"I'll issue the same invitation to you," Mitch said. "Leave my county and don't come back."

Chapter Nineteen

RILEIGH AND MITCH made their way through the protesters back to his cruiser. The protesting crowd had thinned some, but what they lacked in numbers, they made up for in intensity as they yelled and chanted. Rileigh always wondered about that. Where did protesters come up with their chants?

Zeke Wakefield was still on a roll. When they opened the door, they saw him standing out on the roadside just inches beyond the property of the church. As soon as he spotted McPherson behind them, he began screaming again that he was the spawn of Satan, that he was evil incarnate, that God would strike him down with a bolt of lightning. McPherson did not respond in kind, but Rileigh could tell that Wakefield was getting under his skin.

McPherson had a stick in his craw about witches, but Rileigh thought he ought to be a little more worried about the Christians yelling for blood right now.

She slid into the cruiser beside Mitch, who slammed his door too hard.

"That's all I need. Gilbert Pierce, here."

"You guys have quite a history," Rileigh said.

"That man is total pond scum."

"Pond scum, yes, but is he more than that?"

Mitch turned and looked at her. "You're asking me if I think he's capable of violence? The answer is, absolutely yes. If you're asking me, do I think he murdered Annie Giordano, the answer is the jury's still out on that. I suppose it's possible. He certainly got into it with all the witches at that ceremony. According to everyone I've talked to, that was the main event. But it is a bit of a stretch that he shows up, gets into an argument, then murders the person he was arguing with that night."

"True. But he certainly strikes me as a man who would be capable of slitting someone's throat and then using a garden claw to make it look more vicious."

"He did have both motive and opportunity. But still, it's a stretch."

Georgia called Rileigh on her way home and asked if she'd stop by the store and pick up some bananas. That was the equivalent of a 911 call. Because if Georgia ran out of bananas, Mayella would turn life in that house into an emergency.

She pulled up in front of the double-wide trailer on Carter's Mill Road, got out, and watched the kids playing in the yard. She loved all of Georgia's kids, but there was a special place in her heart for Mason because of what they had been through together. She had saved his life, but he had saved hers too. He came running when he saw her, flung his arms around her legs, squealing, "Aunt Rileigh" and the other kids piled on for a group hug. She was Aunt Rileigh to them all. As soon as she got into the house with the bananas, Georgia snatched one, peeled it, and handed it to a squalling Mayella, who shut up like you'd taken out her batteries.

"Thank you so, so much," Georgia said. "I owe you my life. How many times have you saved it? I've lost count."

She said it in the offhand way of a casual remark, but with gut-baring honesty. Rileigh got both messages.

"So, how'd you spend this lovely Saturday in June?" Georgia asked as she loaded dishes into the dishwasher, then searched around under the cabinet until she found some dishwashing soap and started the machine.

"I just came from a protest," Rileigh said.

"Another one?"

"I suspect there are going to be a lot of them around here for a while," Rileigh said. "We've got people with diametrically opposed world views bumping up against each other and sparks are starting to fly."

"And that's different from what's going on in the rest of the country …how?"

"True that."

"Who was it this time?"

"Reverend Zeke Wakefield of the holiness church versus the not-reverend Gilchrist McPherson of the Satanist church. Mitch knows Gilchrist as a con man in Nashville, almost came to blows. But Gilchrist has saved his real ire for the witches."

"So has Wakefield," Georgia said. "Both of them." She opened the refrigerator, got out some ice and plunked two big cubes into a glass, filled it with lemonade, and handed it to Rileigh. Georgia's lemonade rivaled Mama's. In a lemonade Olympics, they would share gold.

"What do you mean, both of them?"

"Both Wakefields. At that summer solstice celebration downtown, it wasn't just the elder Mr. Wakefield who looked like he wanted to strangle the witches. So did the younger. Well, not all the witches, just Jaclyn."

"Ross?"

"Yep, I was walking back to my car and caught sight of them screaming at each other."

"About Jaclyn becoming a witch?"

"No, about the fact that she broke up with him. Of course, he tacked onto it that she'd always been a witch, and now she was just making it official — the kinds of things people say after they break up." She paused. "But I will say I was surprised at how vicious Ross was. He said Jaclyn had deceived him, made him think she was a sweet Christian girl when in reality she was a, what did he call her? A 'cloven-footed demon from the bowels of hell.'"

"Yeah, that's kinda nasty."

"He laid a guilt trip on her, too, that it was her fault he was in a wheelchair. Apparently, she destroyed his life and stole both his livelihood and his masculinity, along with his legs."

"Hard to be a lineman for the electric company from a wheelchair."

"In the beginning, there was talk that maybe it wasn't permanent, but I guess that was wishful thinking." Mayella finished the first banana and Georgia peeled a second. "So how did you happen to be at the protest outside the church? Just passing by and thought you'd drop in?"

"No. Mitch and I were having lunch at that new Mexican food place, Tacosaurus Rex. But I ended up eating my taco out of a napkin in my lap. He got a call in the middle of it that the protest was going on, and that the Satanist minister was demanding to see the sheriff. So, we get there, and turns out the Satanist minister is—"

"Whoa, whoa, whoa. How about we back up to the part where you said, 'Mitch and I were having lunch.' That's the interesting part. How? Give."

"He called this morning and asked if I would go with him to the Moonstone store in Gatlinburg. Gus told him that the fellow who ran the place might recognize the runes that were left in blood on the doors of the witches' houses."

"Describe for me the landscape between the invitation to Moonstone and tacos."

"Mitch said it's a new place and he knows I like Mexican food."

"So, this was a date?"

"I didn't say that."

"I know you didn't say it. I'm asking. Was it a date?"

"Maybe it was something like a date."

"The only thing that's *something like a date* is a fig. Maybe an olive." Georgia eyed the half-eaten banana in front of Mayella and reached for a third one, but didn't start peeling it yet. "When are you going to give up the ghost and admit that you and Mitch are dating? What is so absolutely horrible about that?"

"It's just complicated. I don't know what we're doing."

"You're dating. Trust me."

"It's complicated because we work together." Sort of, unofficially.

"You think you're the first police officers who ever got together? Don't you watch *Blue Bloods*?" Georgia sat back and eyed her. "This isn't about what you are saying it's about."

"Then what is it about? And what am I saying it's about?"

"You're saying it's all complicated because the two of you work together. But I don't think that's it. I think it's complicated because you're making it complicated. Because you're scared."

"Scared."

"Hell yeah. Scared of commitment. You've sailed through all these years without being in a serious relationship because that's what you've chosen. That's how you chose to live. You got away with it when you were in the military because that was a pretty normal way to behave in the military."

"Why would I be afraid of commitment?"

"So you *are* afraid of commitment?"

"I didn't say that."

"What did you say?"

"I said that I don't know what we're doing."

"Girl, you could complicate a one-car funeral procession."

"How about a new topic, no transition."

"Fine. One last point: you don't owe me an explanation of your love life, but you do owe yourself one. If you genuinely don't know what you and Mitch are doing, I think it might be a plan to figure it out." Georgia took a deep breath. "Want a cookie? I got Oreos. I keep a box on top of the refrigerator, to hide them from the kids."

"I'll pass... unless you've got Girl Scout cookies. I'd crawl over ten miles of razor blades and rusty Spam lids for one of those Samoas. I think we stunted the development of our interpersonal skills by not selling those when we were kids."

"My sister Grace was a leader. We coulda joined. Speaking of sisters, how's Jillian?"

"Jillian is ... better."

"Do you ever wonder —"

"Yes, but I don't ask. She'll tell me when she's ready."

"Not *that*, just ... she mentioned to me that she got a good deal on that Nissan because she paid cash. Who pays cash for a car? How much money has she got and how—"

"I don't know," Rileigh said, hating that answer more every time she was forced to say it. "That's the answer to every Jillian question — I don't know."

Chapter Twenty

WHEN RILEIGH PULLED up in front of Mama's house late that afternoon, she took a better look than she had before at Jillian's car. She had assumed, she didn't know why, that it was a rental. Now that she knew Jillian owned it, and not just owned it, but had paid cash for it, she took a better look.

It was a nondescript Honda Accord, light blue.

But Rileigh knew that she had purchased the vehicle in the name of Heather Priest, which was the name that was on all of her documents, including her driver's license and her passport. Rileigh hadn't gotten around to asking how she'd come by the documents, let alone the car.

She went up the steps and into the house, through the house to the kitchen, where Mama was starting supper.

"Where's Jillian?"

"She went for a walk in the woods."

Rileigh smiled at that. Jillian had taken her on many long walks in the woods when she was a little girl. That's how she'd grown to love them so much. Jillian seemed to know the answers to every question she asked. And now, looking back with grown-up eyes, she realized that it wasn't that Jillian was an amateur botanist. It's just that the questions a little girl asks about flowers and leaves and bees and trees and why there are no big fish in the creek were questions that had easy answers. Rileigh shook her head. There weren't any easy answers to the questions in Rileigh's life anymore. And there certainly weren't any easy answers to the questions in Jillian's.

"Which way did she go, Mama?"

Mama pointed out to the west. There were lots of trails out here in the woods, or at least there had been at one time. When Rileigh was a little girl, she'd worn trails up and down these hills. Most of those had grown over now. But where Mama pointed, there was a trail that was still discernible. Because it was the major trail to the place where you could look out over the mountains. It wasn't an overlook, not in the same way the big overlooks were. There was no drop-off. It was just that there were rocks you could climb on at the top of the mountain and get a view all around.

Rileigh went upstairs and changed her shoes. Then she went out the back door, calling over her shoulder. "Give us a honk when dinner's ready," she said.

That was how you called children into dinner in the mountains. You honked the car horn. Or if you had a big dinner bell, that would work. But car horns were universal.

As Rileigh walked through the trees up the trail, it occurred to her that this was a really lonely, empty place. Other than Mama, there was nobody here, not for miles. If you fell down and broke your leg, you better hope somebody knew where you went. Because it's not like another hiker would come by in a few minutes and see you.

She wondered how Jillian felt being out here all alone again. When Rileigh had left in the middle of the night to go to the scene of that murder, Jillian seemed to see danger behind every bush. Rileigh could understand that, given the life Jillian had been leading. But fear was no way to live. As best she could, Rileigh intended to drag her sister, perhaps kicking and screaming, out of a fearful existence and into the sunshine.

Rileigh started whistling as she walked alone so she wouldn't startle Jillian if she happened to come upon her on the trail. She started out with the theme from the Andy Griffith show, which was the universal whistle song in all the world. She went from that to the score for *High Noon*. Rileigh was a good whistler. Another skill that Jillian had taught her when she was a little girl, and every time she whistled, she thought about her big sister.

In fact, Rileigh remembered that when Jillian vanished, she had been trying to teach her how to snap her fingers.

"Hello down there." She looked up and saw Jillian had climbed up on the big boulders and was facing the setting sun, looking out over the mountains.

Rileigh hopped like a squirrel from one rock to the next until she got to Jillian, then sat down beside her.

"It's beautiful," Jillian said.

"No more beautiful place in the world," Rileigh replied.

"I've been to some places that were geographically beautiful. That's the way I thought of it, that the geography was beautiful. The south of France. The Red Sea coast. The world that God made was sometimes a really beautiful place around me. I concentrated on that." Jillian paused for a beat. "Where have you been?"

Rileigh realized that was her cue not to ask any more questions.

"I have been at a protest," she said.

Jillian raised an eyebrow. "Oh, tell me about it."

So Rileigh told Jillian about going to meet Mitch at Moonstone and asking about the symbols that had been drawn on Annie's friends' doors.

"Rupert knew what they were."

"Witches' symbols?"

"They were nothing and everything, a hodgepodge. Some witches' symbols, some Christian symbols, some Satanic symbols. There was no message in them."

"You thought you'd find a message?"

"Hoped we would. Something to point us toward who did this."

Jillian was silent for a few moments, then seemed to be selecting her words carefully. "So, until the sheriff does figure out who committed this murder and makes an arrest, are you going to be running out of the house at all hours of the night and going God knows where?"

Rileigh sensed several different levels of emotion in the question. Mostly she heard fear. Jillian was afraid for her. She was looking after baby sister as she had done her whole life, until her life had been stolen away from her. Somehow Rileigh had to reassure her, but she didn't know how. And in truth, she probably couldn't. Jillian was just going to have to learn to live with the fact that Rileigh was a part-time cop.

"Until Mitch finds the killer and makes an arrest, I'll be helping him whenever he needs it, wherever he needs it."

"So you'll be running off at—"

"I will be leaving here at whatever time he calls," Rileigh said deliberately, slowly. "That's not the same thing as running off in the middle of the night. Jillian, I'm not in any danger. There's a killer out there who committed murder, but he's not after me." Rileigh looked around at the wonderful view. "These are the Smoky Mountains. These are our people. It's safe here."

When Jillian didn't respond, Rileigh said. "If it's not, then you probably shouldn't be out here alone taking a walk."

"I have protection."

"What do you mean you have protection?"

As naturally as reaching into your pocket and taking out your phone to show a friend a cute video of a dog standing on its head, Jillian pulled from her pocket a Ruger five-shot revolver.

Rileigh froze. "Where did you get that?"

"I know a guy who knows a guy."

"I'm serious, Jillian. Where did you get the gun?"

"I'm serious, Rileigh. I got a gun and a whole new identity and all matter of other things I might need. I know where to go. And it's way out there beyond where the rest of the world lives."

"Why do you want a gun?"

"I've been living in hell for three decades among the most dangerous people on the planet who have absolutely no regard for human life or anything else. And you wonder why I would need a gun?"

Rileigh couldn't fault her for that.

"Do you know how to use it?" she asked.

The Ruger 38-caliber revolver was designed to be an alternative to the Smith and Wesson Airweight model. The upside with both those handguns was that they were extremely lightweight and easy to carry and conceal, along with the reliability that comes with a revolver. Of course, the downside was that they were so lightweight they kicked like a mule. The other downside, in Rileigh's opinion, was that Ruger had somehow figured out how to make a mildly-unattractive gun look downright ugly.

"Yes, I know how to use it."

Rileigh didn't know if Jillian knew — or cared — about Tennessee law regarding handguns. It was wide open, permitted citizens to carry a loaded handgun on their person openly or concealed without a permit.

"You carry that gun with you everywhere you go?" Rileigh asked.

"It's always in my pocket," Jillian said.

Rileigh didn't quite know what to make of that. She understood Jillian's fear. She understood her need to find a way to protect herself. But she also understood that carrying a handgun was dangerous. Statistically, it was way more dangerous for the person carrying it than for somebody they might try to shoot with it.

Jillian might say she knew how to fire the gun, and maybe she did. But she'd certainly never had firearms training.

Rileigh sat quiet for a moment, trying to figure out how to frame this. Then she said, "There's a shooting range in Pigeon Forge. How about we go there sometime and shoot? Would you like that?"

Jillian looked at her and smiled. "Translate that. Rileigh wants to see if Jillian really does know how to fire this gun. And if she doesn't, she wants to teach her."

"Pretty good translation. I didn't know you were psychologically bilingual."

"Fine by me," Jillian said. "I'm all over handgun safety."

"My firearms instructor always told me never to pull a gun unless I intended to use it."

"I've never pulled this one unless I intended to use it."

Rileigh looked close at Jillian's face. "Have you used it?"

"You're asking me if I've ever killed anybody," Jillian said. "I could ask you the same question."

"And I'd tell you, yes," Rileigh said,

"I'd tell you, yes, too." Jillian said. A chill went down Rileigh's spine, like ice water dripping from one vertebra to the next.

Chapter Twenty-One

"WE KNOW WHO DID THIS," Jaclyn said.

"No, we don't," Olivia shot back.

"Yes, we do, but nobody's going to believe us."

"*I* don't believe us." Olivia said. "I can't believe you really think that's what's going on,"

"Give me a better explanation, then. Annie didn't have any enemies, nobody wanted her dead."

"Did you have your eyes closed and your fingers in your ears when we were dancing around the fire on Main Street on Thursday?" asked Veronica — Ronnie— Espinosa.

Ronnie chewed on a fingernail that was already chewed down almost to the quick. She was an ordinary looking girl, neither pretty nor ugly, average height, average weight. Jaclyn had always considered her "eminently forgettable." She'd missed her calling holding up liquor stores because nobody'd ever pick her out of a lineup — well, except Ronnie wasn't the kind of person who would take being forgettable lying down. As soon as she got out of high school and on her own, she'd made herself memorable by covering just about every square inch of her body in tattoos. Oh, they were beautiful, she had paid a fortune for some of them. She had a gigantic rose that looked like it grew up between her breasts and lay on her chest just below her neck. She had a dragon, green with fiery red eyes curled around her left arm. And white-tailed deer running through a forest that covered her whole left thigh and most of her left butt cheek. Plus, Ronnie had a nose ring and a tongue stud and other rings in other places that most people didn't know about.

"There were some serious haters in that crowd. Didn't you notice?"

"Of course I noticed," Jaclyn said, "but people yelling at you, getting in your face, is not quite the same thing as ripping your throat out. Those people were pissed off about witchcraft, but they weren't pissed enough to—"

"I can't imagine how pissed you'd have to be to do a thing like that," Ronnie said, shuddering.

"If it wasn't a person who killed her, then *what* did?" She let the words dangle out in the air between them.

"You really believe that?" Olivia said. "You really believe that Annie was killed by a demon?"

"Of course she was," Jaclyn snapped.

Jaclyn had always known that the other girls really didn't believe in what they were doing as much as she did. They hadn't grown up around Granny Milford. They'd never seen the wondrous, magical things she could do. Jaclyn was sure that Ronnie had signed up to be a witch because it was a thing that got you noticed, and Ronnie longed to be noticed. She couldn't figure Olivia out though, couldn't read her. She was into an eclectic variety of philosophies and beliefs. She had a voodoo doll and some kind of skeleton whose outfit she changed like it was a Barbie doll.

All of that was in addition to being a witch. But when push came to shove, Jaclyn didn't know which one of those beliefs really mattered to Olivia. Maybe one of them did matter to her as much as witchcraft mattered to Jaclyn, maybe one or all of them gave her some kind of power. Maybe not. Jaclyn didn't know, but she did know they had royally screwed up, and they had to take responsibility for what they had done and undo it.

"It's not our fault," Ronnie said.

"Stop it, stop it, stop it right now. Just *stop!*" Jaclyn didn't realize she was shouting until the words left her mouth. Her two friends sat staring at her wide-eyed.

"You know what we did." Jaclyn took a deep breath, tried to calm herself. "We were all here, all into it."

It had been a boring Friday night and none of them had dates. Jaclyn hadn't gone out with anybody since she'd dumped Ross, because every time she went anywhere, he suddenly *happened* to turn up there. He was stalking her, at least what passed for stalking for a guy in a wheelchair. He'd get over it eventually and leave her alone. But between now and then, it was awkward to go out on the first or second date with some guy and constantly be running into your old boyfriend.

No, that wasn't really true. That was what Jaclyn wanted to believe. She wanted to believe that Ross was going to get over it and move on. But there was something about Ross and his intensity that wasn't normal. That's why she'd left. His possessiveness grew greater and greater the closer they got and as soon as she agreed to marry him, he acted like he owned her, body and soul. If only she could have broken up with him before the car accident.

The wreck hadn't been her fault, but that didn't change anything. She'd been driving. Ross had been in the passenger seat, and he had awakened in the hospital unable to move anything from the waist down. The doctors argued about exactly what his primary injury was, but it was some kind of contusion — bruise or swelling —on his spinal cord. A couple of the doctors even held out some slight hope that it was temporary, that once the swelling went down, he would regain use of his limbs. But the other doctors blew that off. They didn't want to hold out false hope, they said. Ross would never adjust to being in a wheelchair if he thought any minute now, he was going to get up and walk. And he needed to adjust to what life really was.

She'd tried to help him do that. But Ross was the tar baby from that children's story. You couldn't touch him and not get stuck. He misread the simplest kind gesture. The sympathy you would extend to a total stranger, he saw as a demonstration that you really did love him still. So, she couldn't even be nice to him!

Ross was why she didn't have a date that night. Since Ronnie, Olivia, and Annie were looking for something to do too, they all wound up in Jaclyn's living room, drinking daiquiris and margaritas, smoking weed and casting spells.

It'd been bussin' weed, some of the best she'd ever had. Working in a head shop, Ronnie knew where to get prime stuff. And Jaclyn had enjoyed every lungful of it. It was Olivia who'd suggested that they cast a spell to summon a djinn, and that got everyone's attention. A djinn was Middle Eastern spirit that, in Western culture, would be called a "genie."

Jaclyn had wanted to learn about different spirits from different cultures, so she'd read a little bit about the djinn, but it was Olivia who knew more than anyone. She was the most committed to strange rites and tiptoeing on the edge of evil. Danger in any form intrigued her. She was a risk-taker, a thrill-seeker.

When Olivia said, "Let's summon a genie," the other girls had giggled.

"Yeah, a genie. I want to know how they decide how many wishes to grant," Annie had said. "Every fairy tale tells a different story. There are four of us. If they only grant three wishes, what are we going to do? Flip a coin?"

"Let's summon the genie before we start divvying up the spoils," Olivia had suggested, and so they went online to read about djinns. Jaclyn had three or four witchcraft-oriented magazines and several books about witchcraft and casting spells. All of those warned against trying to summon a demon of any kind, a djinn or any other. Annie started getting cold feet first, pointing out that they were novices at this, and what if they summoned a spirit so powerful they couldn't control it? The other girls laughed. Jaclyn got the giggles, picturing putting a demon on a leash, and she couldn't stop laughing until her sides ached. They had finally settled on a rite, a spell that would work to summon a genie, and had performed all the pieces and parts of it that would make it happen.

Then they waited,

Nothing happened.

None of the four of them were surprised that the spell hadn't worked. No, that wasn't true. Jaclyn was surprised because she had seen her grandmother perform supernat-ural acts so many times — simple things like turning white eggs to brown eggs or making a watermelon ripen overnight — but still, impossible-to-explain magic things, so she knew it was possible. They were just doing something wrong, obviously. It was possible to summon a being from the spirit world to help you do good, and granting wishes was definitely helping you do good.

Jaclyn had been disappointed, but they'd just blown off the whole thing. She hadn't thought of the spell and the summoning a single time since then ... until Jerry Lockhart called her.

She could still hear the note of almost-hysteria in his voice. He was a novice member of the rescue squad, and primary to their code of ethics was that they didn't go to the scene of somebody's misfortune then call all their friends to tell them about it. That was a definite not-done, but he knew who Annie was, he recognized her, and he'd had a crush on Jaclyn since second grade; apparently he'd thought giving her the news would score points. So he had called her in the middle of the night and told her what the two teenage girls had found when they went to Buttermilk Falls. It was the first really gruesome thing he had ever been called to on the squad, and the sight of the body had totally freaked him out.

'There's all these marks around on everything, on the tree and on the rocks, marks made with blood," he'd said.

"Like, what kind of marks?"

He described a couple of them, and that's when Jaclyn's blood began to run cold. Those were the signs of demons. She knew that much. Jimmy's almost hysterical voice still rang in her head.

"Something killed her, it wasn't no person done a thing like that."

"What do you mean?"

"Some kind of animal ripped her whole throat out. You can see the bite marks."

Jaclyn shook off the memory and looked at her two

friends. "We can argue about this and keep arguing until we're all dead."

"Surely you don't believe—" Ronnie began.

"You think that what we summoned singled out Annie and killed her and that's it, it's over? He'll go back to hell and live the rest of eternity satisfied?"

She took a big breath.

"We summoned an *ifrit*. Do you know what an ifrit is?"

She'd thought Olivia would, but she shook her head no, just like Ronnie.

"It is a demon from the bowels of hell, a prince of demons, stands fifty feet tall with a scimitar in one hand and—"

"We summoned *that* and didn't notice?" Olivia scoffed.

"That's an ifrit's being in the spiritual world. I don't know what form it takes in the physical world, but whatever it was, it had canine teeth and ripped Annie's throat out."

That silenced her friends.

"You can explain the rest of it away somehow. I don't know how. Some random act of violence, some vagrant wanderer coming through town, some tourists decided to entertain themselves by killing someone. But that part is *not* explainable. You can't come up with a reason for why or how her throat was torn out, except that it was an ifrit and we summoned it."

She had Ronnie's attention now, and Olivia's too, although she could still see doubt in her eyes.

"So, what do we do?" Ronnie said. "What *can* we do? Do we run away? I can go to my aunt's in California and—"

"It doesn't matter where you are physically," Olivia said. "The spiritual realm and the physical world are not lined side by side. Travel within the spiritual world isn't the same thing. It doesn't matter where you go. If an ifrit wants you, it will come and get you."

"Then what do we do?"

"We send the son of a bitch back to hell," Jaclyn said, and for the first time felt the anger that her grief had been suppressing. "That bastard *killed* Annie. Murdered her!" Her last words rode a sob out of her throat. "And it's gonna come after us unless we get it first."

"Look, we thought we were summoning a genie," Olivia said, "and you're saying that we *accidentally* got the wrong spirit? Like what? Hell gave us chicken nuggets when we ordered a Big Mac? How—"

"I don't know *how.* I just know that it happened, and Annie's death is proof of it. Unless you all want to suffer the same fate, you have to help me send it back."

"But we don't know how we summoned it to begin with," Ronnie said. "We don't know what we did wrong that summoned a prince of evil instead of a genie. So how can we undo it if we don't even know what we did the first time?"

"There are ways to dispel evil that are beyond witch-craft," Olivia said quietly. "But you guys have to be willing to help me."

The other two girls looked at her wide-eyed.

The rest of that evening had been a blur of awful. They performed every spell to ward off evil that any of them knew. Then they descended into the blackness of voodoo that only Olivia understood and only Olivia could find her way through. When they had finished the other rites, Olivia told them the final rite would have to be a blood sacrifice.

"We need a chicken," she said. "Anybody know where we can get one?"

Jaclyn's Uncle Neb had so many, he wouldn't miss a

single pullet culled from his vast flocks. He liked to tell people he had "more'n twenty thousand little peckers." They were on their way to Uncle Neb's, but they had run out of candles and stopped by the convenience store to get some. And that's how the three girls had run into — literally *run into* — Ethel Snodmotz at the Quik Stop convenience store on Harkness Street.

Chapter Twenty-Two

JACLYN PULLED up in front of the Quik Stop convenience store and the other girls hopped out of the car.

"If I don't get my hands on some Red Bull soon, I'm going to have a full menty b," Ronnie said. "I'll spin around and around like a balloon when you let the air out of it."

Inside, the shelves were jammed with the kinds of items tourists needed to have a good time in the mountains, but the convenience store also carried normal foodstuffs, so locals shopped there, too. Oh, it had the obligatory souvenir section, like every other store — the Smokies didn't get to be the Rubber Tomahawk Capital of the world for nothing. In that area, little kids could buy fake coon skin caps, and mamas could buy useless trinkets and key fobs with black bears on them and postcards to send home to Omaha. The candles were located on the back wall next to the pharmacy. Jaclyn had bought them here before. Ronnie peeled off as soon as they entered, in search of Red Bull. She'd buy it by the gallon if they sold it that way.

Jaclyn came around the corner in the small produce aisle, headed for the pharmacy in the back of the store, and literally crashed into someone moving quickly in the other direction. Ethel Snodmotz. The collision knocked the grapefruits and oranges out of her hands, and they went bouncing across the floor.

"Well ... *phooey!*" She cried. "Made me drop my darn —" Then she saw who it was, really looked at Jaclyn.

Jaclyn had seen angry people before. She'd even seen this woman angry. But she had never watched pure rage take over a person's features, totally hijack them so they didn't even look like they had looked ten seconds before.

Ethel pointed her finger at Jaclyn and cried in horrified revulsion: "A *witch!*"

Jaclyn said nothing, just tried to go around the woman, but there was no going around her. She'd seen the woman yell at them on the street when they were doing their summer solstice celebration. But it was one thing to see a woman yelling from a crowd twenty feet away. It was something else entirely to have that woman get up in your face and scream.

"You're bound for hell," Ethel screeched. "You are a creature of foul evil. '*Thou shalt not suffer a witch to live!*' Exodus 22:18."

"Yeah, that was the verse that fueled the whole Spanish Inquisition," came a voice from behind Ethel, and she turned around to see Ronnie glaring at her. Ronnie had an unopened can of Red Bull in her hand but hadn't gotten a fix yet. She also had a temper. A bad combination. A *really* bad combination.

It was possible that Ethel Smodmotz didn't even know what the Spanish Inquisition was. She definitely looked that stupid. But even if she had, she didn't care.

"Both of you are full of ca-ca. Full of excrement. Filthy witches!"

"Actually, I showered this morning, Boomer," Ronnie said. "You should try it sometime. Wash off that pig-shit smell."

Olivia showed up then, holding two bags of chips and a big container of bean dip.

"You're *all* here now." Ethel was repulsed.

"I left my black hat and broom at home, though," Olivia said, then shrugged. "But I have a rat in my purse, I think, and a black widow spider."

"You're the three the devil hasn't claimed and dragged back to hell — *yet*. But he got the first one and your turn's coming."

"Are you talking about Annie?" growled Ronnie. Jaclyn watched her go from zero to sixty in a heartbeat, suddenly just as angry as Ethel Snodmotz.

"I don't know the witch's name, but Satan recognized her and threw her back into the fiery pit where she belonged."

Jaclyn had never met anybody as ugly as Ethel Snodmotz. It was like every one of her facial features had been selected from a list of the ten *worst* — noses, eyes, eyebrows, lips. And she was a built like a coke machine, big and broad and heavy. The combination of her size, her ugliness, and her rage should have been terrifying, but it had the opposite effect on Jaclyn. It pissed her off.

"Listen, bitch," Jaclyn growled, "get out of my face. If ever there was a hound from hell, it's you, not us. What we do is none of your damn business, so hop off."

"Oh, but it *is* my business." Ethel was a pit bull. "It's the business of all Christians to preserve the sanctity of God Almighty. That filthy witch was evil, and she deserved what she got. If I could have, I'd have killed her myself."

Ronnie surprised Jaclyn then, and she thought she knew Ronnie pretty well. They'd gone to school together, elementary through high school, had been friends, though not best friends. They'd spent thousands of hours in each other's presence, and never would Jaclyn have dreamed that Ronnie would do what she did next.

Shoving the can of Red Bull at Jaclyn, Ronnie said, "Hold my drink." Then she launched herself at Ethel Snodmotz and slammed her up against the wall.

"Don't you dare say Annie Giordano was evil. *You're* evil. You're the monster. Take it back." Ronnie grabbed her by the throat and began shaking her.

But Ethel was as strong as a bull, and she flung Ronnie away from her. Ronnie crashed into a bin in the produce department where the owner, Sundeep Singh, had carefully stacked oranges into a pyramid. The oranges exploded in every direction like shrapnel. Ronnie got her feet under her. Jaclyn tried to grab her, but Ronnie shrugged her off and went at Ethel again. Her teeth were bared, her fingers outstretched like claws, and Ethel would probably have lost a good portion of her face in the next few seconds if Ronnie had had any fingernails, but all she could do was claw at the woman with gnawed-off stumps.

Sundeep Singh abandoned the register then. He was a really nice man — was running for mayor, in fact — and Jaclyn liked him. She'd never meant to create a disturbance in his store.

"Stop it, both of you, stop it," he cried. Sundeep grabbed Ethel's arm as she tried to launch herself at Ronnie and pushed her backward. Either he hadn't meant to swing her as hard as he did, or he shared the opinion of every other man, woman, and child in Yarmouth County — that somebody needed to take Ethel Snodmotz down a peg — and was glad to participate in some small way.

Jaclyn didn't know which it was, but the result was that Ethel staggered off in the opposite direction, a lumbering mass off balance and goin' down, tail up like the sinking Titanic.

On her way to the floor, she collided with a display of carefully-arranged tomatoes, which toppled into the display of red onions next to it, and dislodged a smaller display of kiwi, mingling with the already-released oranges making a break for the door.

Sundeep confronted them, "Either learn to get along or get the hell out of my store," he said. "Mitch Webster is a friend of mine and I'm going to call him if either one of you makes another peep."

Jaclyn noticed then that a small crowd had gathered, all of the customers in the store standing wide-eyed and slack-mouthed at a tattoo-covered girl and an old woman in a catfight. With Ethel momentarily put out of commission on the floor, Sundeep seized the opportunity and started giving Ronnie a bum's rush toward the door, with Jaclyn and Olivia trailing along behind.

Ronnie snatched the can of Red Bull she hadn't paid for out of Jaclyn's hand and held it out, but he said, "Keep it, just leave before she gets back up."

He opened the door, shoved Ronnie out, and because she wasn't a fat old woman, she didn't fall down, just staggered a little.

"That was worth the price of admission," Jaclyn said, trying to make light of the circumstance to diffuse Ronnie's anger. "I bet half the population of Yarmouth County, no, the whole population of Yarmouth County, would like to shake your hand."

"That bitch," Ronnie grumbled, "talking about Annie that way."

"Amen, amen. Let's move it along," Jaclyn said, in the

voice of a kindergarten teacher to her students, as she shoved Ronnie gently before her toward the car.

"She had six inches and a hundred-fifty pounds on you, and you kicked her ass. I'm proud of you," Olivia said.

Jaclyn opened the back passenger side door and helped Ronnie inside, with significant force. Olivia got in the passenger seat as Jaclyn went around to the driver's side, got in, and turned the key.

Ethel Snodmotz came barreling out of the store at that moment, looking way more like an angry witch than any of the four of them ever had. Her helmet hair that was never out of place was sitting askew on her head, almost as if it were a wig. When she fell, she must have knocked over one of the bottles of grape juice sitting on the shelf beside the produce section, because the whole left side of her dress was the purple of a day-old bruise. There was a little scratch on her right arm, and she was so angry she had spittle dangling out of the corner of her mouth. Her nostrils flared like a charging bull.

"You will pay for that, you demon from hell!" she screeched, racing toward Jaclyn's car. She was one of those little old ladies who wore square-heeled shoes and she'd lost one somewhere in the melee. Her lopsided gait would have been comical at any other time.

Jaclyn threw the car into reverse and gave it the gas, moving backward away from the monster intent on ripping Ronnie's face off, hoping that there was no one behind her because she didn't even look. She just pulled out of the parking space, swung the car around, and went barreling out of the parking lot, leaving a streak of rubber on the asphalt. She looked in her rearview mirror and could see that Ethel was chasing after her, hobbling on uneven legs down the side of the road, shaking her fist and mouthing words they didn't have to hear to know what they were.

"Demons from hell," that's what she called them. "Emissaries of Satan himself," she'd said.

A chill ran down Jaclyn's spine because she knew, could feel it deep in her bones, that there was a demon from hell stalking Yarmouth County. And if they couldn't succeed in sending it back where it came from, she was terrified it would kill them all.

Chapter Twenty-Three

JEZZIE THACKER HAD LEFT her damn music at home. She couldn't turn around and go all the way back to fetch it neither, 'cause the road 'tween her house and the church was so bad she didn't never drive it unless she had to, afraid she was going to bust an axle or something falling down into them potholes. But it was Sunday morning, and of course she had to be there! She'd come early so she could practice before anybody else got into the building, but then she'd gone and left her damn music at home!

Jezzie wasn't short for Jessica, it was really Jezzie, and it was short for *Jezebel*. Her mama had done her dirty, giving her a name like that, but didn't nobody know the straight of it except her family, and most of them had died off now. She had a brother who didn't know his own name, let alone hers, and a sister who lived in Knoxville, but other than that she'd outlived them all and she wasn't that old, just seventy-six. She felt a helluva lot older than that this morning, forgetting her music. It had got where she was grateful her head was attached to her shoulders or she'd walk off and leave it somewhere.

Jezzie was the pianist at the Mountain Shaker Fire Baptized Holiness Church, and she wasn't very good. She never had been very good, and she never would be very good. But she was the only person in the twenty-seven-member congregation who knew how to play at all. So, for the last three and a half years, she'd shown up every Sunday morning and every Sunday night and every Wednesday night to play hymns so that the congregation could sing praises to the Lord.

She sure hoped there was some sheet music in that piano bench. Otherwise, she'd have to read music out of a hymnal, and the print was so little in them things, she could barely see it. She cursed herself for a fool, then forgave herself, because the good Lord said you had to forgive everybody, especially yourself, and for all her seventy-six years, she'd tried to live the way the good Lord wanted her to. After she'd joined the church about fifteen years ago, her whole life had changed.

She'd grown up Christian just like everybody else, but she hadn't really known the Lord at all until Reverend Zeke started preaching them sermons about who was going to hell and who was going to go to heaven and how God was going to separate the goats from the sheep on judgment day — and she sure as shit didn't want to be a goat.

So she'd changed her ways. She'd stopped drinking. She wasn't no drunk, but she drank more than was good for her. More important, she'd stopped stealing from the drawer of the cash register in that little grocery store on Hartness Ridge. She'd worked for the Pruitt family that owned it for years and they trusted her, never dreamed that she was always putting cash down in her pockets out of the cash drawer. She had better sense than to steal anything big. A five here, a ten there, sometimes a twenty if she needed a bottle and she was broke.

But she'd stopped that altogether. Cold turkey. Never stole another dime. There was other sins that was just as hard to give up. Gossip was probably her favorite thing in the whole world. But the good Lord said that she hadn't ought to say nothing about nobody unless it was a good thing, and since she couldn't break herself of the habit of talking 'bout people, she had to change what she said. She noticed that after a while, folks came and sat by her at the church socials and was nicer to her, 'cause she was no longer telling secrets about people behind their backs.

She pulled her old pickup truck around to the back of the church, had to throw her shoulder into the door twice to get it to open. But she supposed that a door you couldn't open was better than a door you couldn't close. The whole damn truck was held together with duct tape and Bondo, and wasn't no way in the world she'd ever be able to buy another one, living on nothing but a once-a-month gubmint check. But she wouldn't let herself worry about that, because the good Lord said worrying was a sin. Don't you give no thoughts to tomorrow. That's what he said, that he clothed the birds in the air and the flowers in the field and no king on the earth had finery beautiful as theirs.

Jezzie didn't have no finery a'tall — a couple of dresses, two or three pairs of jeans that had holes in them, shoes that was coming apart. But still, she wasn't naked. The good Lord had provided for her. She had washed and ironed the nicest dress she owned this morning to go to church early to practice. Damn, she hoped there was some sheet music in the piano bench!

She stopped herself. She had to quit doing that too, cussing. It'd be a hard habit to break but the good Lord didn't like them words, so she needed to give them up. She was getting on up in years, after all, and she didn't want to get to heaven and accidentally say a cuss word to the Angel Gabriel at the pearly gates.

As she started across the little gravel lot in the back of the building to the handicapped ramp Reverend Zeke had built for Ross up to the back door, she started thinking about a song. Not one of the hymns she had come early to practice, but a song that was on the radio all the time when she was a girl. The Beatles sang it, about a woman named Eleanor Rigby that Jezzie thought she woulda been friends with. She looked after her church the same way Jezzie looked after hers, cleaned up the rice after weddings. But more important, Eleanor Rigby was lonely and so was Jezzie. She liked it that them boys sang about somebody in England that was just like her in the Smoky Mountains of Tennessee.

Jezzie fished her key out of her purse as she walked up the ramp. They'd started locking up the building after them teenagers went in that time, smoking weed and vandalizing benches, writing ugly things on the wall with spray paint. Didn't nobody but her and the Wakefields have keys, but the lock on the front door was busted, had been broke for months now. Reverend Zeke hadn't got around to fixing it yet. She inserted her key in the knob lock and turned it. The door was unlocked, and it swung inward a couple of inches, then stopped, banged up against something. What was behind the door that it wouldn't open? She put her shoulder into it and shoved, but it wouldn't budge.

Damn it to hell in a handbasket. She was already behind. She didn't know if she was going to be able to read the music for services this morning and now she couldn't get the damned door open. She stopped herself, asked the good Lord to forgive her for cussing, then trudged around the building to the front where the door was unlocked. There was a big muddy spot at the bottom of the first porch step, folks walking on it all the time so's grass wouldn't grow. But there was a mat in front of the door for folks to clean their feet before they went inside.

The building was a little shoebox. The front doors didn't even open into a vestibule like a lot of churches had. You opened the door and there you were in the sanctuary — with the little bathroom on one side and the storage closet on the other. It didn't have no stained-glass windows. In fact, there was times when the windows was broke out and it didn't have no windows at all.

There was wooden benches that served as pews. Real pews was expensive. There was also a platform raised up two feet in the front with a pulpit for Reverend Zeke to stand behind when he preached. Nearby was the cross, the altar, and the piano Jezzie played. You could move them things around to sit the way you wanted them to. They wasn't on wheels, but the floor was waxed and you could scoot 'em. At Christmas, they set the piano right in the middle in front, so the congregation could gather around it and sing carols.

Jezzie's favorite part of the whole church was the baptistry back behind the pulpit, where the Lord would wash your sins away. Carl Rufus, who worked for a concrete company, had managed to get enough concrete to build it, and Jezzie didn't think nobody asked him if he'd come by that concrete legal or not. The baptistry was just a big concrete box about ten feet long, five feet deep, and three feet wide. Water to fill it came from a spring-fed cistern up on the hillside and it had a drain that carried the water through a pipe to the creek, which thankfully was downhill from the church. Reverend Zeke and some other men in the congregation had built a contraption that looked a little like shower rods all the way around a clawfoot tub — or like that tent-looking thing they brought out onto the field during the Super Bowl so that injured player had some privacy. They set it up down front when they had baptisms so the recently saved could change out of their wet clothes — used them beautiful velvet drapes they took down off the windows in the summertime to let air circulate through the building.

As a matter of fact, it was right before they filled the baptistry up with water for the first time that Reverend Zeke had done his last service with snakes. That's where he put 'em. Went out into the woods and caught copperheads and timber rattlers, brought 'em back to the church and tossed them into the dry baptistry where they couldn't get out. She'd been sick with the flu that Sunday and missed it, and that was the last one he ever done. Sarah Cumbey told her all about how he'd climbed down them concrete steps to the floor with a drain in the middle and them snakes wiggling around his feet. One of them struck and got him in the leg. But he called down the power of the Lord on high to protect him from the venom. And he never suffered a single ill effect. She didn't know why they stopped having snake services. She thought they was right effective to demonstrate the power of God Almighty. But then Reverend Zeke said folks talked about them like they was crazies when they heard about it. And there was other ways to demonstrate God's power than letting a rattlesnake bite you.

Mary Lou Fenwick's girl had painted a scene on the wall behind the baptistry — hills and trees and the like, with water at the bottom so it looked like the baptistry itself was the River Jordan. Jesse thought the trees and the hills was funny looking. Unless you knew that's what they was supposed to be, you couldn't have told just by looking at it.

The cross that usually stood on the left side of the pulpit was a simple thing. Reverend Zeke said that was way better than all them pretty crosses you seen in all them churches with Jesus hanging on them. He said the cross that Jesus hung on wasn't no pretty thing and he wasn't going to have no pretty cross in his church. It was just two big boards affixed to a sturdy platform on the floor. And at Easter time, they draped a purple cloth around it.

On the right side of the pulpit was the upright piano that Jezzie played. God only knew how old it was, maybe older than her. And finally, in front of the pulpit was the finest thing the church owned — the altar. It come out of some big, fancy church in Nashville or Memphis. Prettiest thing you ever seen. The top of it was smooth as glass and just about as shiny. She helped clean the church with a couple of the other ladies, and they was always sure to put lots of that spray furniture wax stuff on it to make that altar sparkle. It had legs bigger than Jezzie's thighs, all carved up pretty. And they kept a cloth over top of it that Gladys Malone had crocheted with crosses on both ends.

It was still dark outside when Jezzie stepped in the front door, flipped on the lights, and started around the back of the benches to the platform where the piano stood, her eyes fixed on that bench seat, praying for all she was worth that there was sheet music in it.

She stopped before she got to the end of the row of benches because there was something lying on the floor. It was all bloody, looked like chicken guts. What in the world?

Her eye traveled from the thing that was laying in the floor to some slimy thing hanging off the bench closest to the wall, and it looked like ... *blood* was dripping off it. Her eyes were wide when she lifted them up to see that naked girl hanging up there on that cross, tied to it with wires, her guts all spilled out and a dead black cat wrapped around her neck.

Jezzie clapped her hand over her mouth to keep from upchucking, then turned and ran out the front door, trailing a scream behind her so loud it musta rocked the very halls of heaven itself.

Chapter Twenty-Four

By THE TIME Mitch got to the Mountain Shaker Fire Baptized Holiness Church, any possibility of preserving the integrity of the crime scene was long gone.

Dispatch had told Mitch about the frantic 911 call from Jezzie Thacker, who said that there was a dead body in the church building when she went in this morning.

Deputy Billy Crawford lived near Juniper Hollow, and he had arrived first on the scene. He had radioed in that members of the congregation had shown up, probably summoned by Jezzie, and they had cleaned up as much of the "mess" as they could before he got there and told them to leave it all alone.

To say that Zeke Wakeford was a screaming wild-eyed loony-toon would have been a kind description. The man was almost literally frothing at the mouth.

Mitch had gotten out of his cruiser when Wakeford came running at him down the little walkway in front of the church, grabbed him by the arm, and dragged him bodily into the building, screaming at the top of his lungs, "You have to see this, you have to see it to believe the blasphemy. The Lord God on high has been offended and he will take retribution, he will mete out vengeance on those who would do such a thing in a holy place."

The man said various other things as he dragged Mitch along, almost pushing his son, Ross, who was in a wheelchair, out of the way so he could shove Mitch in the front door of the church and demand that he *look, just look at that.*

Deputy Crawford approached Mitch then. He had stationed himself inside the church to keep the congregation from doing any more harm to the crime scene than they already had when he arrived. As he approached Mitch, he gestured toward the sanctuary.

"By the time I got here they cleaned up most of it," he said. "Put it in that bucket over there."

Mitch didn't have to ask *most of what.* It was obvious that the nude young woman who was affixed with barbed wire to the cross at the front of the church with a dead cat draped around her neck had been slit open and gutted. Her internal organs taken out and apparently strewn all over the sanctuary. The cat looked to have been gutted, too. What might have happened to its innards was hard to tell.

"They were right pissed when I told them they had to stop cleaning. They said they'd mopped up bloody footprints from the cross out the front door. Sorry, Sheriff."

Mitch looked down at the floor and realized he'd tracked mud in from outside.

"*Bloody* footprints, not muddy footprints?"

"Bloody," Crawford said. He hesitated, hated to say the rest of it. "They said there were bloody handprints on some of the benches, but they washed them all off. I thought I was going to have to pull a gun on them to get them to stop cleaning."

Mitch tuned in again to Zeke Wakeford, who had

never stopped shouting about the vengeance of almighty God and lightning striking from heaven and unforgivable sin and sacrilege, desecration and blasphemy, irreverence, godlessness, unholiness and... and ... and disrespect for the holy God of the universe. His words and nasty tone of voice were as ugly as the internal organs that had been scattered around the sanctuary.

Crawford had been unable to do what needed to be done, which was to establish a perimeter of yellow and black, do-not-cross-this-line police tape all the way around the outside of the building. But he'd done the best he could, had cordoned off the interior so that Mitch had to step over the tape to enter the single room. Mitch's eyes raked the scene as Zeke Wakeford continued to yell. What was clear from even a cursory examination was that, unlike Annie Giordano, this woman had been murdered here at the scene. And killing her had left the killer's hands bloody. Which meant that anything he touched would likely have some pretty clear fingerprints on it ... which the good ladies of the congregation had taken great pains to wash away. There must have been washcloths, a mop and a mop bucket in the storage closet, or they'd brought their own, had gotten water from the little bathroom on the other side of the front door and had scrubbed the floor and all but two of the benches in the building before Deputy Crawford got there and made them stop.

There were footprints in the blood up near the cross. And Mitch hoped that those were not the prints of the women who had been in here cleaning. But it would be up to Gus, who was on the way, to determine if the prints were the same as the footprint in mud at Buttermilk Falls just two days ago. Gus had nailed it. He'd said then that nobody went to that much trouble to commit a murder in such a showy fashion and only perform a one-night stand.

This was a guy who wanted an audience, Gus had said. And he wouldn't stop with one performance.

Mitch approached the cross where the girl hung and could tell, even from a few feet away, that the killer had done the same thing here that he'd done at Buttermilk Falls. He'd used some kind of implement, Gus suspected it was a garden claw, to make it appear that an animal had attacked her and ripped out her guts.

Mitch didn't know the identity of the girl on the cross, but someone had gone all the way up to the cross — smearing whatever footprints there might have been in the blood there — and draped a sheet over the bottom portion of her body to preserve her modesty. Apparently, it was a greater desecration to be hanging from a cross without any clothes on in the church sanctuary than it was to be a dead body there.

"Papa, you've got to calm down," Mitch heard someone say from behind him and he turned to see that the young man in the wheelchair had rolled up beside his father and had taken his arm. "All your hollering is not helping anything. It's not going to change what is."

Mitch turned to face the minister. "Your son's right, Reverend Wakefield. Yelling is doing no good. You need to calm down so I can ask you some questions."

"What questions could you possibly have for me? Why aren't you out there looking for the monster who committed this unforgivable blasphemy in my church?"

"I will have to find that monster before I can arrest him. And the questions I'm going to ask you might help me find him."

"Papa, he's right. We have to tell him everything we know to help him find whoever killed Ronnie."

"Ronnie?" Mitch perked up. "Are you saying that that girl is—"

Ross finished for him, "Veronica Espinosa. Yeah, that's who it is."

Mitch and Rileigh had gone by her house to question her, but she wasn't home. The neighbor had told Mitch that her father and mother were on a cruise somewhere. Mitch was ashamed that he was grateful he wouldn't have to deliver the news to another grieving mother.

"She's one of them witches," Zeke growled, having gotten enough control of his emotions to stop yelling. "Like them others that was parading around in front of that fire on Main Street, looking like normal folk. But the eyes of God can see through into the heart. The eyes of God see the unseen. He saw the filth and ugliness beneath those pretty girls' faces."

"Papa, please," Ross said.

His father turned on him.

"Well, it's true. She might look pretty on the outside, but she's evil to the core. And it's the best decision you ever made to dump her."

Mitch asked the question, though he knew the answer. "Is your father talking about Jaclyn Milford?"

Ross nodded. "We were engaged. But then I broke it off. I realized what kind of person she was inside. Papa's right about the beautiful exterior and the rot inside. That girl was a monster in a human being suit." He made a bark of laughter. "A monster who summoned a monster."

"What does that mean?" Mitch asked.

"She and the other witches summoned a demon," Ross replied.

"What are you saying?" Zeke roared. "A demon?"

"Yeah, a demon. They were trying to summon a genie to grant all their wishes." Ross curled his lip in disgust. "But they screwed it up somehow. Because the demon they got was not the demon they tried to summon. They all believe it's the killer — that demon."

Now that was an interesting piece of information.

Mitch turned to Ross. "So you're saying these girls got together—"

"Not girls, girls are human. These are witches."

"You're saying these *witches* got together and summoned a demon, and now they believe it killed Annie?"

"I'm sure they'll think it killed Ronnie, too. That's what Jaclyn told me. She's scared shitless," Ross corrected himself. "I'm sorry, Papa."

The man patted his son on the shoulder. "There's nothing more obscene than what has occurred in this church today."

"So tell me, Reverend Wakefield, where were you on Thursday night?" Mitch asked.

"What?"

"Simple question. Where were you Thursday night?"

"You think, you mean, you think I…"

That set him off again and he started railing about blasphemy and sacrilege until Mitch held up his hand and told him sternly, "Be quiet, Reverend Wakefield. I'm not going to listen to any more of your screaming. I want to know where you were on Thursday night."

"I was home on Thursday night."

"Can anybody verify that?"

"No, I was home alone." Mitch looked toward Ross and Wakefield caught the gesture. "He don't live with me. He's got his own place."

"So, you're telling me that there is no one who can verify where you were on Thursday night?"

"Yeah, that's exactly what I'm telling you."

"How about this morning? Where were you then?"

"The same place I was Thursday night. I was at home, reading the Holy Scripture and preparing my sermon for this morning. I get up at three o'clock every Sunday morning and commune with God and the Holy Spirit. Allow Him to inform me what he wants me to tell the people who come here hungry for God's word."

Mitch didn't bother to verify Ross's whereabouts when the murders were committed. Though his upper body appeared to be fit and strong, a man in a wheelchair couldn't have climbed a tree and draped a dead body over a limb.

Mitch noticed on the wall, scrawled in blood, a rune like those he had seen on the door frames of the other girls' houses. He looked around and found one more, but that's all.

"Did the good little cleaning ladies wash off the walls?" he asked Deputy Crawford, who responded, "Scrubbed them clean."

Mitch left the Wakefields and made a slow circuit around the sanctuary that Deputy Crawford had cordoned off with police tape. Apparently, the cleaning ladies had started at the front door of the church and were working their way toward the back, because the closer he got to the girl hanging on the cross, the more of the mess that the killer had made was still visible. There was blood all over the floor and it was trampled with footprints. He looked on the edges of the benches where the girls' internal organs had been tossed and saw splatters of blood everywhere. Maybe one of them was a fingerprint. Gus would have to figure that out.

He stepped up onto the platform and was level with the cross where the girl hung. The cross had obviously been moved to the center of the platform, after the pulpit and altar had been pushed back and the upright piano had been shoved against the back door. Mitch looked at Ronnie, examined her. It appeared to him that, unlike Annie Giordano, either this girl had put up a fight or she had been roughed up after she died. She had scratches and abrasions all over her. Mitch did not think that the fact that the corpses had been nude was anything sexual. But there was certainly no way to tell with this one, since the good ladies had preserved her modesty by covering her with a sheet.

Mitch took a couple of steps and looked over the short concrete wall into the baptistry. There was no water in it, but the walls in the bottom were wet. The killer had tracked blood up the center aisle of the church to the door as he left ... a blood trail the cleaning ladies had taken great pains to obliterate.

"Yo Mitch," a voice called from the back of the sanctuary, and Mitch looked up to see Gus Hazelton standing beside the deputy. He had his satchel with him, and he was looking over the crime scene. Mitch knew that he was seeing things other people didn't even notice. Gus was like that. But the good ladies of the congregation had destroyed so much evidence, Mitch was afraid it was unlikely Gus would be able to get much by way of forensics here to help them find the killer.

Mitch walked to the back of the sanctuary, careful to avoid the puddles of blood, then stepped over the yellow and black police tape. He turned to Reverend Wakefield, who was still standing there beside his son, and told him, "I'm sure Deputy Crawford explained this to you, but let me make sure you understand. The ladies who cleaned up the mess here did a great disservice to the police, to those of us who have to figure out who killed that poor girl. Cleaning up the mess, they removed evidence."

"There's still plenty of mess to clean up before we can conduct services," he said.

"Which won't be this morning," Mitch told him.

Wakefield was off to the races again. "What do you mean we're not going to be having services? This is the Sabbath day. This is the seventh day that the Lord has ordained that we are to worship him."

Mitch so badly wanted to tell him to put a sock in it, but he didn't. He merely said, "Until we have released this crime scene, nobody touches it but one of my officers, or Gus, is that understood?"

"How long will that take?"

"Probably most of the day."

"Fine, then we'll have services tonight." Zeke turned on his heel and strode out of the sanctuary. Mitch could hear him calling out to the small crowd that had gathered, perhaps the entire congregation of the church, telling them that there would be services tonight on the Lord's day.

"Eight o'clock, here at the church. And if they won't let us inside the building, then we'll worship God out here under the stars."

Chapter Twenty-Five

MITCH HAD CALLED Rileigh early this morning with the grisly news about the body that the pianist at the Mountain Shaker Holiness Fire Baptized Church in Juniper Hollow had found. At least the phone call hadn't awakened her from a dead sleep. Or from a terrible nightmare. But she still had her pajamas on and hadn't yet washed her face when the phone rang. After Mitch told her about the murder, she'd gone into her bedroom and sat down on the bed. Not because her knees wouldn't hold her. But she had to admit to feeling a little shaky after he got more specific about describing the crime scene in gruesome detail.

She asked if he needed her help. But he said that Gus had just arrived.

"That is one unhappy coroner, too," Mitch said.

"Because …?"

"Because the good ladies of the Holiness Church cleaned up much of the crime scene before he got there this morning. Scrubbed it spotless."

Rileigh didn't have to ask what it was they had cleaned up. "Was there any evidence left at all?"

"Down in the front of the church around the pulpit and the baptistry. They hadn't gotten that far when Deputy Crawford got here, shooed them out, and used police tape to cordon off the sanctuary. But there probably won't be any good footprints in the blood to compare to the plaster cast Gus got at Buttermilk Falls. One of the 'helpful' church members tromped around under the cross, covering up the girl's body, at least from the waist down. Apparently, it's a greater sin to be naked in church than it is to be murdered there."

Rileigh knew better than to hope that Mama and Jillian hadn't heard about the murder this morning. She'd heard Mama's phone ring even before hers did. Somebody on the telephone tree was a busy little beaver. Rileigh was so preoccupied with thoughts about it that she wasn't a very good conversationalist in the car on the way to church. Rileigh had taken to driving Mama wherever she went, making up some excuse that she needed to go there too. The truth was, she didn't like Mama driving anymore. She could wind up somewhere and not know where she was, or not remember how to get home, or run over some poor soul on the way. She was getting closer to having the dreaded take-the-keys-away-from-Mama conversation. But at least she'd have Jillian in her corner, and between the two of them, they had Mama outnumbered. That's why Rileigh had agreed to take Mama to church today. Jillian wasn't ready for that, and Rileigh certainly wouldn't push her. She could do whatever she felt up to doing at whatever rate she wanted to. Mama was one of the every-Sunday-morning, every-Sunday-night, and Wednesday-nights-too crowd at her church. While Rileigh was in the sometimes-there, usually-not crowd.

She and Mama always sat in the same place — three rows from the back on the left-hand side of the sanctuary, next to the aisle. Had it been a wedding, it would be the bride's side. Rileigh shuddered to think what would happen if a visitor chanced to come to church on a Sunday when every member of the church showed up, because every member of the church had laid claim to some piece of real estate inside the building — *their* pew — and God help anybody who tried to evict them.

Rileigh could hear discussions about the grisly scene at the Fire Baptized Holiness Church all around her. Everybody knew about it. No big surprise there. Nobody had the story right. No big surprise there, either. The accounts varied from something approaching reality to "there were three people with their throats slit, dangling upside down from the beams in the ceiling of the church, and a gutted skunk on the altar."

The crowd was a little slower to settle down when the music leader got up to lead the first hymn. That was unusual. Rileigh felt that sinking sensation in her belly as soon as Reverend Tobias Potter stepped into the pulpit and said, "I had a sermon all written for this morning, but I tore it up when I heard what happened in a house of God in Juniper Hollow."

The rest of the sermon was predictable. Reverend Potter was no hellfire and brimstone preacher. He always emphasized the love of God rather than the retribution that awaited those who didn't accept his love. He stressed grace, and when he talked about the Gospel, it really was *good news* — that God had given his son to ransom the whole world and to pave a way for every person on the planet to connect with God for all eternity.

That's what he usually preached about. Not this morning. This morning, if Rileigh had closed her eyes, she would have sworn she was in a snake-handling church so far back in the mountains sunlight only shone there twice a week.

Reverend Potter talked about the Satanist Church.

"The smartest thing Satan ever did was to convince people he didn't exist," he began.

He went on about Satan's plan to trick humanity into believing he was a little guy with horns and a pointy tail dressed in red long johns who came out at Halloween for trick-or-treating.

"But that's not what Scripture says about Satan," Reverend Potter said, "That's not how the holy word of God describes Lucifer."

His central point was simple: Satan had moved bag and baggage into the neighborhood, and the good Christian people of Yarmouth County couldn't stand by idle and let it happen.

Rileigh was not surprised by the anti-Satanist church tirade. She was a little surprised, though, by the vehemence with which Reverend Potter attacked the witches' coven — saying that witches were the servants of Satan who conjured up demons to attack good Christian families and enabled Satanic forces to take over the hearts and souls of good Christian people.

By the time the minister was finished, there wasn't a man, woman, or child in that sanctuary who would have thought twice about throwing freedom of religion to the wind and freedom of speech right along beside it. The Reverend told them that it was their job to clean the iniquity out of the county. Then he imparted a bit of interesting information about the telephone calls he'd been having with the other Protestant ministers in the county, and even the two Catholic priests, who seldom got together with the Protestants on anything. But they were united in this regard.

"After services today, I'm going to ask all of you to stand up for your Christian faith and stand tall against the Antichrist. We will march to the Satanist church and let the devil worshippers know that they are not welcome in our community."

Rileigh fished her phone out of her pocket and hit speed dial for Mitch as the choir sung the final hymn. "I think you need to know that there's going to be a—"

"A protest? Yeah. You're not the first person who's told me. Apparently, all the ministers got together and planned it."

"If they did, they probably did what Reverend Potter did this morning, which was to tell the whole congregation that if they didn't show up to kick the Satanist church out of the county, God was going to take back their team jerseys."

"At least we got a little warning," he said.

"I'll see you there," Rileigh replied.

Chapter Twenty-Six

RILEIGH ABSOLUTELY DID NOT WANT Mama to go to the protest, but she'd driven her to church.

Before she could decide what to do, Mama's best friend, Mildred Hanover, rushed up to them. The last time Rileigh had seen Millie, the woman had been dressed as Mary Poppins for a party on the Queen of the Smokies riverboat casino.

"Can you help with refreshments?" Millie asked Mama. "We thought protesting might be hot and thirsty work, so we're going to make lemonade and cookies for the congregation in the kitchen in the basement."

Rileigh was grateful to leave her mother to the task. And by the time she got to the protest it was starting to get out of hand. There must have been upwards of five-hundred people, maybe as many as a thousand. Some of them had obviously learned of today's "impromptu" protest in time to make signs. Most of them were black signs with white lettering and the scripture from Exodus 22:18, "Thou shalt not suffer a witch to live." In the King James Translation, of course. It sounded more commanding and authoritative than other translations that merely pointed out "Death is the punishment for witch-craft," or simply, "Do not allow a woman to do evil magic."

Mitch's deputies had set up a line about fifty feet from the front of the little church and were holding the crowd at that point. But Mitch made it clear that it had already gone south.

"I can't lock up every Christian in the whole damn county," he said. "But if they keep threatening violence, I'm going to have to try."

Apparently, it had gotten ugly even before Mitch arrived. Some early birds had shown up and thrown rocks at the church, broken out some of the windows. Gilbert McPherson had been inside and he'd come out to confront the rock-throwers. The Exodus signs set him off because his church, according to his definition, didn't have a thing to do with witches. There had been some roughing up before McPherson made it back into the church and locked the doors behind him. Now he was stuck there.

When the crowd started getting unruly again, Mitch called out to them.

"According to Ordinance 792 of the Yarmouth County code, a crowd of more than fifty people must have prior approval by the council to stage a protest." When a rumble of anger and disbelief lifted up from the crowd, Mitch held his hands up. "We're going to set that ordinance aside today, assuming that nobody intended any harm, since this was not an 'organized event.' I'm sure nobody here knew anybody else was going to show up — right? So, no viola-tion." They didn't exactly cheer, but there was a rumble of approval from the crowd. "For your safety and the safety of this property, I have stationed deputies at both ends of Donner Pike to stop traffic during your protest."

They almost did cheer then, until he continued.

"*But* … I will *not* stop traffic for longer than an hour." Even though Donner Pike wasn't a main thoroughfare, an hour's stopped traffic would back up cars all the way down the mountainside. He looked at his watch. "You have twenty-three minutes. Those of you who choose to remain here when my deputies let the backed-up line of angry tourists loose will be on your own. Good luck."

That was a bluff, of course. Mitch wouldn't let the protestors get run down. But he delivered the threat very convincingly, Rileigh thought, and the crowd seemed to buy what he was selling, allowing him to defuse the situation while still keeping most of his constituents reasonably happy. It was looking like the situation might end peacefully. Until Ethel Snodmotz arrived on the scene.

Everything went to hell in a hand basket after that.

Ethel came marching down the middle of the highway like she owned it, and the rest of humanity had damn well better get out of her way. She had brought with her a contingent of rough-looking men who looked like they'd been culled from the back tables of every seedy bar in Yarmouth County. Unshaven and certainly not dressed for church, they hadn't been sent here by a minister who'd whipped his congregation up into a fury at church this morning.

Her posse muscled their way through the crowd in front of Ethel, though she'd have done the same without them. She came to stand right in front of Mitch with her feet spread wide apart, her arms folded on the shelf of her considerable bosom. She had a speech all prepared.

"The Lord God Almighty sent me a sign last night," she said, "after I was *attacked by witches*."

Ethel didn't exactly have a reputation for truthfulness, so few in the crowd took what she said at face value. But then she rolled up her sleeve and displayed a bandage on her forearm. It didn't look like she'd been attacked by a pack of wild dogs or anything like that, but there was gauze wrapped around it from her wrist to her elbow. "I had to have six stitches in my arm where they come after me with their witches' claws."

That got people's attention. Rileigh leaned over to Mitch. "Who the hell is she talking about? Jaclyn, Olivia, and Ronnie?"

"Are you on a first-name basis with any other witches in the county?" he asked.

Ethel went on, bulldozed through the crowd's disbelief. "There was three of them. Three good, God-fearing girls that grew up here with Christian parents but was turned to the ways of the very devil this *church*—" she waggled an accusing finger at the building "—wants everybody here to bow down to and worship."

The crowd noises died. They all were listening to Ethel now.

"As I was down on my knees by my bed last night, praising the Lord for delivering me from the clutches of those witches, I heard the voice of God speaking. Not that still, small voice we're all used to hearing when we pray. I'm talking about an audible voice from the Archangel Gabriel himself. He commissioned me to rid this county of Satan and his minions."

Clutches. Who used a word like that? And minions. Rileigh couldn't help it — images of little yellow creatures shaped like fire hydrants in blue overalls and construction goggles popped into her mind and she had to fight an urge to giggle.

Ethel suddenly cried, "Thou shalt not suffer a witch to live!" and leapt forward, intent on getting past Mitch to the church. That must have been a prearranged signal, because her gang of hoodlums charged the other deputies at the same time. Scuffling broke out up and down the "thin blue line" of deputies. Mitch grabbed one of Ethel's arms and Rileigh grabbed the other as the enraged woman tried to shove her way between them, but the forward momentum of a body mass as dense as hers carried her on — until Mitch stuck out his foot and tripped her. She went down then, flailing, and her elbow caught Rileigh in the left eye. The blow was stunning, and Rileigh let go of her grip on Ethel and staggered back. Ethel crashed to the ground, and in an adept move, Mitch pivoted his grip on her wrist and twisted her arm behind her. The dust hadn't even settled before Mitch had both her hands cuffed behind her. He stepped over her to Rileigh.

"Are you all right?"

"I'm good," she said as the *whum-whum-whum* rhythm of pain throbbed in her cheek and eye socket.

He lifted her chin, moved her hand away from her eye and pronounced, "You're going to have a shiner."

"Goody."

"You need to put some ice on it."

"Got any in your pocket?"

"You get these poopy cuffs off me," Ethel shrieked from below them, trying to roll over. But her protruding round belly gave her the shape of a stinkbug on its back, and she was helpless to do anything but thrash ineffectually around on the ground.

Deputies Mullins and Rawlings both had prisoners of their own. Deputy Crawford's man had run off into the crowd. The minor uprising was quelled on the spot.

"Let me up, I ain't done nothing illegal."

"We'll start with creating a public disturbance, then make our way through inciting a riot to assault on a police officer," Mitch said. He turned to the shocked-into-silence crowd. "I hereby declare this protest officially over. Disperse now or go to jail. Your choice."

The protestors hastily selected Door Number One.

Once he had dispatched Deputies Mullins and Crawford to haul the prisoners to jail — to cool off, then he'd let them go — Mitch knocked on the door of the church and called out, "The party's over. You can come out now."

Gilchrist yanked the door open and confronted Mitch with much the same look of rage Rileigh had seen on Ethel Snodmotz's face.

"This is a *church!*" he cried. "Not a den of witches. We worship the fallen angel Lucifer."

"Sounds like a distinction without a difference to me," Mitch said.

The angry man let fly a string of artfully constructed profanity. "Those stupid bitches have spoiled everything. It's all *their* fault the community has the wrong impression of Satanism."

Rileigh thought perhaps Pierce had not gotten the news about Ronnie's death.

"Do you know what happened this morning at the Holiness Church up in Juniper Hollow?"

"Did the stupid fools burn me in effigy?"

"One of the young women who claimed to be a witch was murdered last night, Pierce."

McPherson took the news as if Mitch had just informed him that the Pirates had lost to the Seahawks nine-to-nothing.

"Awwww, bummer," he mocked. "Wish I'd shot her myself. That's two of them down and two to go."

Mitch bristled as Pierce stepped back into the building and grabbed the door to slam it. Instead, he turned and fired one final shot.

"I was assaulted this morning." He wiped at what was

now a smear of dried blood under his nose. "I want every one of them arrested. I intend to press charges."

Mitch cocked his head to the side.

"So you're *demanding* I arrest a bunch of fine Christian Yarmouth County residents and take them before the prosecutor where you will *demand* that he press charges." Mitch made a sound that was almost a chuckle. "Good luck with that, Pierce. Let me give you some advice, one old friend to another — don't let the door of Yarmouth County hit you on the ass on your way out."

Chapter Twenty-Seven

RILEIGH CALLED Mama to ask if she could get a ride home from church with Millie so that Rileigh could go with Mitch straight to Jaclyn Milford's house, to give her the news about Ronnie and to ask if she had any idea what had happened. Mitch had been on his way there when he'd been called away to stand between a conman named Pierce and a group of upstanding citizens who had every reason to be pissed at him.

When they got to Jaclyn's town home, the bloody runes that had been painted on her door, door frame, and surrounding walls were gone.

Mitch knocked on the door, and they heard no response from inside, though her car was parked out front. He knocked again. After knocking a third time, he called through the door, "Ronnie, it's me, Sheriff Webster. Rileigh and I need to talk to you."

He heard the sound of movement inside, then the door slowly opened. If Jaclyn had looked bad after Annie was killed, she now looked like what Mama would have called death on a cracker. It was like she'd aged five years, maybe more. Her skin was drawn. There were lines around her mouth. And she had the most haunted look Rileigh had ever seen.

"I know about Ronnie," she said. "You don't have to tell me."

"May we come in?" Rileigh asked.

"Sure." Jaclyn had to move something before she could open the door. When they stepped inside, Rileigh saw that she had placed a high-back chair up against the door, with the back jammed against the knob so it would be hard to open. She was scared to death.

"Is it true what they said?" Jaclyn asked.

"There are all kinds of rumors flying around this county," Mitch said. "And most of them are so far from the truth as to be unrecognizable. Which one are you talking about?"

"That there were claw marks ..." was all Jaclyn could say.

"We're not certain they were claws, Jaclyn," Mitch said, and she looked at him with dull, unbelieving eyes.

"You don't understand," she began.

"No, actually, I *do* understand. But you're wrong. It's not some monster that killed your friend. It was a human being. A monstrous human being. But just a person."

"You don't know that. You don't know what we did."

"What I do know is that the coroner, Dr. Gus Hazelton, ruled in Annie's death that some kind of instrument was used to claw out her throat." Rileigh could see he was reluctant to use the words "garden claw" and she couldn't blame him. "He said it was *not* the bite of an animal. It was meant to look like one, but there was no animal saliva in the wound."

"I don't imagine spirits have saliva," she said quietly.

"May we sit down, Bunny Rabbit?" Rileigh asked the

girl tenderly. She put her arm around Jaclyn's shoulders as she showed them into the living room. It wasn't as neat as it had been the last time they were there. There was a pizza box on the coffee table in the living room. Soft drink cans sitting around the room. And if Rileigh's nose was not betraying her, she could smell the lingering stench of marijuana. Weed had been smoked in this room in the last twenty-four hours. There was no ashtray around with telltale ashes. But Rileigh suspected that as soon as Jaclyn realized who was at her door, she'd dumped them in the toilet.

Marijuana was illegal in Tennessee. Not that there was a single person over the age of fifteen who gave a shit about that law.

Jaclyn went to the wraparound couch and curled up almost in a fetal position in the corner.

Rileigh noted that there was a chair braced against the sliding doors that led out to the patio. It would have done no good. It wasn't a barrier like a chair pushed up under a doorknob. But Jaclyn didn't know that.

"When was the last time that you saw Ronnie?" Mitch asked her.

She barked out a little laugh that became a sob before it left her throat. "Last night. Ronnie and Olivia and I were here, sitting here in this room. The three of us got together to see if we could send it back."

"Send what back?"

"We did a summoning spell, but something terrible went wrong."

"Ross told me about that," Mitch said. Jaclyn actually flinched at the mention of his name. "He said you had been trying to summon a genie?"

"When you say it like that, you make it sound so silly,

but it's not crazy. You don't understand about magic. My grandmother did magic. I grew up around it. It's real."

"She taught you a spell that would summon a genie?" Rileigh asked.

"No, learning to cast spells is something I'm pretty new at. I've been studying up on it since I became a witch. I don't know if Granny Milford cast spells or not. I don't think so. She was just magical."

"So how did you know how to cast a spell to summon a genie?"

"Well, we didn't really. We just tried some things, different ways of summoning spirits from the beyond."

"This is just me, but I would imagine if it were easy to cast a spell that would actually summon a genie who would grant you three wishes … don't you think everybody would be doing it?"

"We were serious about the spells we used. We did everything we knew how to do. But I don't think the others really believed anything would happen."

"Did anything happen?"

Then Jaclyn's face broke. "Nothing happened except Annie got killed and Ronnie got killed." She burst into sobs, put her face in her hands and cried as if her heart would break.

Rileigh got up from where she was sitting and went over to the couch, putting her arm around Jaclyn and patting her like she'd done when she was a little girl and had a bad dream in the middle of the night.

Jaclyn didn't cry for long. Managed to pull herself together. "So, you tried to summon this genie and nothing happened," Mitch said, taking up the questioning where Rileigh had left off.

"We thought nothing happened — nothing happened that we could see. But obviously something did happen.

Our summoning worked, but it wasn't a djinn. It was an ifrit."

Rileigh thought she knew what an ifrit was. Mitch looked like he didn't have any idea. So she asked Jaclyn, "Tell us what an ifrit is."

"An ifrit is a prince of demons. He's made of nothing but evil and rage and murder. We pulled him up out of the bowels of hell into the world. And look what he did to Annie. Look what he did to Ronnie."

"It was not a demon from hell who killed your friends," Mitch said, as calmly and firmly as he could. "Unless an ifrit wears a size ten and a half New Balance running shoe."

Jaclyn looked at Mitch questioningly.

He added, "There was a footprint in the mud beside the oak tree that Annie was hanging from. The killer had to climb the tree to carry the body up there."

"That was just somebody's footprint. It doesn't mean anything. Don't you understand? It's a demon, and it's killed two of us. And it's coming for me and Liv now."

Rileigh couldn't argue that something, some*body* was coming for them. It was no coincidence that the two previous murder victims had been witches. It was no coincidence that the first murder happened after the witches staged their summer solstice ceremony downtown in front of the courthouse. The deaths of both those girls had something to do with witchcraft. But Rileigh didn't believe it had anything to do with summoning demons.

"You were saying that you got together with Ronnie and Olivia last night."

"Yes, we were trying to find a way to send the ifrit back."

Rileigh had this image of a UPS package with a

barcode. Amazon always took it back when you got the wrong thing.

"If you didn't know how to summon it in the first place, how did you know how to send it back?"

"We didn't know specifically, we just knew there are all kinds of spells to banish evil and to banish demons. Protection spells, too. Those are the ones we did."

At that point, a lop-eared bunny rabbit, gray with a big white spot over one eye, hopped lazily into the room and settled itself on the floor beside Jaclyn's furry slipper. She reached down and picked it up, cuddled it like a little girl cuddling a teddy bear.

"Rabbits are very sensitive. They can tell when you're upset. He's been following me around everywhere I go today." She shook her head. "Unlike cats. Charcoal didn't even come when I called him this morning."

Rileigh remembered what bat-shit crazy Ethel Snodmotz had said at the protest this morning.

"You say the three of you were together last night. Did you go anywhere?"

"Yes," she said, and seemed reluctant to say more.

"Where?"

"It sounds crazy. I know you'll think we're crazy."

"Try me."

"We did all the magic that we knew to do, all the spells we knew, and then Olivia said that we needed to try voodoo. But to do a voodoo spell, you need blood." Rileigh's eyes widened, and Jaclyn held up her hand. "No, no, no. I don't mean like human blood or anything. Chicken blood works. So we went out to my Uncle Neb's chicken farm."

"So, you went from here to your uncle's farm, and then where?"

"Well, we didn't go directly to his farm. We had to have

candles too, and we were out, so we stopped by the Quik Stop Convenience Store on Harkness Street to get some." Jaclyn sat back against the back of the couch. "And guess who we ran into there?"

"Ethel Snodmotz," Rileigh said.

"How did you know? Did Mr. Singh call the police?"

"No. Ethel mentioned it."

"I'm surprised he didn't. Ronnie just went off on her." Then Jaclyn stopped and really looked at Rileigh's face.

"What happened to you?" she asked, and for a moment Rileigh didn't know what she was talking about. Then she glanced in the big mirror above the couch and caught sight of her swollen eye, tinged with shades of purple, yellow and green. A shiner.

"Ethel Snodmotz's elbow."

"I'm not surprised. We ran into her in the store, and she started screaming awful things. When she said she was glad Annie got killed, Ronnie just lost it, jumped on her and was trying to claw her face off. Would have, too, if she'd had any fingernails."

"Did Ethel get hurt?"

"Hurt? No. Well, maybe she scratched her arm on the side of the produce case when she fell. But she didn't get *hurt*. Then Mr. Singh came out and told us all to leave, or he would call you. He said you were a friend of his."

"I am," Mitch said.

"We made such a mess of his store. He had all these displays of fruit and vegetables, and Ronnie and Mrs. Snodmotz knocked them all down. Apples and oranges were rolling everywhere."

"But she didn't get hurt, like, have to go to the emergency room?"

"Lord, no. She probably didn't even need a Band-Aid."

"You say it was Ronnie who attacked her?" Mitch asked.

"She wouldn't stand there and listen to the woman say she was glad Annie was dead. Ronnie's got a temper. And she lost it."

"How did you find out that Ronnie was dead?"

Jaclyn cringed. "Ross texted me this morning. He told me somebody had dragged her in the back door of the church, wired her to the cross and then ... cut her open and *threw* her—"

Rileigh held up her hand. "You don't have to describe it to me."

"It doesn't sound like you and Ross are on the best of terms," Mitch said.

"He was crazy," Jaclyn replied.

"How?"

"It sounded like he was glad, like he was gloating that she was dead. Not sympathizing."

"I understand you were engaged — how long ago did he break up with you?"

"Break up with *me*? I dumped *him*."

Mitch had already told Rileigh what Ross had said about breaking up with Jaclyn. Typical he-said, she-said.

"He was so controlling. He wanted every minute of my time. Then he started demanding to know where I was when he wasn't around. I couldn't live with that. I mean, it wasn't my fault he's in that wheelchair. I was driving the car, but the wreck was not my fault. For months he tried to use being paralyzed to get me to stay with him. But after a while, I couldn't stand it. It was Olivia and Annie and Ronnie who urged me to dump him and get on with my life."

She shook her head. "That was an ugly scene," she said, remembering. "I wanted to tell him in public, so he'd at least have to be polite. We went to the park, and he slid out of his chair onto the bench to sit beside me. I told him I didn't love him and didn't want to marry him. I took the engagement ring off and handed it to him. He started screaming at me and threw the ring down on the ground. He'd have stomped it if he could have gotten up off that bench. Then he grabbed my wrist and started twisting … I broke free and ran away, left him sitting there yelling obscenities."

Rileigh and Mitch had talked on the way to Jaclyn's house about the possibility of offering her and Olivia police protection. But Mitch had said he couldn't justify it. The only connection between the two of them and the two women who had been murdered was that they all four were witches. Right now, Mitch didn't have a single suspect and wasn't even sure that witchcraft was the motive.

Rileigh wondered whether he'd change his mind if another witch died.

"Are you going to be alright here?" she asked Jaclyn.

Jaclyn tried to put a good face on it. "I'll be fine." She held up the furry little creature in her lap. "I've got Ernie to protect me. Nothing meaner than a mad rabbit."

"If you need anything," Rileigh said, "anything at all, I gave you my card. Call me."

"Thanks, Rileigh. But the only thing I need is my friends back."

Chapter Twenty-Eight

UNFORTUNATELY, Mama did not take the sight of her daughter's black eye with the same equanimity Mitch had displayed when he noticed it forming after Ethel Snodmotz elbowed her in the face.

Mama caught sight of her and cried out, "Baby, you're *hurt!*" in such an obvious overreaction, it would have been humorous under other circumstances.

Actually, Rileigh had forgotten all about the black eye after Jaclyn mentioned it, until Mama acted like it was possibly a fatal injury.

"Mama, chill out. It's a black eye, not a broken femur."

Oh, how she wanted to point out that the worst injury she'd received since she got out of the military, worse than getting shot in the leg on a domestic disturbance call once in Memphis, was when her hand was crushed with a sledgehammer last summer by Aunt Daisy.

Aunt Daisy — those two words were not spoken often in Mama's household anymore.

Jillian knew that Aunt Daisy had sold her into bondage, stolen twenty-seven years of her life. Why? To cover up her father's sexual assaults on Jillian, and then Georgia — because Daisy had been in love with her father.

Rileigh had always known that Aunt Daisy was different from all the other flowers in the bouquet of girls born to Elmer and Frances Gillespie. She was a dandelion. No, she was a Venus flytrap.

Aunt Daisy had stopped taking her meds as soon as Mama came to her room waving around that postcard that had been mailed from Black Bear Forge and jumping for joy that Jillian was coming home. In so doing, she had unleashed the monster within Daisy. She'd come very close to getting Rileigh and Jillian both killed. And by the time Rileigh and her sister had recovered enough to hold the old woman accountable, there was nobody home anymore. Every time Aunt Daisy stopped taking her meds, she slid down into psychosis and had to be restrained. It took weeks, sometimes months, to get her medications to the right levels in her blood again to stabilize her personality. Right now, she was in the psychiatric wing of the Carrington House Hospital, literally in a rubber room. Of course, with Aunt Daisy, you never knew, but it appeared to the doctors and staff that she didn't even know who she was. Convenient that whenever she got caught with her hand in the cookie jar, bada-boom, bada-bing, she wasn't responsible for the consequences of her behavior.

Mama didn't have any idea what had been going on between her sister and her husband or what her husband had been doing to young girls the whole time they were married. Mama believed he was a saint so devastated by Jillian's disappearance that he committed suicide. She didn't know that Sheriff Mumford had murdered him to keep him from outing Mumford as a pedophile, too. And that, in Rileigh's view, was the best possible outcome. There was no sense in destroying her poor dementia-stricken mother by telling her the truth about her husband and her sister, or telling her that everything that had happened to Jillian for the past twenty-seven years was Daisy Gillespie's fault.

When Daisy was functioning as a rational human being, thanks to the right concoction of drugs in her system, she called her sister Lily every day — and used Lily as a vending machine to bring her anything she wanted.

But Mama didn't seem to have noticed that Daisy never called anymore. She had been so caught up in the absolutely euphoric delight of having her oldest daughter home that very little of anything else penetrated her consciousness, certainly nothing unpleasant. And that's how it needed to be. In fact, Rileigh was surprised by Mama's concern over her black eye until she realized that Mama was just mirroring Jillian's concern for her little sister. Mama knew that Rileigh strapped a gun on her hip and went to work every day for nine years as a police officer. Mama knew she had been in war, in combat, had killed people, had almost been killed. Mama had watched her and Mitch go out time and time again since Rileigh had come back home to the mountains to work on one case or another. But now, since Jillian was concerned for Rileigh's safety, Mama jumped on the boat with her.

"Let me get some ice to put on it, it's so swollen. Does it hurt bad?"

"Mama, it doesn't hurt at all. I'd forgotten I had it."

"What happened to you, baby? Who hit you?"

"Nobody hit me on purpose."

"Nobody hit you? What... did you run into a door?"

"There was a scuffle and Ethel Snodmotz accidentally elbowed me in the face."

"You got into a scuffle with Ethel Snodmotz?" Mama said. Just then Jillian came downstairs where she'd been painting in her studio, took one look at Rileigh, and it was same song, second verse. "Rileigh, honey, what happened to you?"

Though Rileigh was trying desperately to hold onto her irritation, it was really annoying to have these two women fluttering around her like twittering birds when there was no reason for concern.

"I'd like to say that I got into a fistfight with Ethel Snodmotz, because then I could claim I hit her back, but actually I got the black eye from her elbow in my face. It was an accident."

"An accident that wouldn't have happened if you hadn't been there," Jillian intoned, sounding way more like Mama than Rileigh liked. True that, but Rileigh let it go. Hoped both her mother and her sister would forget all about the black eye, but unfortunately, they couldn't seem to let the matter go.

Mama made it clear that Rileigh never should have gone out to that protest in the first place, and Jillian made it clear that Rileigh was not a police officer, and that she didn't understand why she kept putting herself in harm's way as if she were.

When Jillian left the room for a moment, Mama went to Rileigh and spoke in her ear in a harsh whisper: "You need to be staying home more with your sister. She needs you to be here, and you're out running around getting black eyes and fighting with Ethel Snodmotz. Jillian's been gone for almost thirty years. Can't you just stay home for a few nights with her?"

Jillian came back into the room then, and Rileigh managed to smile while grinding her teeth at the same time.

"I've got an idea," she said. "How about we have game night tonight? Doesn't that sound like fun?"

She had vague memories of playing Monopoly or some other board game when she was a child.

Mama lit up like a Christmas tree at the prospect, and even Jillian looked thrilled.

Rileigh, on the other hand, could think of very little in life she would enjoy less. What she really wanted to do was to go help Mitch.

Chapter Twenty-Nine

THE REVEREND EZEKIEL WAKEFIELD felt so filled with the fire of the Holy Spirit that he wondered: if he turned off all the lights in the sanctuary, would he glow in the dark?

He had never — not in his entire ministry, not in his entire life — felt the kind of holy wrath he felt right now.

There was something very freeing about the righteous rage that burned in his breast. There was no gray area here, no compromising, no sliding down some slippery slope of uncertainty. The light of truth and right shone so bright it was almost blinding. It cast out all the shadows, made the path forward easy to see.

The world was indeed an ugly, dangerous place. He had always known that. That's why he had retreated to the mountains, to find solitude, to grow closer to God, and to gain the blessing of a congregation of other righteous Christians who tried to live by God's holy ordinances, who would stand with him in this fight against the devil himself.

It was a life-or-death battle.

Zeke understood that more clearly than anyone else.

Like the Apostle Paul on the road to Damascus, the scales had fallen from his eyes and he could see. He could *see!*

"Thou shalt not suffer a witch to live." God didn't make suggestions. That was a command, a simple, emphatic, *undeniable command* from almighty God.

The foul creature who had been left to hang on the cross in the sanctuary of his church had got what she deserved. She had been dispatched back to hell from whence she came. But the defiling of his sanctuary with her blood had him incensed.

Oh, Zeke had always known that Jaclyn Milford was evil. She was not a good Christian girl. She wasn't who Zeke wanted his son to be involved with, certainly wasn't who he wanted to be the mother of his grandchildren. Her grandmother had been a witch, everybody knew it. Oh, they could put pretty words on it, color it up with flowers, spray a little perfume around it, and make it seem not as awful as it was. But the stink of the rot beneath would still come out. He could see it in her eyes that she didn't love the Lord right, and he'd been so grateful when his son came home and told him he had broken up with that girl that Zeke had fallen down on his face before the cross in the sanctuary and wept.

It was her fault his son would never walk. *Her fault.* His son was bound to that wheelchair, and for a while, he had feared that maybe the two of them would hang together because of that shared misfortune. But Ross had better sense than that. Ross had seen with the clear eyes of a Christian young man and known she wasn't for him.

Zeke looked at his watch. The congregation would start filing into the little church in half an hour. He and three of the sisters in the church had spent every moment since the black-and-yellow police tape had been taken down on their hands and knees, using bristled scrub brushes to remove the filthy blood of that abomination from the floor of this holy church. He'd been working so hard, he hadn't had time to write his sermon for tonight, had not hammered out the words he ought to speak to move these simple people to action.

It was clear what they had to do. It was clear they were all that stood between the evil that had come upon them and the good Christian people of this county. And though there were many who would claim to be on their side, there were few who would lock arms with them and stand beside them when the time came.

But he and his would stand tall against evil — including the newest abomination that had been unleashed on Yarmouth County. Zeke learned this morning that not only were the forces of evil arrayed against him in the form of witches and a church of Satan in his very community, but those witches had *summoned a demon from hell* to live here among them on the earth.

This was a hill he had to die on. He begged God to put the right words in his mouth to move his congregation to action. If they didn't do what was right, that demon would take over one soul after another until there wasn't a Christian, God-fearing person left in Yarmouth County, Tennessee. But Zeke would stand with God against the onslaught, and if he died in that effort, he would be taken on the wings of angels to glory.

He heard the front door of the church open and turned to see his son Ross rolling his wheelchair down the center aisle of the church. The wheelchair that a witch had set him in.

"Papa, are you alright?"

And Zeke realized that he was lying face down on the floor in front of the cross. He had been in such a rapture of communion with the God of the universe that he didn't know when he'd gotten up from the bench where he'd been sitting writing his sermon, didn't know when he'd collapsed to his knees and fallen on his face.

"I have never been better in my life, son," he said. "Tonight, we are going to stand together, united against evil. God is on our side. We will rid this county of evil." He paused, emphasized his next words. "*By. Any. Means. Necessary.*"

Chapter Thirty

MITCH WAS PULLING into the parking lot behind the courthouse when the radio in his cruiser crackled.

"Unit 1, this is dispatch. Ten-twenty-six reported at 2098 Harkness Lane."

A ten-twenty-six. Shit, the Fallen Angel Church was on fire.

Mitch whipped a U-turn in the parking lot and headed back out, lights and siren, to Harkness Lane. He could see the smoke rising as he drove and knew that the fire would attract a considerable number of rubberneckers and looky-loos. So he radioed the dispatcher to send Deputy Rawlings to the north end of Harkness Lane and Deputy Mullins to the south end for traffic control.

He knew there would be people already gathered there. Everybody loves a fire. But he hadn't expected the size of the crowd to be what it was when he rounded the last bend and saw the people standing in front of the church. There were more of them than there had been at the protest that morning. And those people had been siphoned from every church in town to go to the protest on Harkness Lane.

When he pulled his cruiser as close as he could get, Fire Chief Pete Brady and his entire department were already there, shooting plumes of water up into the air to land on the roof of the old building. When Pete had finished giving instructions to the firefighters, he turned to Mitch.

"Total loss," Pete said. "No way in hell to save that building. It's a tinderbox, old wood, termite-eaten. It'd be my guess that there was an accelerant used. When we arrived, it appeared that the whole structure was involved in the flames, which meant somebody spread something around inside, probably gasoline, and lit a match."

Goody.

Mitch turned when he heard voices and saw what was probably the entire congregation of Zeke Wakefield's Mountain Shakers Fire Baptized Holiness Church standing with the light of the flames flickering on their faces, cheering and yelling and chanting.

Mitch left Pete and walked over to where Zeke Wakefield stood, his face bathed in a huge smile.

"I don't suppose you had anything to do with this fire," Mitch said.

Wakefield looked surprised. "No, I did not, but if I'd thought of it, I would have. If it had occurred to me, I would have come here and burned this building to the ground. But by the time I got here, somebody had already beaten me to it."

"You have an alibi for the last few hours?"

"You can ask anybody." Zeke made a sweeping gesture at the people around him. "We all got here at the same time, and we could see the smoke from half a mile away."

So, Wakefield did have an alibi. This time. He hadn't had an alibi for the times that the two girls were butchered.

Mitchell scanned the huge crowd of people. There were plenty he didn't recognize. He suspected they were tourists stopped by to see the fire. But there were familiar faces in the crowd, too. And one of them was as ugly as a buffalo's ass. Ethel Snodmotz was yelling and cheering with everyone else. It was like a football game. Homecoming. And our team just won fifty to nothing.

Mitch walked to where Ethel was standing. She'd gotten here fast, had barely enough time to go home and change clothes after Mitch had her released her from detention.

She saw him and grinned. "You bring your hot dogs and your marshmallows?" she asked, then threw her head back and laughed. It sounded like a witch's cackle. "Ain't this the finest thing you ever seen? Ain't this the most beautiful fire that ever graced the earth?"

"When did you get here, Ethel?" Mitch asked. Obviously, she'd gone home to change clothes. She'd come to the afternoon's protest from church and had been hauled away with her dress soiled and wrinkled and a big snag in her pantyhose. It had occurred to Mitch at the time to wonder if she was the only woman in the county who still wore pantyhose. He didn't know that that was a thing still.

She looked at him and straightened herself up taller. "I went home and had to get cleaned up after you locked me up for no good reason, and by the way, you will be sorry for that. I'll be pressing charges for unlawful detention." There was no such crime. And if there had been, the prosecutor, not a private citizen, would have to file them. "And I'm going to lodge a complaint against you with the county council. I'm going to have me a talk with the right honorable County Mayor Rutherford Abernathy. I'm going to tell him how you've ridden roughshod over the rights and privileges of the people a sheriff is elected to serve. I'm going to—"

"I asked when you got here."

"I went home and changed clothes, then came right back to town."

There was absolutely no way to tell whether what she was saying was true. The pair of jeans she had on were filthy.

Mitch knew about how long it took to get to her farm from town. He might have been a card-carrying Away from Here, but he was slowly getting the lay of the land. Ethel had barely had time to get to her house before she came back.

"What was your hurry to get back to town? You didn't dress to go church tonight."

"Why would I? I done missed services, thanks to you. And I don't have to give you an explanation of my comings and goings. I come back to town because I wanted to come to town."

"So you didn't put on a pair of pants maybe because you didn't want to get gasoline on a good Sunday dress?"

She fixed him with a cold stare.

"You ought not to be making accusations like that that you can't prove," she said. "And you can't prove nothing."

Then she turned away from him and started cheering again.

Mitch wandered the perimeter of the tape that Pete Brady's firemen had set out, looking for familiar faces. Arsonists almost always showed up at the scene of the fire they had set. Otherwise, it would be like cooking a big dinner and leaving the table before you ate it.

Of course, this fire wasn't set just for the joy of watching a building burn. The person who set this fire did it for a reason, and right off the top of his head, Mitch could name at least half a dozen people who had demonstrated within the last forty-eight hours that they had a reason to torch this church. He could picture the faces of a couple of dozen more whose names he didn't know.

Mitch was standing on the edge of the crowd near the corner of the building when he saw with horror that a little boy had ignored the don't-cross-this-line tape and climbed up a huge tulip poplar tree to get a better view of the blaze. Just then the wind shifted, fanning the flames toward the tree, and the boy started screaming.

Knocking people out of the way, Mitch ran dead out, as fast as he could, toward the tree. The little boy was terrified now, the heat turning his face red. The bark on the trunk of the tree beneath him had been set afire by the whipping flames, so he couldn't climb down. But he couldn't stay where he was or the fire would toast him like a hot dog on a stick.

Mitch saw two firemen running toward the boy from the other side of the building, but he was much closer than they were. He'd get there first and seconds mattered. All it would take was one more gust of wind from the wrong direction and it would set the whole tree — and the little boy in it — on fire. Mitch reached the trunk of the tree and started scaling it on the back side, away from the flames, listening to the screaming child shrieking above him.

"Hey, son, this way," he cried. "Climb around to this side of the tree, can you do that? Climb around the back here where it's not burning."

The little boy turned and scooted on his butt along the limb where he'd been sitting to the bigger limb that protruded out from the trunk of the tree. Mitch was about fifteen feet below him, had climbed as far as he could reach without going around onto the other side of the tree where the limbs were easier to climb — but also happened to be on fire.

The fireman had reached the bottom of the tree by then. Pete was one of them and he yelled up to Mitch, "Can you get him?"

There was no time for Pete to get a ladder.

"Get ready in case he falls," Mitch called back to Pete, then turned his attention to the boy, who'd made it to the big limb but was still on the side of the tree facing the fire. The heat of it was burning his skin like a sunburn.

"Son, you gotta be brave now. Can you be brave for me?" Mitch yelled. "You have to jump from that limb down to the one below it. Can you do that?"

"I'm scared," the boy cried.

"There are firemen down on the ground who will catch you if you fall."

The boy looked down to the fireman standing below him. "What if they miss me and I hit the ground?"

"They won't miss you because you're not going to fall. It's harder to climb up a tree than down it, and you were strong enough and big enough to climb up. Now, you've got to get around to this side of the tree to get away from the fire. Come on. Jump to that limb!"

The boy got carefully from his butt up to his feet, crouched on the big limb and looked down at Mitch.

"I'm scared," he said.

"Of course, you are. Everybody gets scared when scary things are happening. It's *brave* people who do what they have to do anyway. You're brave enough to jump from that limb to this limb. Do it now, son. Do it *now*." The boy paused for an agonizing moment, then leapt toward the limb just above Mitch's head. He almost made it.

But instead of landing on his feet, he was off balance and tipped forward. Mitch scrabbled up a few more feet and grabbed the boy's leg with one hand before he could topple off the limb toward the ground. The kid was screaming now, had totally lost it.

"It's okay. It's okay, I gotcha," Mitch said, though he didn't have a good grip on the boy at all. Mitch let go his own grip on the tree, balancing precariously on the limb where he stood, so he could use both hands to hold onto the boy. Mostly upside down, the boy was wiggling and squirming in panic, threatening to knock both of them out of the tree.

"Be still!" Mitch commanded in his sternest voice, and the boy froze. That's all it took, a second or two. Mitch lurched backward, slamming his side into a limb behind him as he dragged the boy around to the back side of the tree. The kid seized Mitch in a choke hold and there was a terrifying, off-balance moment when they both could have gone down, before Mitch grabbed the tree again with his free hand while pulling the boy to him with the other. The little boy clung to Mitch, sobbing. Mitch looked down at the ground to the fireman. Pete had sent two of them back to the truck and they had just returned with a ladder.

Leaning the ladder against the tree, one of the firemen scrambled to the top of it like a monkey. Mitch leaned over as far as he could and handed the boy into the fireman's arms. There was so much smoke now, it was hard to see anything. The other side of the tree had caught fire. Pete had not directed fire hoses at the tree before because he feared that the water would knock Mitch and the boy out of the tree. But as soon as Mitch handed the boy off to the fireman on the ladder, Pete let loose, squirting the side of the tree that was burning, dousing Mitch like he'd been dropped into a dunking pool. Pete kept the hose directed on the no-longer-burning tree as Mitch climbed down to where he could get his feet on the top rung of the ladder, then went down it the rest of the way to the ground.

"Jody, get over here," Pete called.

Mitch didn't understand why Pete had called one of the paramedics until he looked down at his left arm, at the huge splinter protruding out of it. He must have jabbed his arm into it when he lurched backward, trying to keep his hold on the wiggling boy. It was a three-inch-long piece of bark. He only became aware of it when he saw it, as the adrenaline dump into his bloodstream subsided and the tunnel vision, feel-no-pain effects of it began to wear off.

"You okay, Mitch?"

Mitch nodded, but Pete wasn't taking his word for it. Mitch watched Pete's eyes as they traveled over his body, checking for other injuries. The boy had been whisked off by the other firemen to an ambulance, and Jody Mills arrived at that time with a satchel.

"Come back to the truck with me," Jody said, "and we'll get this bandaged."

"Please tell me you're not going to cut the sleeve of my uniform off. It's just torn in this one place. It is a brand-new uniform," Mitch said.

Jody looked at him. "I'm going to cut the sleeve of your uniform off. Cope."

Pete walked along beside Mitch and tried to act like he wasn't hovering in case Mitch suddenly collapsed on the ground, injured in some way that couldn't be seen.

Mitch appreciated the concern. It felt good to see that he'd made that kind of genuine friend, even though he was an away-from-here. He sat down on the bumper of the ambulance, listening to the chaos around him. Firemen yelling. People chanting and cheering. The crackle of the fire and the whoosh and sizzle of the water hitting it. As he watched in dismay, Jody took a pair of scissors and snipped off the sleeve of his uniform, then cut it lengthways to ease it away from the splinter that had slid into his arm at an angle.

"You're gonna need a couple of stitches to close this."

The wound was bleeding profusely now, the blood running down Mitch's arm to his side and staining the pants of his uniform.

Mitch shot a look at Jody, who said, "What? The blood will wash out. Of course, the shirt won't likely grow a new sleeve, but like I said—"

"I know," Mitch finished for him, "cope."

Mitch heard the character of the crowd's grumbling change and turn ugly. People were shouting now at the man who was striding through their midst, head held high. Rileigh was right. He did look for all the world like Gavin Newsom.

McPherson stalked up to Mitch and growled in an angry voice. "Somebody set fire to this building on purpose, surely to shit, you know that."

"It would seem so," Mitch said as Jody cleaned the wound before he stitched it up.

"What are you sitting here for? Why aren't you out there finding whoever did it?"

Mitch looked down at the paramedic preparing to put stitches in his arm and back up at Gilchrist McPherson, aka Gilbert Pierce, and shook his head. "I'm on it, give me a minute."

"It's going to be a complete loss," Pierce said, his hands on his hips, staring at the burning building. "Insurance will have to write the whole thing off." Mitch's eyes clicked up to the man's face, but Pierce didn't notice. "It'll take more than the insurance money to build it back, though. I'll need contributions from the community."

"You could get very old very fast waiting for the good

people of Yarmouth County to contribute to a church that worships Satan."

"I had followers, you just didn't know who they were. They didn't have a chance to come out into the open before somebody poured gasoline on our church and burned it down."

"How do you know somebody poured gasoline on it?" Mitch asked, and he saw an instant of hesitation in McPherson's eyes before the glib autopilot took over.

"A fire this big, surely somebody used gasoline to start it."

But Mitch had caught it. Just that little spark, that second or two before McPherson got his shit back together. And that was all he needed. Now, Mitch had another name to add, and it would move immediately to the top slot on the list of suspected arsonists — McPherson himself.

Chapter Thirty-One

MAMA MADE POPCORN. Game night with the family all gathered around the crackling fire as snow fell delicately outside the window required hot chocolate and popcorn to seal the Currier and Ives ambience—

Stop it, Rileigh, she chided herself.

Mama was only trying to recapture some measure of the time that they had lost. All those years of Monday mornings at breakfast and Thursday afternoons at the baseball park, Sundays at church, and Saturdays hiking in the mountains — thousands of days gone that were unrecoverable. Mama was just trying to do everything she could to squeeze as much family-ness into the time they now had together.

Rileigh understood it all. It was just that she also understood it wouldn't do any good, that there was no recapturing the lost moments, that trying to jam happy Currier and Ives scenes into this family that had been fractured and broken years ago by her scumbag father was an impossible task. But then Mama had never been daunted by impossible tasks. She had, after all, been dating Rhett Butler.

Rileigh had always rather liked games. She couldn't recall playing them often, but it seemed like she'd enjoyed herself when she did. She was lousy at cards. Board games were games of strategy, but she never played any of them long enough or often enough to get good at them. But tonight wasn't about the games Mama had set out. Pictionary, a brand-new unopened box of Monopoly, and something else called Chutes and Ladders. Mama flitted around from Jillian to Rileigh and back to Jillian like a butterfly in a meadow of flowers. And Rileigh loved seeing the look of peace on her face that Rileigh hadn't even realized was missing until she saw it back there again. Mama had all her chicks in the nest, and she was a happy mother hen.

"I think we should play Monopoly, don't you?" Mama said.

"It's fine with me," said Rileigh.

Jillian shrugged. "I'm good with Monopoly."

"I bought this game. When was it? Oh, I know. About a year ago, back when Rhett was coming to call. He loved Monopoly."

"Rhett who?" Jillian asked.

"His last name was Butler, I think," Mama said. Jillian looked at Rileigh with her eyes opened too wide, and Rileigh just shrugged.

"Yeah, but you broke up with Rhett Butler, didn't you, Mama?" Mama nodded and Rileigh continued. "Even Scarlett O'Hara couldn't say that."

"Who's Scarlett O'Hara?"

The three women sat down at the kitchen table, put the game board out flat on it, picked up the dice, got the little cards, the houses and the hotels and the money, and Mama began dispensing it all.

"So, tell me about your day," Mama said to Rileigh, and Rileigh swallowed hard.

Well, she could start off by describing the phone call from Mitch to let her know that there was a dead body in the sanctuary of the Holiness Church in Juniper Hollow. The dead body had been mutilated and wired to the cross with a gutted black cat draped around its neck — and its internal organs had been scattered around the sanctuary.

"Oh, nothing particularly interesting," Rileigh said.

Jillian had stayed home that morning, so Rileigh asked, "What did you do today?"

Jillian got a strange look on her face and answered too quickly, "Nothing, nothing at all."

Alarm bells went off in Rileigh's head and a sinking sensation filled her belly. What was it that Jillian didn't want her and Mama to know? Rileigh supposed the list of possible answers was legion, since there was almost nothing they *did* know about Jillian's life before she'd come home, and what little they did was a horror movie rated R for violence and sexual situations.

"Actually, what I spent most of the morning on was a picture," Jillian said with some pride, and Rileigh smiled. She loved that Jillian was using the paints Rileigh had gotten for her makeshift art studio upstairs.

"What's it a painting of?"

"It isn't a painting of anything."

"What does that mean?"

Jillian took the dice that she had been about to roll and set them carefully on the table. "I've been trying for over a week to paint simple things like bowls of fruit or flowers or a scene of the mountain tops or the hills. But I couldn't do any of it. Nothing I paint looks anything like the scene I painted."

"It takes time, Jilly honey," said Mama. "You can't expect to just become an artist overnight. You know what Aunt Daisy always said?"

The mere mention of the woman's name made both Rileigh and Jillian tense, but Mama didn't notice. "She always said, 'If you want to do something good, you got to be willing to do it bad first.'"

"Well, this morning I was starting on a picture of the creek running along down beside the meadow. The view out the window. But I couldn't make anything on the canvas look like that. So I stopped trying, and I just painted what I felt."

"You painted what you felt instead of what you saw?"

"I set the brush down, closed my eyes for a moment, and thought of a time, a situation, a sensation. Then I picked up the brush and tried to paint it."

"There's a name for that kind of art, but I don't know what it is," Rileigh said. "Impressionistic or expressionistic, maybe."

"I don't care what its name is. I just care that I felt free when I painted it, like I was cleaning out something inside me and getting rid of it by putting it there on the canvas."

"Well, I want to see it," Rileigh said, and started to scoot her chair back.

"You can't, I destroyed it."

Rileigh sat still where she was.

"It was a scene from a dark place inside me. That's why I didn't want to tell you what I did this morning, because I didn't have a painting to show for it. I took it out into the backyard, poured some kerosene on it and set it on fire. I enjoyed watching it burn."

Mama didn't quite know what to say about that.

Neither did Rileigh.So she jabbed her hand down into the big bowl of popcorn, grabbed a handful, and shoved it in her mouth.

"Your turn, Mama," she said with her mouth full.

And so they played. Mama was surprisingly good and unbelievably cutthroat. She got all the utilities the first time around the board. And as soon as she had Park Place, Rileigh knew she and Jillian were destined for a long, slow death.

When Mama got up to take the half-empty bowl of popcorn into the kitchen, her phone rang. They heard Mama talking for a few minutes and when she came back into the room, her phone was back in her pocket.

"There was some excitement downtown tonight," she said.

Rileigh perked up. "What kind of excitement?"

"You know that church where they was going to worship Satan? Well, tonight somebody burned it down."

"Burned it down," Rileigh said, her voice airless.

"Yep, I think all the way to the ground. Mary Lou talked to Phillip, who's a fireman, and he said by the time they got there it was already a total loss. That old building, somebody poured gasoline on it probably." Mama looked at Rileigh. "He said Mitch was sitting on the back of the ambulance getting bandaged when—"

"Bandaged," Rileigh said, getting to her feet. "Getting bandaged for what?"

"I didn't ask."

Rileigh snatched her phone out of her pocket, hit favorites, and punched Mitch. The call went to voicemail. She hung up and looked at Mama. "Tell me what she said about Mitch."

"I done told you everything she said. Apparently, he hurt himself, but wasn't nothing bad."

"I should have been there." Rileigh couldn't stop grinding her teeth.

"You mean, if you'd been there, he wouldn't have got hurt?" Mama asked.

Rileigh realized how absurd her statement was. Mama was right, of course. Rileigh's presence wouldn't have spared Mitch whatever minor injury he had incurred. It's not like she could have *saved* him. But dammit, she should have been there. She understood that it was totally irrational. She felt like a mirror image of Mama when she saw Rileigh's black eye, totally overreacting, as if it were somehow a life-threatening injury instead of a bump. And she was sure Mitch's was no more than a bump. If Mitch's injuries had been serious, whoever Mama had talked to would've said so.

Mama went on playing, rolling the dice and moving her piece and buying some little property. Rileigh didn't even notice what it was. Her mind was somewhere else.

"Your turn."

"What?"

"It's your turn," Jillian said and handed Rileigh the dice.

"Oh." She rolled the dice, got a six, picked up her rubber duckie and moved it six spaces down the board. She landed on the electric company, and Mama demanded her rent. As Rileigh picked up her pile of money, she realized that she was angry. She didn't want to be playing this stupid game. She was mad at having to be here. She was mad at being emotionally blackmailed into staying at home tonight. When she should have been—

No, it wasn't where she *should have* been. But it was where she *wanted to be.*

Her phone jangled in her pocket. She stood up so quickly, she upended the board. The houses and hotels

Mama had set up so carefully slid to the edge of the table and toppled off, making clacking sounds on the floor.

"I'm sorry, I'm sorry, I didn't mean to. I'll clean it up."

Grabbing her phone out of her pocket, she felt enormous relief when she saw caller ID.

"Hello there, I hear you were at a bonfire tonight," she said.

"News travels fast in this county."

"So, what happened?"

"I don't know. All the usual suspects were there, certainly enough people who had demonstrated not only motive, but opportunity and willingness to burn that building down. And they were all standing there cheering like it was a football game and our team had won."

"I hear you, um, you got hurt."

"You heard that?"

"Well, did you?"

"Yeah, I got a splinter in my arm."

"How'd you get a splinter in your arm?"

"Climbing up a tree."

"Are you going to make me drag this out of you one question at a time?"

"A kid had climbed up a tree so he could see the fire better, but the wind moved the flames that way, so I had to help get him down."

Rileigh was certain it had been way more dramatic and dangerous than Mitch tried to make it seem.

"Is the kid okay?"

"First-degree burns, like a sunburn on his face. And scared shitless. But that's all."

"So, did that splinter in your arm need stitches?"

"How do you know about all this?" But before she could answer, he said, "Never mind. I know how you know.

The same way your mama knows everything. Have you ever heard of the hundredth monkey?"

Rileigh had no idea where he was going with this. "The hundredth monkey?"

"Yeah. It is said that if ninety-nine monkeys in the jungle learn a thing, the hundredth monkey knows it without having to learn. That's kind of what Yarmouth County is. Everybody here is the hundredth monkey."

"You didn't answer my question."

"A couple of stitches, yea, and I'm good to go. The only real casualty of my encounter with the fire tonight was my uniform. Jody had to cut the left sleeve off to get to the splinter."

That told Rileigh it was more serious than Mitch wanted her to believe. You don't cut off a piece of clothing to get to a scratch, but she let it go. She could tell by his voice he was fine, and that's all that really mattered. He was fine.

"Just wanted to let you know that I'm going to be out first thing tomorrow morning talking to the usual suspects about this fire. I want to know where they all were, and I want to be able to corroborate those alibis. I could use some help."

"You got it. I'll be there," she said. She told him goodbye and shoved her phone back into her pocket.

Mama and Jillian were looking at her. Just looking at her.

"What?" she said.

Jillian looked at the pile of little red hotels and little green houses in the center of the board where Jillian had put them after she picked them up off the floor. They'd been Mama's, and they'd been set around where they were supposed to be until Rileigh knocked them down.

"Oh, Mama. I didn't mean to mess it all up. I'm sorry."

Mama said nothing. Not "it's okay dear" or "don't worry about it" or "no problem". She didn't say anything at all. Neither did Jillian.

And for the first time in her life, Rileigh felt like odd man out in her own home — Mama and Jillian on one side and her by herself on the other. It was a feeling she very, very much did not like.

Chapter Thirty-Two

RILEIGH WAS JARRED from sleep before dawn by the ringing of her cell phone. She felt around blind on the bedside table, trying to grab it before it rang again and woke up Mama and Jillian. Her fingers were clumsy though, and she knocked the phone off onto the floor and had to scramble to pick it up. Milliseconds before it rang a second time, she panted, "Hello."

"She's gone! Oh, dear Goddess in heaven, she's *gone!*"

For a moment, Rileigh had no idea who she was talking to. She hadn't had a chance to look at the caller ID screen, and it sure as hell wasn't Mitch. The female voice on the other end of the phone let out a cry that was part scream, part keening wail. "It got her, oh gods, it got Liv."

Her voice had been so distorted that at first Rileigh had not recognized Jaclyn Milford. Rileigh sat up in bed, swinging her feet off the side and into her slippers as she told Jaclyn, "Calm down, I can't understand what you're saying."

"It got Olivia."

Rileigh shuffled in her house shoes into the bathroom

and ran some cold water in the sink while she tried to talk Jaclyn Milford off the ledge.

"Honey, you have to talk more slowly. Are you saying that something has happened to Olivia?"

"Not *something*, the ifrit. It got her and it's coming for me, too, and there's nothing I can do. If a demon comes for you, there's nothing you can do."

"No demon is coming for you, Jaclyn."

At this point, if she had been in Jaclyn's presence, she probably would have slapped her to get her attention. But there was no equivalent slap that a cell phone could administer. The best she could do was to shout Jaclyn's name and get her attention. But she couldn't shout her name without waking up Mama and Jilly.

Rileigh pushed images out of her head before she could even think them. Well, before she could think much about them. The disappointed faces of Mama and Jillian when they looked down at the ruin of the Monopoly board after Rileigh had jumped to her feet. Mama had been winning, had a pile of money in front of her. And once you got on that kind of roll with all the utilities and all the rail-roads, nobody else had a chance. It would merely be a slow march to death for her and Jillian to the end of the game. But none of that made any difference to Mama and Jillian.

As she was brushing her teeth for bed last night, Rileigh analyzed it and realized that both Mama and Jillian had been *disappointed* in her. And maybe felt a little betrayed. Certainly Mama wanted Rileigh to stay home and babysit Jillian 24/7. And Jillian….

Rileigh sighed. Jillian was an enigma wrapped in a conundrum.

She shook off those thoughts and concentrated on how she could reach Jaclyn. Then Rileigh stepped into the shower stall, grabbed a huge fluffy towel, and put it in front of her face behind the cell phone. Muffling as much of the sound as she could.

"Jaclyn!" she shouted. "Jaclyn, stop!"

There was silence on the other end of the phone.

"Jaclyn? Are you still there?"

"I'm here." The girl sounded like a mouse caught in a trap.

"Now tell me why you called me."

Jaclyn let out a sigh of such defeat it broke Rileigh's heart.

"We were going to run away, Olivia and I. But Olivia said it didn't matter where you were on the planet, that the spirit world and the human world didn't line up side-by-side. If a demon wanted to come at you from the spirit world, it could find you anywhere. But we were so scared we had to do something. So last night we agreed to meet early this morning and go to Nashville. To a big city where there are police that answer a 911 call."

Rileigh suspected that at this particular point in American history, that was definitely not a foregone conclusion. But she didn't point that out to Jaclyn.

"So I packed my bags and I got Ernie and put him in this little cage. I couldn't go anywhere without Ernie."

She'd said that Ernie was her familiar, that most witches had familiars. Olivia had said that the barn owl was hers ... so had she put the owl in its cage to run away with her? Dragging an owl and a rabbit into the lobby of a hotel would just about guarantee you wouldn't get a room.

But the girls probably hadn't been thinking about that.

"I couldn't sleep last night. All I did was pace around and around and around. I went from the front window to the back window. From the front door to the back door. I checked the locks a thousand times. Ten thousand times. But can a lock even keep a spirit out?"

Rileigh had absolutely no idea whether demons abided by the rules of the universe. Locks and bars and such. "So you stayed up all night, and then…"

"We were supposed to meet at five o'clock this morning. I was dressed and ready to go at three. So, I called Olivia to ask if maybe I could come by early. But she didn't answer her phone. That scared me. So, I dropped everything and went to her house. Left my suitcases and Ernie at home" She let out another sigh. "Olivia wasn't there, Rileigh. She was gone. Nobody was there."

"Was her car in the parking lot?"

"No. Yes. I don't know. I didn't look."

"Did she take her purse with her? Suitcases, maybe."

"I didn't look at that either, because her house was such a mess. It was all torn up. Cedric was perched on a curtain rod. His cage was lying on the floor and the door was open. I started screaming for Olivia, but nobody answered. So I ran back out and got in my car and just drove up into the mountains. I wanted to go see Granny Milford. Granny Milford would have known what to do."

Granny Milford had died ten years ago.

"I have nowhere to go and you gave me this card and said I should call if I needed anything. I need somebody to keep me from being eaten alive by a demon from hell."

The last few words revealed the incipient hysteria just under the surface.

"Where are you now?"

"I'm sitting in the Walmart parking lot. It's lit with those big sodium lights like it's daylight outside. And there are people around, some. Who in the hell goes to Walmart at five o'clock in the morning? But I couldn't stand to be alone. I don't know if a demon can come for you if there are people around. Maybe the demon doesn't care. Please come, Rileigh, please." Then Jaclyn Milford burst into tears.

"I'll get dressed as fast as I can. Lock all the doors of your car."

Locking the car doors wouldn't keep out a demon, at least not a determined one. But a girl sitting alone in an almost empty parking lot could invite the attention of other creatures just as evil as an ifrit, but concrete and substantial and from this world.

Rileigh put her cell phone down, washed her face with cold water, and looked into her own eyes in the bathroom mirror. She and Mitch weren't any closer to figuring out who had killed these girls than they had been when Mitch had called Rileigh in the middle of the night to get two teenage girls to tell her what they'd been doing at Buttermilk Falls.

Unlike in the other cases that they'd worked, this time they had more suspects than zits on a freshman. You could count as a suspect every single member of Zeke Wakefield's church. There were ... what? Two or three dozen? And any other fanatical Christian anywhere in Yarmouth County. Then, more specifically, was Gilchrist McPhearson, because he blamed the witches for the demise of his church. And there was Ethel Snodmotz, because she believed that all witches should be dispatched to hell summarily. So far, Mitch and Rileigh hadn't managed to eliminate a single suspect from the list.

Do not pass Go. Do not collect $200.

That thought stopped her. Was she neglecting Jillian? She'd spent three decades desperate to have her sister back. And now she found herself begrudging the time she was spending with her because...

Go on, finish the sentence, said that annoying voice of the essential Rileigh.

Because she'd rather be spending it with Mitch.

Rileigh didn't like how that admission felt. Maybe Georgia had put her finger on it. Maybe Rileigh was afraid of commitment. Was that why she just couldn't seem to relax and let herself be open to … to … well, to whatever this was.

And what is it, do you think? asked the essential Rileigh.

"I don't have any idea," Rileigh whispered aloud.

She dried her face. Brushed her teeth. No makeup. She almost never wore it.

Rileigh stepped out of the bathroom into her bedroom to find Jillian standing in her nightgown at the foot of her bed. She jumped in surprise, then let out a sigh.

"You know what I said about you being able to sneak dawn past a rooster? I take it back. You're quieter than that. You're more silent than a mouse in house shoes walking across a cotton ball."

If she'd said something like that to Mitch, to Ian or Georgia, there would have been the pleasant banter of whether or not you got points for it. But Jillian didn't even smile. She just looked at Rileigh.

"You're going out on some kind of police business, aren't you?"

Rileigh squared her shoulders. "Yes, I am. I just got a frantic phone call from Jaclyn Milford saying her best friend is missing."

"And it's your job to go find her?"

Frustration rose up in Rileigh like bile in the back of her throat and she swallowed it down with an effort. "If I can help, I'll help. This is serious business and Mitch needs all the help he can get."

"So, you're going to go running out here to go looking for a missing girl?" Jaclyn said.

Rileigh sighed. "Yeah, that about covers it."

She turned and opened her sock drawer and pulled out a pair, then sat down on the edge of her bed and kicked off her house shoes.

She was surprised to see that Jillian had come to sit beside her.

"I'm trying really hard," Jillian said. "Please believe that. I am. I'm just so scared for you. I've seen how ugly the world can be. I've watched it playing out in my own life for decades. And I don't want anything to happen to you."

In a surprising display of emotion, Jillian threw her arms around Rileigh and hugged her tight. "Please. Please promise me you'll be careful."

"I promise," she said.

_____

Chapter Thirty-Three

MITCH WAS awake when Rileigh called him Monday morning to tell him about the frantic telephone call she'd just gotten from Jaclyn Milford. He'd been up most of the night, unable to sleep. It was his job to find the murderer who had savagely killed two young women and he had lots of suspicions, but no clear winner.

Mitch and Rileigh were operating on the assumption that the motive here was witchcraft, because there were certainly a whole lot of people in the county who were pissed off at the girls for being witches. Even the minister of the recently-burned-to-the-ground Fallen Angel church was angry at them for—and this was rich—maligning the character of Satan.

Mitch thought that was probably a pretty difficult thing to do.

Somewhere around 3:30, Mitch had forced himself to stand back from the evidence that he was working with and abandon the suppositions he was basing his theories on, to see if he couldn't look at it from a new angle. Was it possible that there was some other reason these young women had been murdered? That someone had a motive that didn't have anything to do with them being witches?

He had been mulling over that interesting concept when Rileigh called.

"I'm on my way to the Walmart parking lot," Rileigh said. "I'm going to get Jaclyn and bring her back home with me."

"I'll go to Olivia's house and see what I can find there."

Mitch had dressed in an old uniform, because his brand-new uniform was missing a sleeve. He looked down at the bandage on his arm and decided that the wound had not been worth destroying his uniform over.

When he pulled up in front of the small trailer house where Olivia Booth lived on Postal Clerk Lane, Olivia's car was parked out front of the trailer. Wherever Olivia had gone, she hadn't driven herself there. There were lights on in the living room, but nowhere else in the trailer. Mitch climbed the steps to the porch.

He knocked. No answer. He knocked again. Still no answer. He reached down and turned the doorknob, and it turned easily in his hand. The door wasn't locked.

Mitch stepped into the living room, and the first thing he noticed was Olivia's purse hanging on a hook beside the door, with the car keys attached by a carabiner to the strap. Stepping farther into the room, he realized that Jaclyn had not exaggerated when she said that it looked like there'd been some kind of struggle in Olivia's living room. It hadn't been pin-neat when he was here last. There had been clothes and other things scattered around on the floor and dirty dishes on end tables and in the sink. But this was way more than just a messy house. The most telling evidence that there had been some violence in this room was the fact that the cage where the big owl — he thought Olivia had said its name was Casper — had been perched when they were here before was lying on its side on the floor with the door hanging ajar.

Suddenly Mitch heard a sound, like flames or the fluttering of wings, and the huge owl swooped down at him from where it had been perched on the curtain rod, talons out. It snatched Mitch's hat off his head and flew around the room a couple of times with it, finally dropping the hat in the floor and landing again on the drapery rod.

Casper sat perched there, looking down at him. It wasn't like seeing an escaped parakeet perched on a lampshade. The big barn owl was more than two feet tall, with piercing eyes. As Mitch stared back up at the owl, it began to turn its head slowly around. Mitch knew that owls could turn their heads almost 360 degrees. It was something about their eyes being in fixed sockets so they couldn't move them and having to move their whole heads to look around. But knowing the bird could do it and watching it do so, Exorcist-style, in order to look at Mitch over the other wing, was unnerving at best.

Mitch crossed the room carefully, keeping one eye on the big bird. He had no desire to feel those talons scraping across his scalp. He placed his hat back on his head and pulled it down tight against his ears, then continued to look around.

The altar where Olivia kept her witch's implements, including her wand, had been knocked aside, pushed to the edge of the table. And the voodoo doll that had been lying next to the statue of a red-robed skeleton was lying on the floor. The skeleton lay next to it, skull disconnected from its body, big empty eye sockets staring up at him … as the eyes of the owl stared down at him.

Olivia Booth was a big girl, almost six feet, and looked to be strong. Even if a demon from hell that came after her, she would have fought back ferociously. That there

234

were no tables knocked over, no furniture shoved out of place, seemed to indicate that whoever it was had subdued her quickly. There was no blood. Had the killer gotten to Olivia?

He searched the rest of the small trailer and found no evidence that anything was amiss. In the back bedroom an open suitcase lay on the bed, half full of clothes and shoes. A woman's dopp kit lay beside it. A drawer with lingerie in it stood open in the dresser.

Clearly, Olivia was packing to go with Jaclyn to Nashville, but somebody had gotten to her before she had a chance to run away. They must have taken her by surprise — but the door showed no signs of forced entry.

Had she willingly opened her door to her attacker?

Chapter Thirty-Four

MITCH WAS HALFWAY to Jaclyn Milford's townhome when the radio in his cruiser crackled to life.

"Unit 1, this is dispatch. Report of a ten-nineteen at the Mountain Shaker Fire-Baptized Holiness Church in Juniper Hollow." A ten-nineteen was "shots fired."

Mitch wheeled a U-turn in the middle of the road, turned on his lights and his siren, and headed towards Juniper Hollow. He told the dispatcher to send Deputy Crawford to serve as backup because Crawford lived in that neighborhood. Then he called the dispatcher on his cell phone so that everything he said wouldn't go out over the radio.

"What's up in Juniper Hollow?"

"It was a 9-1-1 call, sir. Reverend Zeke Wakefield says that somebody's up in the woods, shooting at his church."

Mitch killed his siren about a mile away from the church but left his lights on. He came rumbling up the gravel road to the building that sat among the trees, where he saw Wakefield's pickup truck and the handicapped van that was driven by his son, Ross.

"About time you showed up, Sheriff," Zeke shouted from inside the building after Mitch risked rolling down his window. "There's some crazy fool up in the trees yelling that we're murderers. I think he's drunk."

A man who was drunk before nine o'clock in the morning had serious issues, was Mitch's first thought. His second thought was that a drunk with a rifle was a very dangerous situation.

Before Mitch opened his car door, he reached up and unhooked his service rifle from the clasp on the ceiling above him. Then he opened his car door and rolled out onto the ground, then moved in a crouch to the back of the car and peered around it.

Bam. The sound of a gunshot broke the morning stillness.

Then Mitch heard a voice from far up the mountainside.

"Dirty sons of bitches, she didn't never hurt nobody." The far-away voice drifted down to Mitch. "You killed that poor girl just because you didn't like them tattoos on her arms and them body piercings. I thought you Christians was s'posed to be all about God seein' what's on the inside and not judgin' what's on the outside. And that poor girl was good as gold in her heart."

The man fired another shot and continued his rambling babble about Veronica Espinoza, whose body had been found wired to a cross in the church building on Sunday morning.

Mitch knew who was up in the woods. It was Ronnie's neighbor, Festus Herndon.

"Mr. Herndon," Mitch called out as loud as he could. "This is Yarmouth County Sheriff Mitch Webster. I need for you to put that gun down and come out of those woods with your hands up." There was a pause —

237

maybe he hadn't heard Mitch. He was pretty far up the hillside.

"I ain't putting this gun down till I empty it into that building. I'm going to shoot out every window and turn them walls into Swiss cheese."

That remark sounded like Festus hadn't come here intending to hurt anybody. It was possible he didn't even know anybody was inside, had simply come here to shoot the windows out of the church to vandalize it.

"Mr. Herndon, don't make me come up there after you. You're going to hurt somebody if you don't put that gun down and come out."

"I ain't going to hurt nobody," the voice called back down the hill. "But I am gonna hurt this church."

He fired another round and Mitch heard a window shatter.

Mitch shouted to Zeke Wakefield.

"I don't think he intends to hurt anybody. He's just pissed and wants to vandalize the church and is using a gun to do it. Stay down. Don't go anywhere near the windows. I'll get him."

Moving in a crouch back to the front of the cruiser, Mitch looked up the hillside toward the trees, then made a dash for the nearest piece of cover — a large oak tree trunk on the side of the driveway leading to the church. He moved slowly up the hillside, leaping from one piece of cover to another, higher and higher, until the church building was just a little box sitting in the trees at the end of a gravel driveway.

Mitch was above Herndon now. The old man was firing a .30-06 deer rifle, and he had three boxes of shells arranged on the ground in front of him. He had come here to riddle that church with holes and he'd brought enough ammunition to do it. Given his current state of inebriation, it was a miracle he'd managed to drive his truck out here. He had to have disabled the breathalyzer device somehow. Mitch figured if he had to take a test right now, he'd blow a 2.0. Maybe more.

"Mr. Herndon, do you know there are people in that church that you're shooting into?" Mitch called out.

Herndon looked around in surprise. He hadn't taken cover behind a bush or tree, was just sitting on a rock out in the open.

"Bullshit. Ain't nobody in there."

"So, you think the cars parked in front of the building were delivered by a UPS truck?"

Mitch heard no reply, then "I don't see no cars. You're lying."

Apparently, Herndon had climbed to his position above the church from the other side of the mountain. From where Mitch crouched on the mountainside, he could only see his own cruiser, parked beside the church building. He couldn't see the front side of the church at all.

Mitch began to make his way slowly down the hillside, holding his service rifle in his hands and praying he wouldn't have to use it.

When he got close, he saw Herndon put the rifle down and begin to reload it. That was his chance.

Mitch yelled, "Herndon, get your hands above your head. Drop that gun and get your hands above your head."

The man was so startled, he dropped a box of shells and bullets scattered out on the ground around him. He tried to turn around, and it was a good thing he couldn't manage it, because if he'd swung the barrel of that rifle in Mitch's direction, Mitch would have had no choice but to fire. But the man was apparently so drunk that he got off-balance trying to turn all the way around and look up the hill. Then he fell over on his side and dropped the rifle in front of him.

Mitch was on him two seconds later, kicking the rifle out of his reach.

Festus Herndon lifted his face to Mitch with a look of sadness and desolation.

"They *killed* her," he said. "I hear they strung her up on a cross and killed her — just 'cause she had tattoos and went around telling folks she was a witch. Poor thing done nothing to nobody, and they killed her." Then Herndon sat back on his haunches, put his face in his hands, and started to cry.

Mitch hauled the drunk man down the hill with his hands cuffed behind him. He got to the church building as Deputy Crawford pulled up in his cruiser.

"This is Festus Herndon," Mitch said as he placed Herndon's abandoned deer rifle on the hood of his own cruiser. "How about you give him a ride into Gatlinburg?"

Crawford asked, "Put him in the drunk tank?"

"No, this poor asshole is going to have more charges against him than just public drunkenness."

Herndon was still sniveling and snorting, staggering under Mitch's grip, his eyes leaking down his face. Mitch handed the man's arm to Deputy Crawford, then opened the back door of Crawford's cruiser. Crawford eased the man into the back seat. He promptly fell over on his side and began to throw up.

Crawford shot Mitch an aggrieved look. Mitch just shrugged. Then he went to the front door of the church and knocked.

"Reverend Wakefield, this is Sheriff Webster. You can come out now. The man has been arrested and is on his way to jail."

Reverend Wakefield opened the door of the building and Mitch could see Ross sitting in his wheelchair in the middle of the lone aisle that led to the pulpit, the cross, the piano and the baptistry.

"So, you're sure it's safe?" Wakefield said and his tone and manner surprised Mitch. He had expected anger at the very least — probably rage, given the state of Wakefield's irrational behavior in the past few days. But what he found was a man who seemed slightly disoriented, like he wasn't quite sure what was going on.

"Are you okay Reverend Wakefield?" Mitch asked.

"Oh yeah, sure, we're both fine." He turned and looked back at his son and smiled broadly. "Yes sir-ee, me and Ross is just fine."

"Well, I'm glad to hear that nobody was hurt."

"Windows is just glass. They can be replaced. We can patch them holes in the outside of the building. It takes a whole lot more than a drunk with a rifle to shut down the forces of almighty God."

Mitch was reasonably sure that Herndon hadn't come out to the church to stand down almighty God.

"The man's name is Festus Herndon," Mitch said. "He lives next door to Veronica Espinoza's house on Turtle Run Road and she was a friend. Apparently a much more special friend than I knew."

The pleasant look on Wakefield's face vanished. "That woman was a witch, and she has been dispatched back to hell where she belongs."

Mitch didn't bother to argue with him.

"She and the rest of them witches has unleashed a demon from hell on this county, prowling around looking for souls to steal and it will be up to the forces of almighty God to stop it."

"Exactly what do you mean by that, Reverend Wakefield?"

The Reverend looked at him and shook his head.

"We're talking about spiritual warfare here, son. Ephesians 6:11 says we must put on the 'full armor of God' to stand against the schemes of the Devil — the belt of truth, the breastplate of righteousness, the shoes of peace, the shield of faith, the helmet of salvation and the sword of the spirit. With God's help, we will crush the witches and the devil they've summoned under our heels."

Thinking of Olivia Booth, who'd been taken by force out of her home as she packed to run away, Mitch asked, "So tell me — where were you and your son early this morning?"

Ross' head snapped up, but his father just waved his hand in the air as if he were shooing away a pesky fly. "We was doing the work of almighty God."

"*Where* exactly were you doing God's work?"

"Where I was every other time you've asked about my whereabouts. I was at home."

Mitch's eyes flicked to Ross. "Can you verify that?"

"Sure, he was home," the young man answered and hooked a smile on his face like a surgeon attaching a mask. "I was with him, spent the night at Papa's last night."

"But you said you were home *alone* when the other two girls disappeared."

"*Other* two?" Wakefield said, looking genuinely surprised.

"Olivia Booth is missing."

Wakefield looked up at the ceiling of the church, lifted his hands, and cried, "Hallelujah, thank the Lord. The God has shown his mighty glory in this county, coming to the aid of his followers, protecting them against the evil one."

He looked back at his son and smiled an odd smile, but said no more.

Mitch tipped his hat. "Good day to you both." He turned and went back out to his cruiser and considered what the look that had passed between those two men had meant.

Chapter Thirty-Five

JACLYN MILFORD WAS as close to a total meltdown as Rileigh had ever seen anybody. And she couldn't blame her. The girl's three best friends had been murdered over the course of three days, and she believed the demon responsible was coming after her.

Rileigh pulled into the Walmart parking lot and parked beside Jaclyn Milford's car. As soon as Jaclyn saw her, she leapt out and threw herself into Rileigh's arms, sobbing.

"I just know it's got her," she said. "It's got Liv. It's killed three of the four of us, and I'm next."

"How about we dial the hysteria back just a little bit?" Rileigh suggested as she held the girl in her arms. She was more than trembling, she was vibrating.

Rileigh knew that Mitch could not put this girl in protective custody, but Rileigh could provide the same kind of "police protection" Mitch had given Rileigh when the former sheriff had been trying to kill her. It had been nothing official, just *here I am, nobody's going to get at you*, which, unfortunately, had turned out not to be the case.

Still, Rileigh couldn't just pat this poor girl on the

head, tell her everything was going to be fine, and drive away. Jaclyn was terrified and Rileigh believed she had a really good reason to be. Oh, not because she and some friends had summoned a demon from the bowels of hell that was now coming after them, but because two young women had been murdered, and the third was missing. If Rileigh had been the fourth, she'd have been scared shitless, too.

"I called my parents," Jaclyn said through her tears. The Milfords had been in California for the past two weeks. " I told them they had to come home *right now*. I guess Mama heard the hysteria in my voice, because she said they'd catch the first flight. She called back a little later and told me that I could pick them up in Nashville this evening at about six." She drew a shaky breath. "And when I pick them up, we're not coming back here. We'll just get in the car and drive somewhere. I don't care where, just not here."

"Well, you have to do something between now and when you pick your parents up at the airport. So how about you and I have a girl's day out?"

Jaclyn looked at Rileigh like she had lost her mind.

"You don't want to be by yourself right now. You're scared to death, and you're not going to get police protection. But I'm *almost* police. I'm a pretty protective sort. I have been a soldier. I think if push comes to shove, I can keep you safe."

She was trying to make light of it, but Jaclyn's eyes filled with such gratitude, it made Rileigh uncomfortable.

"You'd do that for me?"

"Yup. And I won't even charge for … babysitting. Bring your hiking boots."

"What … why?"

"There are some great trails behind my house. I

haven't been up there in a long time, and I bet I can talk my sister Jillian into joining us. We'll have a great time."

Rileigh could tell that Jaclyn got the subtext — they'd be out in the woods where nobody could find them.

When Rileigh showed up at Mama's with Jaclyn it was not yet noon, but Mama was already sitting in the rocking chair on the porch doing something that approximated knitting — at least, it used up a bunch of yarn. Jillian was nowhere to be seen. Mama got up when she saw Rileigh, and her face burst into a beatific smile when she saw Jaclyn. "Well, hello there, sweetheart. I haven't seen you in ages."

Mama wrapped the girl up in her arms. Rileigh could tell that a grandmotherly hug was exactly the medicine Jaclyn needed.

Rileigh found Jillian in the backyard with an easel set up and paints on a nearby table. She hadn't yet started painting when Rileigh came out the back door.

"Hey, Jillie, you in the mood to go for a hike?"

"Right now? I was just getting ready to start."

"I brought Jaclyn Milford home with me and she's kind of in a bad way."

"I think she earned it," Jillian said, beginning to put her paints and brushes away.

Rileigh was thrilled. "There's nothing better to do on a beautiful summer day in the Smoky Mountains than go for a hike."

Jillian smiled, then surprised Rileigh with her serious tone. "You've grown into a warm, compassionate person, Little Sister. I'm proud of you."

As Rileigh tried to sputter out a response, Jillian hooked her arm in Rileigh's and the two of them went up the back porch steps together.

Rileigh checked in with Mitch by phone, told him that

she had Jaclyn under her watchful eye. He said he intended to spend the day on his list of suspects, corroborating alibis — for the murders and the church arson.

"I'm going to start with Ethel Snodmotz," he said, "because of what your Aunt Daisy told me once."

"And what was that?"

"If you have to eat a frog, don't look at it too long."

Rileigh burped out a giggle and finished for him, "And if you have to eat two frogs, eat the big ugly one first."

Rileigh hung up, cruised through the kitchen to pick up the picnic lunch that Mama had packed for them. Then the three of them crossed the backyard and headed up into the woods. They went up the side of Tucker Mountain where they crossed the ridge, then headed up to Tucker Peak, which really wasn't the peak, but it had been named Tucker Peak at some point, probably by the Tucker family, and since it was their mountain, they could call it whatever they wanted. Though there was no "overlook," there were breaks in the trees where they could look down on the valley stretched out below them. The air was as fresh as if it had been scrubbed with lye soap and hung out on the line to dry in the sunshine. The shade under the trees was cool and refreshing, the meadows were full of wildflowers, butterflies, and bees. It was a Currier and Ives *summertime*, a balm to their souls for all of them, each needing it for a different reason. Such was the power of the Smoky Mountains to heal and restore.

Then Rileigh's phone rang and she saw on Caller ID that it was Mitch, calling to see how they were doing. Or not. Maybe he was calling to tell her something. In the instant between that thought and touching the little green phone-shaped icon, her gut told her which.

"We found Olivia," he said.

Chapter Thirty-Six

MENTION FRANK SNODMOTZ to any Yarmouth County native and you got the same response — sympathy. You had only to meet Ethel Snodmotz to know why.

Nobody knew the story of how Ethel had managed to go out into the wide world and snag a man, given her glorious good looks and her charming personality. All anyone knew was that she'd returned to Yarmouth County when she was in her late twenties with Frank on her arm. As soon as you met him, you understood what he saw in Ethel — nothing. Frank Snodmotz was blind.

A kind, gentle soul, Frank Snodmotz had been born without eyes, had never seen a cloud or a flower or a bird or a smile. Or the face of his bride, Ethel, who brought him home to live on the farm her parents had bequeathed to her, along with a herd of Holstein cattle to milk, along with Hereford beef cattle, sheep, goats, chickens, ducks, and pigs. Over time, Ethel sold off all the farm animals and used the proceeds to buy the kind of livestock she preferred to raise — pigs.

To live downwind of the Snodmotz pig farm was to die a thousand deaths with every breath. Though she didn't seem the kind of woman who'd raise cute little lambs or baby goats, Ethel was a conjury of contradictions, and also populated her acreage with all manner of avian life, large and small, from swans to ducks and geese. Her flock of peacocks grew into huge birds that were as mean as Ethel was, according to the mail carrier who finally refused to deliver mail to the house at all. She put up dozens of purple martin houses all over the farm, along with sugar-water bird feeders for hummingbirds, which some said hummed around her back yard like bees. She even put up houses for the bats.

Frank Snodmotz had lived only a few years after he married Ethel. He'd had other birth defects besides lacking eyes — severe congenital heart problems. It was surprising to all of their neighbors that a man like Frank Snodmotz had been able to purchase life insurance, but Deputy Mullins had it on good authority from his brother-in-law, Craig, who was an insurance agent, that Ethel had collected almost half a million dollars when Frank died. She invested it in the farm, making renovations and hiring farmhands to do the "grunt" work, no pun intended, of taking care of pigs. Soon she had one of the largest herds in the state.

Mitch pulled his cruiser into the driveway leading up to a neat frame house with grass that needed mowing and no flower beds. It wasn't a dump, but neither was it one of those little storybook houses you saw so often in the mountains that looked like somebody dreamed them up in a fairy tale. He got out of the car, walked up onto her porch, took a deep breath, and rapped on the door.

"Who is it?" called a grumpy voice from inside that reminded Mitch of the cawing of a crow.

"It's Sheriff Webster, Mrs. Snodmotz. I need to talk to you."

The door was instantly flung open and Ethel stood before him in full-on attack mode. "Well, I need to talk to you, too, so you get yourself in here and sit your ass down, because you have been derelict in your duty to the citizens of this county and I for one am not going to stand for it any longer."

Mitch took his hat off and stepped inside. "Ma'am, I didn't come out here for you to—"

"I don't care what you came out here for. You're in my living room now, son, and you're going to hear me out."

What followed was at least a ten-minute spiel in which Ethel described, without ever pausing for breath, the various ways in which Mitch had shirked his primary duty as sheriff, which was to protect the citizens of the county from harm. If there was anything more harmful than the devil, she didn't know what it was, but witchcraft was a close second. He had turned a blind eye to the wickedness, depravity, and maliciousness of witchcraft, and had allowed a whole coven of them to come into the county, to nest here and *breed* — whatever that meant.

She finally paused to draw a breath and Mitch leapt at the opening.

"Mrs. Snodmotz, I want to know if you had anything to do with the fire at the Fallen Angel Church."

She smiled, a cat-that-swallowed-the-canary smile. "You don't have no proof that I had anything to do with that." Then the smile drained off her face. "And the reason you don't is because I didn't. I didn't burn that crappy church down. I should have. I could have. I *would* have. But somebody beat me to it."

Mitch switched gears.

"I understand you got into an altercation yesterday

evening in the Quik Stop Convenience Store with three women."

"*Witches*, you mean. They gave up their rights to call themselves women when they gave up their humanity, and they gave up their humanity when they swore allegiance to the hound of hell."

"So, you admit you got into a disagreement with Jaclyn Milford, Veronica Espinosa, and Olivia Booth?"

"Disagreement? I didn't get into no disagreement with them. That's the poopiest thing I ever heard. That girl, that *witch* with the marks of Satan all over her—"

"Tattoos?"

"Yeah, tattoos. She come after me. She attacked me."

"That's not what the others say—"

"A totally unprovoked attack. I just told her and the others what was the truth of God, and if the truth of God provokes you, then that's your problem. I told them how all the saints in heaven and all the angels was going to come after them and drive them like sheep to slaughter into the bowels of hell itself."

"I was told you said you were glad that Annie Giordoni was murdered."

"I did tell them that. I am glad. I'm glad that tattooed harlot witch is dead, too. They all deserve to die. Every poopy one of them."

"Did you have anything to do with their deaths?"

"No, I did not, but I wish I had, and if I'd had the opportunity, I would have. If you had given me a gun and told me I could put it to their foreheads, they'd have had their brains on the wall behind them before they could say jiggity jig. They don't deserve to live. The God of the universe loathes their kind. He—"

"Did you have anything to do with the disappearance of Olivia Booth?"

She did pause for a beat, but didn't really act surprised that Olivia was missing.

"If she's gone, good riddance. Now there's just one left."

"Where were you last night, Mrs. Snodmotz?"

"I was right here at home, drawing up petitions that I'm going to hand out and make everybody at church sign. I'm going to go up and down Main Street getting every man and woman in this county above the age of fifteen to put their name on the dotted line and tell the county council that they will not put up with a church of Satan in their community and that the witches who have lit here on their broomsticks—"

"They didn't light here on their broomsticks." Mitch didn't mean to let it out, but it flew anyway. "Jaclyn Milford has lived here her whole life. So has Veronica Espinosa, and Annie Giordoni. They didn't burst full grown from an oak tree like Tecumseh."

"Who's Tecumseh?"

Her eyes were squinted shut, reduced to slits between her fat cheeks and her Neanderthal forehead. He had no doubt that given the opportunity, she would have butchered the witches and eradicated the church, that she would have stood on Main Street with her bloody sword in her hand and her foot on the fallen while demanding that the good Christian citizens of the town bow down to her righteousness.

Ethel Snodmotz would have killed Annie and Ronnie in a New York minute. She *would* have … but *did* she?

Was Olivia here, maybe, stashed somewhere on the farm? It didn't seem likely, but Olivia was *somewhere* and *somebody* had taken her.

"Would you mind if I searched the premises?" Before Ethel could speak, Mitch said, "That's just my polite way of saying I *am* going to search the premises. Now, you can put up with me sitting on your porch until I can get a search warrant — a couple of hours, maybe more. Or you can just give me permission and we can both avoid the delay. And if, as you say, you haven't done anything wrong, then there's nothing for me to find and you shouldn't care if I search."

She opened her mouth. Then closed it. Looked a lot like an angler fish with its own bait dangling out in front of it. But when unsuspecting prey took the bait, the angler fish opened that maul with razor-sharp teeth and ate them alive.

"I ain't got time to fool with you today, Sheriff, and the reason I don't is because I am calling everybody I know and telling 'em that they have to sign this petition I'm going to take to the county council. You look anywhere you want. You can start under my bed if that suits you. You're not going to find nothing. I am a fine, upstanding Christian woman, praise the Lord, and there is no stain of sin on my soul."

"You wait here," he ordered her, then left the living room and searched the house. Nothing. He left the house and went around to the back to several storage sheds of various sizes and a huge barn with its adjacent pigsty, where the grunting animals that stunk up the entire valley for five miles in every direction wallowed around in the mud.

Mitch's uncle had kept pigs.

THE STINK IS UNBEARABLE, so foul it makes you want to vomit, but vomiting won't make the stink go away. And vomit stinks, too. All those thoughts fly through Mitch's mind as he and Hank follow their uncle around to the back of the barn, where a truck has just delivered three huge sows. The animals are in a small pen, grunting and shoving their noses through the space between the slats on the fence.

"There's shovels in the shed," his uncle says. "Get to it."

He and Hank have been assigned the task of digging out a recessed area in the center of a big, fenced enclosure, to turn the area into a pigsty.

Mitch had always assumed pigs smelled bad because of their environment. They lived in mud, ate slop — of course they smelled bad. But these pigs were merely standing in a pen, looking at him with their beady little eyes. They didn't have a sty yet — that's what he and Hank would be providing. So how did they already stink? And they did, a putrid odor that would curdle new milk. Skunks didn't stink — they had this spray kind of thing that shot out stinking liquid to keep their enemies away, but the skunks themselves didn't smell bad. He'd seen a baby skunk once when his uncle had torn up its den with his tractor. Mitch held it and petted it… until his uncle saw, marched over, yanked the little animal out of Mitch's hand and stomped it into the ground.

He and Hank pick up the shovels and start digging up the hard-packed dirt, they work all afternoon in the boiling sun. Mitch won't let Hank take his shirt off, although he wants to, because he knows Hank's fair complexion will sunburn, and his aunt certainly won't have any aloe vera to take the sting away.

About nightfall, their uncle returns to where they've been working, carrying a water hose. He dispatches Hank to turn on the water, then he fills the dug-out area with water.

"Now get in there and mix that dirt with the water," his uncle commands. "Make mud out of it."

The boys do as directed until they are knee-deep in goo.

Their uncle goes to the pigpen, then turns to Mitch and Hank.

"Run!" he cries and opens the gate. The boys drop their shovels and take out for the fence, reaching it only seconds before the nearest sow. Their uncle is laughing uproariously.

"That 'un nearly gotcha," he cried. "You shoulda seen your faces."

"My hat!" Hank cries. His Pittsburgh Pirates baseball cap is lying in the mud.

"Go on, go get it," their uncle urges, but Mitch grabs his brother's arm and won't let him move. Suddenly the biggest sow spots the hat and goes for it. Another pig goes after it too, and the animals quickly rip the hat to shreds.

"Pigs'll eat anything," his uncle says. And Mitch is certain that if the pigs had eaten him and Hank, their uncle would have stood by laughing.

MITCH METICULOUSLY CHECKED THE OUTBUILDINGS, not really expecting to find Olivia, but hoping. He looked for cans of gasoline that Ethel could have loaded up in her pickup truck and taken to town to douse the foundations of the Fallen Angel church. He looked in the garage, then in the utility shed, where there was a lawnmower and a weed eater and several other pieces of lawn equipment that looked like they hadn't been used in a quarter of a century. But there was no gasoline can. The lawn mower was electric.

That left only the pig barn. Mitch didn't intend to spend any more time in that pig barn than he absolutely had to. He would get in, look around, and get out.

He stepped from the relatively clean air outside into the reek of the pig barn and would have gasped for breath, but that would have drawn the air into his lungs through his mouth, and he was sure air that smelled that bad tasted even worse as it went by. He searched the barn itself, moving as fast as he could, casting a glance now and then to the pigsty that spread out for fifty yards around the barn building, a loblolly of mud. There were troughs in the front of the pigsty closest to the barn where Ethel's field hands tossed slop to the animals three times a day.

Mitch passed by the trough and turned to hurry out of the building when he saw something that caught his eye. He turned back around, knowing that he couldn't have seen what he thought he saw. Moving closer, resisting for all the world the urge to vomit at the stench, he got closer and closer to the pigsty. Then one of the sows bit into what was lying in the mud beside the feed trough, and Mitch was so horrified he couldn't breathe.

Chapter Thirty-Seven

MITCH STOOD silent beside Gus as they watched the farmhands herd the huge, stinking, grunting animals out of the enclosure so the rescue squad could recover the body.

"Explain to the city boy," Mitch said to the medical examiner, "what's the difference between a pig, a sow and a hog ... and which are these?"

"I studied *human* biology, not veterinary medicine. But I've hunted wild boar, and I am here to testify that I'd rather face a charging bull elephant with a sinus infection, toe fungus, and a rash on his privates than a wild boar in a good mood."

Gus made a sweeping gesture across the expanse of stinking mud at the animals that the hands were trying to corral on the other side of the pen.

"I think *sow* and *hog* may be about sex, but I could be wrong. I do know that *pig* is a generic term for all of them, the way *horse* is a generic term for everything from Secretariat to a kid's pony. I have heard, though, that domestic pigs released or escaped into a wilderness are more dangerous than wild species. Those suckers are murderous. They'll eat anything — *an-y-thing* — that doesn't eat them first. Grass, vegetables, birds, fish, the young of any species from ferrets to armadillos. And they'll instantly attack anything they perceive as a threat or a meal."

"I can give you an amen on that, brother," said a nearby farm hand who had overheard the conversation. "Domesticated pigs ain't gentle or docile neither. They just tolerate us 'cause we're the hand that feeds 'em. They's mean as a snake, so don't never turn your back on one. I seen boar hogs that weigh a thousand pounds, and there's teeth in that mouth that'd shame a pit bull."

Mitch glanced up toward the farmhouse, where he had just dragged a handcuffed Ethel Snodmotz *literally* kicking and screaming out to his cruiser — and considered that the man's description fit the owner of the animals as well as it did the beasts themselves.

Mitch had seen a lot of death, in all its grizzly forms. You sign on for that when you become a police officer. When he'd worked traffic, images from fatal traffic accidents haunted his nightmares for weeks afterward. Eventually those images faded. Rileigh said she'd had flashbacks after she got back from Afghanistan. She said those images faded, too. But as Mitch stood beside the pig pen on Ethel Snodmotz's farm in the bright June sunshine and watched rescue squad members look for … the *remains*… of Olivia Booth, he didn't think he would ever get over that sight.

"She just let you come out here and find it," Gus said. "Is that what you're saying?"

Mitch tuned back in to the conversation that the images had booted out of his mind.

"I'm sure she thought that by now there wouldn't be anything left to find," Mitch said. What Ethel Snodmotz had done so staggered Mitch's mind he couldn't get his head around it. The murders she committed had expressed the evil of a human heart too rotten to countenance.

The farmhands had finally cleared the livestock out of the area to allow the rescue squad to finish the grisly task of retrieving Olivia Booth's body. Gus would examine what they put into a black body bag when he performed the autopsy. Mitch was still trying to figure out how she'd done it. Oh, Ethel was an extraordinarily strong and stout woman. It was she, not her husband, who farmed the land that she had inherited, cared for the livestock, plowed the fields, did everything that all farmers do. He supposed that if she had the strength for those tasks, she was up to climbing a tree and draping a dead body over a limb. What about the shoe print, New Balance, size ten-and-a-half? She couldn't have worn old-lady shoes to climb a tree — but she could have gone out and purchased more appropriate foot attire just for the occasion. Gus had said the shoes were brand new. Mitch and his deputies would come back and conduct a thorough search of her house to find them.

And now he knew what the killer had done with all that blood.

Ronnie Espinoza had been small. Mitch was sure she'd been an easier kill than six-foot-tall Olivia Booth. There'd been evidence of a struggle in her apartment, so the girl had not gone gentle into that good night. She had put up a fight — and that was another thing he couldn't work out in his head. How had Ethel Snodmotz managed to subdue the murder victims before she killed them?

As if answering his unspoken question, Gus commented, "I'm sure I'll find ketamine and/or rohypnol in her system as I did in the others. Date rape drugs, AKA Grievous Bodily Harm, Liquid Ecstasy, Somatomax, Cherry Meth and Easy Lay."

"Did you tell me that and I just don't remember?"

"No, I haven't had time to file the official reports — you keep bringing me fresh meat." Gus reached into his pocket for the cigar he always carried in case he had to examine a floater, the body of a drowning victim who had been in the water for a long time. He pulled the cigar out, put it under his nose, inhaling, but he didn't light it.

"There are days, Sheriff Webster, when I wish I had picked a different line of work."

"Copy that," Mitch said.

It should have been very satisfying to arrest Ethel Snodmotz and charge her with the murder of Olivia Booth. Let the prosecutors figure out all the additional charges later, including, but not limited to, kidnapping maybe, and certainly several counts of desecrating a corpse. It should have felt good to slap the cuffs on the old witch, but the juice hadn't been worth the squeeze on that one and all he had felt was sick to his stomach listening to the old woman rant, so distraught she had white spittle at the corners of her mouth.

The rescue squad had gotten Olivia Booth's body up onto a gurney and cleaned as much of the slime off of it as they could. She was … missing body parts — that's all Mitch would allow himself to know. As they wheeled the gurney past, Gus held up his hand.

"Take a look at that," he said and pointed to a ring on the filthy hand of the murder victim. It was on the third finger of her left hand, and what made it remarkable was that it was stuck on the knuckle, embedded in the flesh, as if it either wouldn't go down any farther or wouldn't come off.

"What's that about?" Gus asked nobody. That was 100% freeze-dried Dr. Gustav Hazelton. Nobody else would have noticed that ring. Not in the shape that body was in right now — maybe after the corpse had been cleaned up and ... Mitch wouldn't allow himself to think the word "reassembled", but that was what he meant.

"What do you make of it.?" Gus asked. "You think the killer wanted the ring, tried to take it, and couldn't get it off — a trophy maybe?"

"To my knowledge Ethel didn't take any jewelry from the other two victims, so why this ring?" Mitch shrugged. "Figuring that out is above my pay grade. That, *Dr.* Hazelton, is what they pay you the big bucks for."

Mitch turned his back on the grisly scene as the rescue squad members loaded the black bag into the ambulance and closed the doors.

"I have to call Rileigh. She picked up Jaclyn Milford in the Walmart parking lot and has been keeping her in 'protective custody.'"

Gus laughed. "Took her to Lily's and said, 'She followed me home, Mom, can I keep her?'"

Mitch rolled his eyes. "Jaclyn *still* believes the killer is a demon that she and the other 'witches' summoned from hell."

"I heard about that. They put their quarter in the machine, punched magical genie, but demon-ifrit dropped into the tray."

"Something like that." Mitch shook his head. "The brutality of these murders ... it sure looks like a demon from hell committed them. I'm ashamed to admit I'm glad Rileigh's going to have to tell Jaclyn the news and that I don't have to." He paused. "I just have to call Olivia's parents."

Gus reached over and patted Mitch on the shoulder. "And that, *Sheriff* Webster, is what they pay *you* the big bucks for."

Gus turned and walked toward his car, a Mercedes

town car with the words "Yarmouth County Coroner" written in dignified small script on the door.

"I'll get you the results of all the toxicology reports as soon as I can," he said over his shoulder. Then he stopped and turned back to Mitch. "I'm glad you finally stomped this spider. I'm tired of looking at beautiful young women lying on an autopsy table, gutted before I even pick up a scalpel."

Chapter Thirty-Eight

Zeke Wakefield had to hold it together until the stupid sheriff left.

Had to wait until after the sheriff dragged that crazy drunk who had been shooting holes in Zeke's church down out of the woods, making it sound like the whack-job just had a minor lapse in judgment because he was so distraught over the death of that witch.

Zeke couldn't allow the joy to rise up into his heart, feared some kinda golden light would shine out from his eyes and his ears and his mouth if he did, so bright the sheriff would surely see.

But when the sheriff was finally gone, Zeke turned, speechless, to his son Ross, and held out his arms.

Ross stood up out of his wheelchair, walked to his father, and grasped him in a fierce, loving hug.

Ross had saved Zeke's life. When that crazy man started shooting, a bullet came flying through the window and came so close to Zeke's head that he could feel the air rearranging itself after it passed. Ross had jumped up out of his chair and tackled his father, shoving him to the floor as more bullets came crashing through the windows.

If it hadn't been for Ross, one of those bullets probably would have lodged in Zeke's head and he'd have been standing before Almighty God's judgment right now instead of holding onto his son so tight and hugging him so fiercely that he was afraid he was hurting him, but he didn't let go and Ross didn't act like he wanted him to.

Oh, the doctors had said in the beginning that Ross's paralysis *might* not be permanent, that Ross might one day walk again. But Zeke wasn't a fool to cling to false hope, and all the doctors had made it clear that the most important thing he could do for his son was to help him accept the reality of being a paraplegic, not dangle walking again as a carrot in front of him so he was always grasping for it, always reaching for what he couldn't have, a miserable wretch, despondent and despairing. Zeke had let go of all hope a long time ago.

But now ... *now!*

"You can walk, you can stand, you can walk, why didn't you ... how long have you..." He sounded like such an idiot, babbling, only able to form half sentences, not even realizing that there were tears streaming down his cheeks until he felt them drip on his shirt.

He finally let Ross go, held his son out in front of him. He felt like laughing and crying and shouting and jumping in the air all at the same time, but he had shut his mouth so that Ross could answer the questions he'd been firing at him like the bullets out of the rifle barrel of the stupid drunk up in the woods.

"It didn't happen all at once, Papa," Ross said. "It was slow. One night I was lying in bed and I wiggled my toe, just my big toe. I ripped the covers off the bed and sat up. I turned on the bedside lamp and just stared at it, wiggling it for all I was worth." Ross's handsome face burst into a grin that so filled his father's heart with love, he could barely stand the pressure of it.

"I wanted to put a flag on it, Papa. One of those little four-inch flags people put on their desks at work, or maybe an umbrella, a Japanese umbrella like they put in Mai Tais in a bar, just anything on it to wiggle when I wiggled my toe."

"But why didn't you tell anybody?"

All of the joy and happiness drained out of his son's face, and he spit out a single word like it tasted foul in his mouth, "Jaclyn."

"What about Jaclyn?"

Ross began to pace back and forth as he spoke — and the joy of watching him walk again was so overwhelming that Zeke had trouble concentrating on what the boy was saying.

"That was about three months ago. I was still a fool then. I hadn't looked down into the soul of that woman and seen her black heart. I still wanted her. God help me, I still loved her. I hoped, stupid as it sounds, that maybe she would come back to me because I was paralyzed, that she would feel guilty about what she did to me and come back and I could convince her that she really did love me as much as I loved her."

Ross made a sound in his throat that might have been a stifled laugh or a bark of disgust.

"That was before I understood. Before she threw the ring I'd given her into the dirt, walked away and left it there. I shook hands with reality then, and after that, there was only one emotion left in my heart for her. Hate. I hated her and I was not going to let the bitch whore get away with dropping me like you toss away a candy wrapper on the ground. Oh, no, no, no, no. She wasn't going to get away with *that*. That's when I started dreaming about putting my hands around her throat and choking her, watching her eyes go blank as she died."

Zeke stood, staring at his son whose handsome face was twisted into a mask of hatred and rage, and he didn't quite know what to think.

"Then I'd lie in bed at night and do exercises, moving my ankles, then my knees, getting the strength back in my legs. All of it was fueled by Jaclyn, by hatred of her." He turned back to his father with the fiercest look Zeke had ever seen on his face, "fueled by the solemn oath I pledged to myself that I would *kill the bitch*."

Ross's loathing of the girl was not the same as Zeke's. Zeke loathed her and all the other witches because they were an abomination in the sight of God, an evil that had to be wiped from the face of the earth. But that's not why Ross hated her.

And then an awful thought occurred to Zeke. Unbelievable, unthinkable, but it crystallized as reality in his mind. It was truth. And his daddy always told him that you can't un-know the truth. Once you see it, once you know it's true, you have to do something about it.

Ross had turned from his father and was staring out through the broken glass at the woods, answering the question Zeke had been unable to ask.

"Everybody would have known, Papa. I'd have got caught. I *had* to kill her. But wasn't no way in hell I was gonna spend the rest of my life in prison for it. I'm doing a service to all mankind by gutting that bitch." He turned back toward Zeke. "But everybody knew about our breakup. I didn't keep it no secret that I hated her. I even said stupid things in public, told people what I dreamed of doing to her. Them people would cheerfully sit down in a witness chair, point their bony fingers at me and repeat every word."

Zeke's head was reeling. He could see where all this was going, understood his son's words a few beats before he even said them. He knew what Ross had done.

"But what if she wasn't the only one who died?" Ross continued. "What if there were other murders at the same time? So the police were out looking for people who wanted to kill those other women, not just me standing there in the glare of a spotlight. Me, who didn't have no reason in the world to kill them other three. I figured out that if I could tangle her death up with other deaths, I could get away with it."

"And so you killed ..." Zeke didn't have enough air in his lungs to finish the question. But he already knew the answer.

"Hell, Papa, they dished it up on a platter and set it right down on the table in front of me. That solstice cele-bration, them out there dancing — wicked, ugly, vile witches. I looked at the faces of the people who were watching them, the disgust, the revulsion. And there it was. I was looking at the faces of a dozen different people who wanted to see those girls dead. Lots and lots of suspects. All I had to do was make it look like it was all about witchcraft."

Zeke felt a gigantic hole open up in his chest. Like the scientists talk about black holes out there in the universe that eat up stars and suns. That's how big and voracious was the hole in Zeke Wakefield's chest. His son had murdered three innocent women so he could get away with murdering the woman who had dumped him.

Zeke couldn't hold onto that. He could think it in his head, understand the absolute truth of it. But when he tried to believe it in his heart, it fell down into that black hole and was consumed in everlasting darkness.

Something happened to Zeke Wakefield then. He could feel it, could almost hear it. There was a ripping sound. The shroud in the temple ripped from top to bottom when Jesus was crucified. It was a sound like that. A sound like the ripping of heavy cloth. The sound accompanied the sensation of his whole being tearing asunder. His soul ripping apart right there in his chest.

Some part of him fell away then, some part of his humanity was gobbled up in that black hole. But not all of it. Not all of who Zeke Wakefield was. Not the man of God. Not the soldier, the crusading soldier commissioned to right the wrongs of the world. Not the man singled out by God Almighty to rid this county of evil. No, that part didn't fall into a black hole.

That part was all that was left when the rest of him did.

And that part turned a zealot's eyes on his son and saw the deeds that he had done in the light of God's understanding. God had used Ross as an implement of death to destroy Zeke's enemies. It had been God's hand in all of it. God had fashioned Zeke's son into a sword of retribution and had cut down the filthy, slimy evil of those four witches.

He stepped up to Ross, who was still staring out the broken window, and put his hand on his shoulder.

"I'm proud of you, boy. Not never one time in your whole life have I ever been more proud of you than I am right now."

Ross turned to him, a little surprised, as if maybe he had thought admitting what he'd done to his father would make his father think less of him.

"Oh, no, no, no, son," Zeke said, took hold of his

shoulders and turned him around to face him. "You are a saint in the army of Almighty God and you have risen up in the time of need. God has lifted you, picked you, out of all of his children, to be his mighty hand of retribution to smite the wicked. You are going to save this county from the ravages of that demon summoned from hell, rescue God's people from the carnage of its attack on their very souls."

Zeke felt warm tears running down his face again.

"I'm gonna kill Jaclyn, Papa."

"Of course you are, son. And I'm gonna help you."

Chapter Thirty-Nine

RILEIGH FOLLOWED Jaclyn in her car from the Walmart parking lot back to her house. The girl had been so shaky, she didn't really want her to drive. But Jaclyn assured Rileigh that she'd be fine.

"I just need to get home where I can have a good cry. Let my hair down and come apart for a little while. Then I'll pull myself back together and go pick up my parents at the airport."

Rileigh went inside with her when she got home, to get her settled and to make sure she really was okay to stay by herself until her parents arrived.

Jaclyn walked into her little town home and looked around like she didn't know where she was.

"Jaclyn, are you alright?"

"No," she said, "absolutely not. I don't know when I'll ever be alright again." She dropped down onto the love seat and looked at Rileigh with eyes full of desolation.

"I've lost my three best friends. I know that people live through things like that. In wars and disasters, sometimes people lose everyone they know. So, I get it intellectually that it's a survivable tragedy. But I just feel so lost."

Rileigh sat down beside her and took her hand. "I knew a woman in Afghanistan who lost all five of her children when the vehicle they were riding in hit a landmine. She and her husband survived, but their five little kids died. The youngest of them was a two-month-old baby." Rileigh paused. "She was nursing, and she said she had to take medicine to dry up her milk."

Jaclyn shook her head. "I know people have lived through worse—"

"I didn't tell you that story to prove that there are people who've suffered more than you. I told you that story because of what the woman said to me. She told me, 'I feel so overwhelmed. How can I grieve for all five of my children?' And she decided that she couldn't, that she would have to grieve for them one at a time. So she'd say, 'today I'm grieving for Amir.' And on that day, she would grieve for her oldest son. The next day, she would grieve for one of her daughters. You get what I'm saying? I don't think it's possible for you to grieve the losses of Annie, Ronnie, and Olivia all at one time. But you can grieve for them one at a time. And you have to grieve for them. It's not a thing you can just decide not to do. You have to walk through it and go on."

Jaclyn sniffed, squared her shoulders, and wiped the tears off her face.

"I'm going to be fine," she said. She glanced then at the altar that she had built on the little table by the window. She got up, walked to it, picked up the stick she had made into a magic wand, and used it to scrape the altar and everything off onto the floor. Then she stomped it, breaking it all into pieces, making little grunting sounds.

"That's not what killed them."

Jaclyn sat down with an exhausted sigh and Rileigh continued, "One day, you'll understand that the fact you girls decided to become Wiccans is not the reason three of you are dead. They're dead because there's evil in the human heart. Ethel Snodmotz was consumed by anger and rage and hatred. And it finally ate her alive. Religion was her weapon. Almighty God was her club, and she used it to beat up everyone near her. There was absolutely nothing real about her faith in God. But I think you really did believe in magic."

"Of course I did. I watched it happen as a little girl, over and over."

Rileigh didn't argue, because maybe she had. Certainly, Rileigh believed that she had seen magic the day she was at Granny Milford's house.

"Magic doesn't have to be a thing in and of itself. The supernatural exists in the realm of God. And in the realm of God, anything is possible."

Rileigh could see that the grieving young woman was devastated but functional. She would fall into her mother's arms at the airport, finding the healing she needed in her parents' embrace.

Rileigh drove home thinking about the wonder of family. It was how God knit the world together, family by family by family. Hers had been shattered by the evil of her father. But she still had pieces of it. And she would cling to those pieces. Hold them close to her heart.

Finally, the whole ghastly murder case was *over!* She could go home and spend time mending fences with Mama and Jillian. She might even suggest they play Monopoly tonight.

Late that afternoon, Rileigh sat at the kitchen table with her mother and sister, the aroma of fresh baked bread making her mouth water. Mama was making homemade rolls for dinner. Rileigh was helping to knead the dough for the second batch, constantly glancing at the timer on her phone to see when the ones currently in the oven would be ready to come out. The timer on the stove hadn't worked in a decade.

Mama's random babble buzzed pleasantly in her head, as Lily hopped from one topic to another like she hopping from one stone to the next to cross a creek. Rileigh figured that was a pretty good description of her mother's mind. She did have stones — memories and understanding and beliefs. They just weren't connected one to the other anymore. There was flowing water between. And to get from one to the next, you had to leap up into the air.

She tuned back in and caught the end of what her mother was saying.

"... and Jezzie said she couldn't even get in. She drove all the way there in that rattledy-bang old pickup truck of hers and left her music at home. It'd take too long to go back and get it, so she pulls up behind the church, gets her key out to unlock the back door, only it's already unlocked."

Rileigh realized that Mama was talking about Jezzie Thacker, the woman who had found Veronica Espinosa's body in the Holiness Church sanctuary. Rileigh didn't know how Mama found out all these tiny little details about things. But if you asked her, and she started tracing back who told who what, you would get so tangled up you'd be lost.

"The door was unlocked, but it wouldn't open because something inside had been shoved up against it. So she had to go around the building to the front door. And what did she see when she opened it? She saw—"

"Mama, what did you just say?"

"I said Jezzie went around the building to the front door and—"

"No, no. Before that."

"I don't remember what was before that."

"You talked about how she left her music at home, and she pulled up behind the church, unlocked the door."

"No, she didn't unlock the door. It was already unlocked. She went up that handicapped ramp and put her key in the lock, but the door wasn't locked."

Mama dusted flour on top of the lump of dough on the cutting board, picked up the rolling pin and began to roll it out flat. "And I said the door was unlocked but it wouldn't *open* because something was shoved up against it. The piano, I think she said. It's one of them big ole uprights, probably weighs more than my car. So she had to go around the building to the front door."

"Was it locked?"

"She said the lock on it was broke. Now is that all you want to know? Because now you totally ruined my story, and I can't remember what I was telling."

Jillian jumped in to change the subject. But Rileigh sat very still, her mind whirring. The lump of dough forgotten in her hand.

"Excuse me, I'll be right back," she said, got up, dusted flour off her hands into the sink and picked up her phone off the counter.

"Don't you go runnin' off with that timer, now," Mama said.

"It's still got eleven minutes, and this won't take long."

Walking out onto the front porch, she dialed Jaclyn Milford's number. The girl answered on the first ring. "Hello?"

Her voice sounded so tear-clotted. Rileigh wanted to reach out and hug her through the telephone.

"I'm sorry to disturb you, honey. I just need to ask you something."

"What do you want to know?"

"Would you mind going back through your texts and reading to me the one you got from Ross Wakefield about finding Ronnie's body?" She could hear a little squeak of beginning protest.

"You want me to dig that out, and *read* —"

"I'm really sorry. But this is important. Please understand that it's important."

She heard Jaclyn heave a resigned sigh, then there was silence. A few seconds later, she said, "okay, here it is," then she began to read. 'Jezzie Thacker was the one who found her body. Somebody dragged Ronnie in the back door, killed her right there in the sanctuary, hung her body up on the cross, cut her open and scattered her guts all over the room.'"

Rileigh heard Jaclyn gasp out a sob.

"Let me make sure I heard you right. 'Somebody dragged her in the back door of the church.' Is that what it says?"

"Yeah, that's what it says. I—" She started to say something else, but then Rileigh heard the distinctive ding-dong of Jaclyn's doorbell.

"Never mind, sweetie. That's all I needed to know. Drive safe picking up your parents."

Rileigh punched the little red phone icon and sat down in the porch swing, the *silent* porch swing, an anomaly among all porch swings in the Smoky Mountains. She used her toe to swing it back and forth, back and forth, her mind rearranging the furniture of her thoughts, putting things together she hadn't put together before, trying to make the room look like what Ethel Snodmotz must have seen.

The murderer drives up to the Holiness Church building with Ronnie, either unconscious or dead already. Now, if she takes the body in the front door, she'll have to carry it up four steps. But take it in the back door and she can drag it up the handicapped ramp there. Ethel takes the body inside, moves the pulpit and the piano up against the back wall, out of the way so that she can put the cross and Ronnie's body right in the center. Then she guts Ronnie, takes out her internal organs and walks up the aisle to the front door, throwing pieces all over the sanctuary as she leaves.

There'd be bloody footprints on the floor, leading from the back of the church to the front, but no *muddy* footprints — because the killer didn't come into the building through the mud puddle in front of the porch. Well, either that, or Ethel paused on the porch to wipe the mud off her shoes as she carried a dead body into the building.

When Jezzie arrives, she goes to the back door, gets out her key, but it's already unlocked. She tries to open it, but there's something blocking it on the other side. So, she goes around the building to the front, careful to wipe the mud off her feet on the mat in front of the door.

And the rest, as they say, is history.

Sooooo…

How did Ethel Snodmotz unlock the back door?

Where did she get a key to the Mountain Shaker Fire Baptized Holiness church?

There were probably only a handful of people who had keys — Zeke and Ross, of course, and Jezzie. She doubted Ethel Snodmotz was numbered among them.

Rileigh swung slowly back and forth, listening to the hum of bees in the flowers beside the porch. She didn't like the itch that was wiggling around in her mind. It was a familiar itch. It was an I-have-to-make-the-puzzle-pieces-fit-together itch, and there wasn't but one way to scratch it. Getting up out of the swing, she stuck her head into the living room and called out to Jillian and Mama in the kitchen: "I need to run an errand. I won't be gone long. I need to talk to Zeke—"

"Bring that timer back in here, them rolls is about done."

There were six minutes ... five minutes left on the timer. If she stood there waiting, she'd have to explain where she was going and why. More police business. That would go over like sour milk. So she hurried into the kitchen, put the phone on the counter, and hurried out, calling over her shoulder, "I challenge both of you to a game of Monopoly tonight when I get back."

"I accept," Jillian said.

Mama's cheery voice carried behind Rileigh as she went out the door. "Go ahead, punk. Make my day."

Chapter Forty

It was a hike from Mama's house at the base of Tucker Mountain to the Holiness Church in Juniper Hollow. They were at opposite ends of the county, with Black Bear Forge in between them. Look at the two places on a map and you'd decide "you can't get there from here."

As Rileigh drove along the steep winding mountain roads, she mulled over the suspicions that had propelled her to go have a talk with Zeke Wakefield. By the time she got to the gravel road that led from the main road up to the church, she could feel her Spidey sense kicking in. That's what she called it, because that sounded cooler to her than just her "gut." But every police officer knew what that was. You developed it over time. Gut feelings were really more than just guesses. The mind subconsciously picks up all kinds of cues and information that the conscious mind blows right by. That's what her Spidey sense was. It was her subconscious mind telling her to be careful for reasons it knew, but she didn't. She listened.

Instead of driving up to the church like she was a welcome wagon lady with a basket of flowers, she parked on the side of the road down the hill and advanced toward the church through the trees. The sun had gone down behind the mountain and its shadow covered the trees, the puddles beneath them growing darker and darker. She could see the lights on in the building through the windows that had been shattered when Ronnie's drunk neighbor had taken potshots at it earlier in the day. Then the building went dark. No, not dark. There was flickering light — candles.

Rileigh could hear voices coming from inside, but she was too far away to hear what they were saying. She walked slowly toward the building straining to hear the words to make some sense of them.

" ... blood sacrifice ... " Zeke Wakefield's voice. "... evil witch." A pause, then, "... the *last* one."

Rileigh pulled her Glock from its holster beneath her t-shirt and advanced slowly toward the building, moving from one tree to the next stealthily. She got to Ross's handicapped van and edged along behind it, then peeked around the end of the vehicle to the front of the church. She hurried quietly up the porch steps and put her ear to the door and listened. But she could hear no voices now. The men had stopped talking.

Jezzie had said the lock on the door was broken, so she turned the knob and pushed the door slowly inward. The door opened directly into the sanctuary with no anteroom or vestibule before it.

In the flickering candlelight, she could make out Zeke Wakefield on the raised platform, standing in front of the huge ornate altar that was the single defining piece of architecture in the building. She turned her eyes to the altar. What she saw there would have made her gasp if she hadn't been trained to be *silent*.

Jaclyn Milford.

She was lying on her back on the altar, dressed in what looked like a choir robe.

Zeke Wakefield stood looking down at the girl. Ross had scooted out of his wheelchair to the bench on the front row, doing something with a handful of candles.

Rileigh eased quietly into the building. Once inside, she lifted her gun in the two-hand grip and called out, "Freeze! Everybody freeze!"

In surprise, Zeke dropped what he had been holding. She'd only caught a glimpse of it, but it appeared to be some kind of ornate knife, like a dagger.

Ross whirled around on the bench and gawked at her. But Jaclyn didn't move at all. She just lay there.

Either she was tied down or unconscious. Or dead.

Rileigh moved slowly and carefully down the center aisle of the church, with her gun pointed at Zeke Wakefield.

"What are you doing here?" he sputtered.

"I got a better question. What is *she* doing here?" Rileigh nodded to Jaclyn Milford's still body lying on the altar. "She's supposed to be on her way to Nashville to pick up her parents at the airport."

Ross sat mute, his eyes wide. Had he been sucked into this with his father?

He spoke then, his voice tremulous.

"Thank God you're here Rileigh. I didn't know what to do, how to stop him." He nodded toward his father, standing silently beside the altar. "You're not going to believe this, but it was Papa. Papa killed those girls."

Actually, Rileigh didn't find that hard to believe at all.

"I found out about it tonight when he showed up with Jaclyn. He *kidnapped* her. He's planning to *kill* her.'"

"Well, we're changing his plans," Rileigh said. "She's safe now."

She walked up the center aisle, stepped around where Ross sat on the bench, and took another step toward Zeke. Gesturing with the barrel of her gun, she said, "Now, I want you to use that knife you just dropped to cut the —"

There was the sound of movement *behind* her, but there was no time to respond before the whole world went black.

Rileigh opened her eyes and blinked them shut again. Looked out at the world through almost-closed eyelids. The back of her head and neck pounded with pain.

Through the forest of eyelashes, Rileigh could see Ross Wakefield helping his father move the cross so that it was at the head of the altar... Ross Wakefield *walking*. That's when all the puzzle pieces slid into place. Ross. Of course. It made perfect sense. Jaclyn had been the target all along. The others had been ... what? Practice shots? Collateral damage? No, camouflage to direct suspicion away from the poor guy in the wheelchair who couldn't walk.

She couldn't tell what Ross and Zeke were doing without moving her head, and that would hurt. She also did not want them to know she had regained consciousness. She needed time to listen and look and figure out a way out of this. She was lying on her side with her hands and ankles bound next to the altar where Jaclyn was laid out like a body on a slab in the morgue. Probably not dead. Yet.

It appeared to Rileigh that Zeke and Ross were putting together a structure around the altar that sat in front of the pulpit, some kind of makeshift frame from which to hang drapes. Perhaps they were building something that approximated the tabernacle in Jerusalem where sacrifices were made to God — the Holy of Holies. It was clear what ... *who*... the sacrifice was intended to be. The witch.

Of course, if they killed Jaclyn, they'd have to kill

Rileigh too. They couldn't leave her walking around with what she'd seen and heard.

Her hands were bound behind her. She pulled on her restraints as furtively as she could, so they wouldn't see the movement, and instantly realized they had used the restraint of choice for all criminals these days: Ziplock ties. There was no way she was going to get her hands out of those. Or her feet.

Looking around through her eyelashes, she tried to see if she could locate her gun, but it was nowhere within her sightline.

What was she going to do?

She remembered when she and Jillian had been dropped into the well, she had felt such rage at Sheriff Mumford for taking away what little bit of life Jillian had found.

But she supposed there wasn't really any good time in anybody's life to get murdered. She shook off the pain at the thought of losing Jillian and Mama. And an image loomed up huge in her mind, though she stubbornly refused to give the face a name, as if, in refusing to call him Mitch, she could totally ignore that he was who she thought about when she feared she was going to die. That it was his face and the thought of leaving him behind that stabbed such anguish into her heart.

Damn it, damn it, damn it, she thought. Not now, please, not now.

Chapter Forty-One

It seemed to take a long time for Ross and Zeke to complete whatever it was they were building around that altar. From what she could see now, it was clear that they had hung drapes from some kind of makeshift structure so that the altar itself was surrounded on four sides by curtains.

"Papa, can we quit now?" Ross said.

"Quit?"

It was clear from the little bit of conversation she'd overheard that Zeke was on some kind of spiritual journey and he hadn't taken his son along for the ride. Obviously, Ross just wanted to kill Jaclyn. It was Zeke who was determined that somehow her death would wash her soul clean and she could go to heaven and in so doing would return to hell the demon she and the other witches had summoned. Something inside Zeke Whitfield had snapped. You could see it in his wild eyes — the man's dipstick didn't touch oil anymore.

"Don't you see, son? This is the only way. But for the spilling of blood, there is no remission of sin. That's what scripture says. We must spill her blood. There will be such power in this blood sacrifice that it will expel that minion of hell that the witches summoned, and the whole of Yarmouth County will be clean again."

"Yeah, whatever, Papa. But we need to get this over with. We got two bodies to get rid of when we're done. We can collect the blood in this bucket and wash it down through the baptistry like I did with the blood from Annie's body, wash it clean out into the river and it's gone for good. But the bodies ain't going to be that easy. And we ain't got all night."

"Son, God has all eternity."

"Yeah, but we don't. Who knows who Rileigh told she was coming out here? When's somebody going to start looking for Jaclyn? We need to get done with this and gone."

Something of a plan had formed in Rileigh's head as she listened to the men discuss committing murder like they were butchering cows. The plan was lame, a BTN plan — better than nothing. But anything *was* better than simply lying there on the floor and watching these two men sacrifice a twenty-year-old girl. Followed by Rileigh.

While the men were outside of the drapes, they couldn't see her movement. She rolled over twice, positioning herself next to the pulpit, then got to her knees, leaned her shoulder against the pulpit and, using it for balance, rose slowly to her feet to crouch behind it. She could hear Ross's footsteps coming down the center aisle of the church.

As soon as he stepped up onto the platform, Rileigh tensed, trying to make her legs into springs to propel her upward. Ross moved down the side of the altar to hang up the final curtain. As soon as he had his back to the baptistry, she leapt up at him. Crashing through the makeshift curtains, she slammed into Ross's chest and knocked him backwards. He staggered. The concrete wall of the baptistry caught him behind his knees. He tried to keep his balance, pinwheeling his arms frantically, but couldn't, and toppled over backwards into the concrete baptistry, falling head-first onto the concrete floor five feet below. At the very least, he cracked his skull. Maybe even broke his neck.

Zeke cried out when he saw. "Ross! Ross!"

He ran down the steps into the concrete box where, every time they got the opportunity, the congregation took a new disciple down into the water and washed away their sins.

With her feet tied together, Rileigh fell to the floor after crashing into Ross, landing with a bone-rattling jolt on her side next to the baptistry wall. Scrambling up to her knees again, she made her way to the other side of the altar, looking around frantically for the knife that Zeke had intended to use on Jaclyn. If she could find it, she could cut the plastic zip-ties binding her hands. Where was it?

Then she saw it lying on the edge of the altar above her head. There was no way to inch up to a standing position by leaning against the altar the way she had leaned against the pulpit. The pulpit had a flat side. The altar was four legs and then a tabletop. All she could do was knee-walk back to the pulpit as fast as she could and shimmy her way up it to a standing position.

Zeke had stopped crying out now. She didn't know what he was doing. She had only seconds. As soon as she got her balance standing, she started hopping toward the altar. One hop, two. She began to topple and threw her weight forward so that she fell toward the altar. Twisting around in the air, she struck the altar with her back and tried to grab the knife with her bound hands on her way down. Her fingers grazed it but couldn't grasp it as she hit the top of the altar, bounced off, and banged down onto the floor again. Though she couldn't grab the knife, she did knock it off onto the floor. And now she looked around for it frantically, saw it and—

"My son's dead."

Rileigh looked up into the cold eyes of Zeke Wakefield.

"You killed him." In the flickering candlelight, the man's eyes were black, like dark pools where some small animal had fallen in and drowned.

"You can't do this, Zeke. You can't—"

"Oh, yes, I can, Missy. And I'm going to. You killed my son." With a strength she would not have believed he had, Zeke Wakefield grabbed her by the shoulders and hauled her up to her feet, then picked her up and plopped her down beside Jaclyn. The altar was just wide enough for the two of them to lie side by side on their backs. She hadn't noticed the belt until that moment, when Zeke picked up the buckle end of it. Before she could wiggle free, he grabbed the other end, put it through the buckle and pulled it tight round Rileigh's neck, pinning her down on her back with her hands crushed painfully beneath her. It was stretched over Jaclyn's neck too, barely long enough to stretch over the two of them, making the fit so tight that even the slightest movement choked them both. Rileigh couldn't see what he did next because she couldn't move her head, but then she felt him pull a second belt tight around her ankles.

Rileigh was totally immobilized. She could do absolutely nothing to defend herself or Jaclyn.

Wakefield reached down to the floor and picked up the dagger that Rileigh had knocked off the altar. She thought it might possibly be just a letter opener, but it had an ornate handle whose intertwined snakes with their heads forming the top of the handle. The blade looked very sharp indeed. If it was a letter opener, Zeke had sharpened it.

Stepping to the head of the altar, Zeke moved out of Rileigh's line of sight, but she could hear him just fine. He began to mumble some kind of prayer. Rileigh lay helpless beside an unconscious Jaclyn in a choir robe.

"Zeke, listen to me. I know you didn't kill those other girls. You're not a murderer. You—"

"But you are! You murdered my innocent boy."

Innocent? He murdered in cold blood three young women just to divert attention away from him so he could kill the girl who ditched him. Yeah, he was innocent, all right. She said none of that, of course, just looked at Zeke, scrambling around in her mind for something else to say, something she could do. Only one of the long drapes they had hung around the altar had been knocked down when she hit Ross and sent him flying. The room beyond them was dark. Candles on the pulpit that stood taller than the altar provided the only light, casting flickering shadows dancing around Rileigh and Jaclyn, like little dark fairies leaping and cavorting.

Zeke moved to stand behind Rileigh's side of the altar and looked down at her with dead, black eyes.

"Wicked bitch," he spat. "Spawn of hell. It is a privilege, an *honor* to be selected by God to send you back to the fiery pit to burn for all eternity."

Rileigh had time to feel a great wash of indescribable gratitude that Wakefield did *not* serve the God of the universe. In his perversion and hatred, he had recreated God, shaped him into his own image, changed and distorted reality until it was unrecognizable. Zeke Wakefield had turned the "god" he served into a creature more evil than the Satan he reviled. The *real* God of the universe was a God of love and grace who even now looked on his poor misguided child with compassion.

Zeke lifted the dagger slowly up into the air above her, holding it in both hands. Rileigh had only seconds, another breath or two, and oh how badly she wanted to *live*.

"Please..." she whispered.

"May God have mercy on your soul," he said, then plunged the dagger down toward her heart.

Chapter Forty-Two

MITCH HAD NOT BEEN EXPECTING a call from Gus until tomorrow. He didn't know how much time it typically took to perform an autopsy, but he had supposed that simply getting the corpse clean in this situation would have elongated the process considerably.

He answered the phone with, "That didn't take long."

"Oh, I'm not finished. I just thought I'd call and give you preliminaries because you said you wanted to know."

"Wanted to know what?"

"The toxicology reports. You mentioned them and I should have gotten them to you sooner. You wanted to know how Ethel had overpowered the girls before she killed them. And I suggested that perhaps they'd been drugged. Well, the first two were, but the last wasn't."

"You mean Olivia Booth wasn't drugged?"

"Nope. But her jaw was broken. Somebody punched her in the face. And there was human skin under her fingernails."

Mitch kept himself from asking how Gus could

possibly have figured out what was under the fingernails of that girl's hands, given where he'd found her.

"Could we get a DNA match?"

"Indeed we could, if I could get the state lab to run the test in anything approaching a reasonable amount of time. I'm considering getting the equipment to run my own DNA tests."

Mitch didn't know a whole lot about that kind of thing, but he was sure that whatever that equipment was, it didn't come cheap.

"There really isn't a rush on this one. It's just more evidence to present in court. It's not like we're looking for the killer. We've got her locked up in Gatlinburg right now."

"You want to know about the ring?"

Mitch had forgotten about the ring stuck on the knuckle of Olivia's hand when the killer hadn't been able to get it off her finger.

"That part doesn't make sense. The ring was way too small, would never have fit Olivia Booth's finger. And when I got a closer look, I saw that it was stuck above the knuckle. So, it didn't get stuck being pulled off. It got stuck because it wouldn't fit over the knuckle in the first place."

"Why would she try to jam a ring on her finger that didn't fit?"

"All such 'why' questions should be directed to the man who gets paid the big bucks to answer them. The sheriff, not the lowly coroner who gets paid a pittance for his time."

"What do you do with those pittances anyway?"

"Give it to the animal shelter. The last one anyway. The one before that went to the senior citizens center. And the one before that—"

"I get it. So, about the ring... you couldn't tell much

about the ring covered in muck the way it was. What's it look like now that it's cleaned up?"

"It looks like an engagement ring."

"Well, it was on the third finger of her left hand, but Olivia Booth wasn't engaged. Or if she was, it was a secret."

"Just telling you what I saw. And on the underside in the band, there was a little figure engraved. I had to get a magnifying glass to make sure I was seeing it properly. It was a rabbit."

"I don't remember Olivia having a rabbit. Jaclyn did, one of those lop-ears rabbits. She said it was deaf. Olivia's familiar was a barn owl that could turn its head all the way around in a circle."

"There's one more thing, Mitch," Gus said.

"Please don't confuse me with something else unexplainable."

"Just giving you the facts, man. I finally got around to checking the cat that was draped around Veronica Espinosa's neck."

"You did an autopsy on the cat? Now, that's what I call above and beyond."

"I didn't do an autopsy. The cause of death was obvious. Its head was facing almost backwards. An owl can pull that off, but a cat can't."

"Somebody twisted the cat's neck to kill it."

"Right."

"So why are you telling me about the cat?"

"It wasn't Olivia's cat. It belonged to Jaclyn Milford."

Mitch sat very still then. "How do you know that?"

"Because it had a microchip in its ear. People do that with pets, so if they get lost, their owners can be found."

"There was a microchip that said the cat belonged to Jaclyn Milford?"

"No, that's not what it said. The microchip simply provided a number. You have to call a registry that stores numbers with names and addresses to match it up. I called the registry. That cat was Jaclyn Milford's cat."

"Any other bombshells?"

"I doubt it, but stay tuned."

Mitch hung up the phone and began to drum his fingers on his desk.

A ring with a rabbit on it.

Jaclyn Milford's nickname was Bunny Rabbit. According to Rileigh, everybody called her that. And her hand would have been smaller than Olivia's. So, was the ring Jaclyn's? Then why had Olivia tried to jam it on her finger when obviously it didn't fit?

Then the rest of what Gus had said rose to the top of Mitch's mind like a bubble in a fish tank. He'd said the ring had looked like an engagement ring.

Rileigh told Mitch that when Jaclyn broke up with Ross Wakefield, she gave him back his engagement ring, but he just threw it in the dirt.

The cat belonged to Jaclyn. She mentioned the morning they talked to her that the cat hadn't come when she'd called her that morning. Which means the killer had taken the cat even before kidnapping Ronnie.

The cat. Where had Jaclyn gotten the …?

Her words again. He'd blown by them at the time.

My boyfriend got me a little black kitten for my birthday …

Her boyfriend — Ross Wakefield.

Mitch kept drumming his fingers on the table, not liking where his mind was taking him, not liking it at all.

Annamaria Giordano's body was discovered draped over a limb of an oak tree near Buttermilk Falls. And Buttermilk Falls is where Ross Wakefield had proposed to Jaclyn Milford.

Veronica Espinosa was found with the cat draped around her neck that Ross had given to Jaclyn Milford for her birthday.

And Olivia Booth had an engagement ring on her finger that didn't fit ... because Ross Wakefield had given it to Jaclyn Milford.

All the tumblers fell into place. The curtain rose up, leaving Jaclyn Milford centerstage with a spotlight shining in her face. This was all about her. Jaclyn Milford was the original target, probably the only target. Everything pointed back to her, to her and Ross Wakefield.

That didn't make any sense. Ross Wakefield was in a wheelchair.

But his father wasn't. His father was hale and healthy. And his father didn't have an alibi for the times that any of the three girls were murdered.

Mitch got up from his desk quickly, grabbed his hat, and headed out the door. "I'm on my way to the Fire Baptized Holiness Church up in Juniper Hollow," he said to the dispatcher. "I've finally been there often enough. I don't have to use my GPS."

As he pulled his car out of the parking lot behind the courthouse, he called Rileigh to tell her what he was thinking, hoping she would convince him he was crazy. Rileigh's phone rang twice and then a voice answered — not Rileigh, but her mother.

"Well, hello there, Sheriff Webster," she said sweetly. "Oh, how I do like that caller ID thingy. You know who's called you before you even answer the phone. Ain't that amazing."

"Indeed, a wonder of modern technology," Mitch replied.

"Me and Jillian was talking about you just a minute ago. Do you like to play Monopoly?"

"Excuse me?"

"You know, Monopoly, the board game. Get out of jail free? Park Place? Community chest? Monopoly."

"Oh, sure, the game."

"Do you like to play it?"

"Yeah, I guess. I haven't played it since I was a kid."

"How would you like to come over to our house tonight and play with me and Rileigh and Jillian? It's more fun with four people. I made yeast rolls this afternoon."

Mitch's mouth actually watered at the words. Pavlov's dog. "If they're anything like as good as they were the last time—"

"Well, the first batch is a little too brown. Rileigh left her phone so we could use the timer on it, but I had the oven turned up a little too hot."

"Rileigh left her phone?"

"Yeah, she set it on the counter before she went to talk to Zeke Wakefield."

The cold lump he so hated, but was so familiar with, instantly formed in his belly. Rileigh was going to talk to a serial killer. Had she figured it out too, and decided, as Rileigh was constantly doing, to go check it out *on her own*?

Mitch flipped on his lights, but not his siren, and began driving way, way too fast on the winding mountain roads.

Chapter Forty-Three

MITCH PULLED his cruiser up beside where Rileigh's car was parked on the side of the gravel road leading up to the Holiness Church building.

She'd parked far from the building so she could approach it unseen. She suspected something, too. He didn't know whether to be thrilled that she hadn't walked blindly into a trap or pissed because she'd walked into it at all.

The cold lump of fear in his belly had swelled up as he careened around corners until it was so big he could barely breathe and the cold of it had seeped out into the rest of his body, so chilling him he was almost shivering. Then his mind had flashed to the day he had eaten tacos with Rileigh at the Mexican food place in Gatlinburg, Tacosaurus Rex.

"YOU KNOW that time I invited you to dinner? Right before—"
"The guy tried to kill me. Yeah, I remember."

· · ·

MITCH HAD TRIED to sound offhanded and casual, didn't want to push. But he also was unwilling to just let the whole thing go, pretend it never happened.

"THE INVITATION IS STILL OPEN. I'd just like to have dinner together, you and me, and not talk about dead bodies or blood or witches or any other ugly thing. Just enjoy."

HE WAS sure she'd been about to say yes, but then his radio had crackled and they'd been called to deal with the protest in front of the Fallen Angel Church. The first protest. The second one had been uglier. And the third — he supposed you could call setting the building on fire a "protest."

The protest had hijacked the conversation about going out to dinner and he'd never managed to maneuver his way back to it. But he *should* have. He should have pressed the invitation. He was certain she wanted to say yes. To a *date*. Not sitting in Mama's kitchen playing Monopoly, but a for-real date.

Why had he let the opportunity slip out of his fingers?

And now... He flat out would not let his mind form the words *too late.*

Leaping out of his cruiser, he ran toward the building. It was dark, but a full moon hung in the night sky, painting everything it touched with a silvery glow. He could see light shining out through the broken glass. Candlelight. Not just one, several, the light flickering and dancing against the darkness around.

As he ran, he drew his service revolver. Leaping up onto the porch, he opened the door and shoved it inward. What he could see didn't make any sense. The room was completely dark, but at the front of the sanctuary on the raised platform, the pulpit and the altar were surrounded by an enclosure of some kind where drapes hung down to the floor from a rod frame above.

The only light source, candles, was inside the drapes, and he could see a backlit figure, a shadowed silhouette standing beside a table ... the altar. And on the altar, he could see...

Was that...?

Slowly, the silhouetted figure lifted something with both hands high above his head. It was a *dagger*.

"May God have mercy on your soul," Zeke Wakefield's voice intoned.

Mitch raised his gun and fired.

RILEIGH HAD SUCKED in a gasp as if to scream, but there would be no time for a cry. The dagger was raised above her, the candlelight sparkling in the shiny blade. She froze but didn't close her eyes. She'd watch death come for her, recalling that she'd sat up and squared her shoulders when Aunt Daisy advanced on her with a chain saw all those months ago, thinking that a person ought to die with as much dignity as the circumstances allowed.

She tensed, waiting to feel the agony of the pointed end of that dagger stab into her chest and rip open her heart.

Then she heard the *bam* of a gunshot and Zeke Wakefield collapsed onto the floor beside her like a marionette when the strings were cut. The dagger clattered onto the side of the altar and then fell to the floor. A heartbeat later, the curtains that Jake and Ross had so meticulously hung in place were ripped apart and there stood Mitch with his gun in one hand.

"Rileigh?" His voice was ragged, as if he had just run a long way. She watched his eyes rake over the scene, trying to make sense of it. She would explain it to him. She would tell him everything that had happened. But right now, she couldn't do anything but cry, "*Mitch!*"

He stepped to her side, holstering his weapon. After a moment's examination, he unfastened the belt that Zeke had strapped around her neck and it dropped away. Then he picked her up into his arms in a hug that was too tight, too long, and absolutely glorious. He was speaking, too, but she couldn't understand what he was saying, couldn't really hear him over the sudden buzzing in her head, and the thud, thud, thudding of her heart in her ears. The adrenaline that'd dumped into her veins was still firing, and all of her senses were tuned up high like a speaker turned up to full volume.

She could feel the exquisite pleasure of his arms around her, smell his aftershave and feel the scratch of his whiskers on her cheek. He finally moved her out of the hug and held her at arms' length. It wasn't until then that she realized he was crying, or maybe she was crying. She had tears running down both cheeks anyway.

"What ...?"

Mitch couldn't finish the sentence.

"Untie me," she said. "Just untie my hands." He rolled her over, reached down and picked up the dagger that Zeke Wakefield had dropped, then sliced the zip tie. Rileigh didn't wait for him to slice the tie around her ankles, just turned on the altar and threw her arms around him.

"Hold me," she said. "Just hold me."

Chapter Forty-Four

MITCH LOOKED DOWN at the Monopoly board and thought to himself that it was genuinely demeaning to be a grown man and get your ass kicked so totally by an old lady who'd been dating Rhett Butler — until she'd dumped him and was now expecting Taylor Swift and Travis Kelce to drop by for dinner.

He looked into Lily Bishop's face and saw such warmth and kindness. A child's face. Happy beyond measure, just because this was the day that the Lord had made and she would be glad and rejoice in it, though she probably didn't remember that particular Scripture. But maybe. Rileigh said she'd heard Lily talking once as she sat out on the porch swing, then listened in awe as Lily quoted all one hundred seventy verses of Psalm 119 from memory.

Not only was Lily kicking his butt, but so were Rileigh and Jillian. He was pathetic.

"Your turn, Mitch," Lily said, and handed him the dice. He plopped them down onto the middle of the board. One landed on a five, the other a four. Nine. He picked up his thimble from Kentucky Avenue and moved it past Chance to Indiana and Illinois Avenues, both red ones. Nobody had houses or hotels on any of the red ones. Then came B&O Railroad. Lily had the utilities, but not the railroads. All the yellows belonged to Jillian — Atlantic, Vintner, and Marvin Gardens, but he didn't land there. No sir, he hopped over them, over the Water Works, and came to a stop in the corner square where a cartoon figure in a blue uniform informed him that he must go to jail. Mitch picked up his little thimble and moved it across the board to the orange block on the opposite corner where an inmate looked out through the bars.

"No professional courtesy for a fellow officer, huh," Rileigh said, shaking her head sadly. She owned the green ones and the purple ones, had houses on them all. But it was Lily, who had hotels on Park Place and Boardwalk, and on the pale blue Oriental, Vermont, and Connecticut Avenues, *and* on the pink ones — St. Charles, State and Virginia Avenues. She was cleaning everybody's clocks. Mitch had landed on Park Place once. If he landed there again, he would be totally bankrupt. That is, if he ever got out of jail.

Jillian asked for a timeout to go to the bathroom. Mitch stretched, enjoying the feel of no tension in his shoulders, enjoying the comfort of sitting here with Rileigh and Lily and Jillian. It felt like sliding a foot into a comfy old house shoe.

"I'm thinking about taking flying lessons," Lily said, plopping the non sequitur out into the middle of the Monopoly game as she plopped most of them out into the world. "Or scuba diving. I haven't decided which yet."

He looked into her clear blue eyes and thought that inside Lily's head must be like a house that had once been full of life with kids running up and down the hallways and the smell of beans cooking on the stove and the sound of a football game coming from the television. But then slowly, over time, all the people moved out. And one by one the rooms began to empty until there wasn't a whole lot left in there anymore.

Old age seemed a terrible thing to do to somebody just because they stopped being young.

When Jillian came back into the room, Rileigh told Mitch, "You should see Jillian's latest painting."

Jillian held up her hands. "No, no, no. I'm not showing any of them to anybody. You weren't supposed to look."

"You didn't tell me I couldn't go in there."

"I didn't think I had to tell you. It's my studio. You said it was."

"I didn't realize it was holy ground."

When Rileigh saw that the remark had hit wrong with Jillian, she backed up so fast she almost fell over her own thoughts.

"I didn't mean it wasn't okay. It's fine. If you don't want anybody in there, nobody's going in there. If you don't want anybody to see your paintings, nobody will look at them." She paused. "It's just, you know, when you create a painting, I would think you'd want somebody to see it."

Jillian sat back down. "I'm sure I'll get to that point, but right now the paintings are mostly for me, mostly therapeutic." She gave Rileigh a conspiratorial look. "And for burning in the backyard — bring your marshmallows and hot dogs."

Mitch liked watching the two sisters interact. It was bumpy going a lot of the time, but he could see that the road was beginning to smooth out.

Neither Jillian nor Mama knew about Rileigh's brush with death at the hands of the Wakefields a little over a week ago. They knew only that Ross Wakefield had murdered the three witches, that he and his father had kidnapped Jaclyn and tried to kill her, and that they had both died in the attempt. When Mama asked if Rileigh had killed anybody, Rileigh had dodged the question by assuring her mother that she had drawn her weapon but had not discharged it. That satisfied both Mama and Jillian. And it was true, of course. She hadn't shot Ross Wakefield. She'd pushed him into the baptistry where he had broken his neck.

There was a knock at the door, and Jillian got to her feet. "I'll get it."

She walked out of the kitchen through the dining room toward the front door. Mitch turned his gaze on Rileigh, who was watching her sister with a look of, what would he call it, relaxed joy, he supposed.

"I think she's doing better," she said quietly. "Don't you?"

"Do you realize that you say that to me every time you see me, that Jillian is doing better?" Rileigh looked surprised. "You don't have to, I can see for myself. She does look like she's doing better. Has she started going to counseling yet?"

"Nope, she's still kicking that can down the road. But we'll get there."

Jillian walked back into the room with a small box, about four inches square. Typed on a label on the front was: "Rileigh Bishop, 639 Bent Twig Road, Black Bear Forge, Tennessee."

"Did you order something from Amazon?" Lily asked.

Rileigh shook her head. "Nope, I'm not expecting a thing."

Rileigh picked up the box, tried to tear the tape off and couldn't manage. Lily got up, got her a knife, and told her "don't cut your thumb off" as Rileigh sliced the tape that held the top shut.

Rileigh lifted the top off and looked into the box. She appeared confused, like she couldn't tell what she was looking at. Then Mitch saw realization — and revulsion — register on her face. Mitch snatched the box out of her hands and looked into it. Then he reached down and pulled out what was inside.

It was a bone. A human bone. From a little finger.

Beneath the bone was a small, folded paper. He opened it. On one side was a crudely-drawn frowny face, the mouth turned down in a sneer. On the other side was the number 5.

THE END

THE END

About The Author

Lauren Street has always loved a mystery. As a kid growing up in bible belt country she devoured every whodunit book she could get her sticky little hands on and secretly investigated all of her (seemingly) normal boring neighbors. Sometimes their pets and farm animals too. All grown up now and living in the UK with her thoroughly unsuspicious (and often unsuspecting) husband, she writes domestic psychological thrillers about families torn apart by secrets and lies. And she sometimes still peers over garden walls to check up on the neighbors.

Also By Lauren Street

The Bishop Smoky Mountain Thrillers

Hide Me Away

Fuel To The Flame

Closer By The Hour

A Gamble Either Way

Calling My Children Home

Too Far Gone

Here You Come Again

Replaced with Nolon King

Replaced

In Her Place

Irreplaceable

The Salazar Redwood Forest Thrillers

The Girl Who Couldn't Stop Dying